Dead Draw
Book Three of the Sophie Lee Saga

by Stormi Lewis

STORMI LEWIS

Dead Draw
Book Three of the Sophie Lee Saga

ISBN: **979-8-9856999-2-0**

Library of Congress Control Number: 2021917510

For information, contact Stormi Lewis

cspresspublishing@gmail.com

Discover us online:

www.chasingstormi.rocks

Find us on Instagram and TikTok:

@chasingstormi

To the OG Storm Chaser, who gave me my love of stories and books, always made sure that I knew she loved me, was always proud of me, and the spirit to all of my writing. I will see you in my dreams whenever you can take a break from chasing around Elvis and drinking coffee with your loved ones in Heaven.

To Shyera McCollugh Thomas, who convinced me to go back to my roots, and gave me the greatest gift I could ever ask for. Pure happiness, pandemic and all.

To Booktok and Authortok, who are forever teaching me new things and helping me reach my author goals.

To Katherine, who took the time to help me get Sophie into even more hands, and keeps me going when I get overwhelmed.

To my Instagram Support Team, who let me reach out for the good, the bad, and the breakdowns to help build me back up and get me back on track.

To my beta readers, that gave me valuable feedback to make this book the best version of itself for you.

Lastly, to my Storm Chasers, who never stop conquering their personal storms while supporting my passions and personal growth. I would not be here without you.

Dead Draw: A term in chess that means a drawn position in which neither player has any realistic chance to win.

Let the games begin....

MATURE LANGUAGE AND CONTENT 18+

PSYCHOLOGICAL WARFARE AND MANIPULATION

VIOLENCE, KIDNAPPING, AND OTHER PSYCHOPATHIC AND ASSASSIN TENDENCIES

SC
SEXUAL CONTENT

<u>**One**</u>

S ophie's breathing was scarce. Ben grew pale as he checked her vitals.

"She's barely got a pulse," he whispered.

"We need to get her to the hospital!" James shouted. His body felt like it was overwhelmingly on fire. The walls closed in. James either needed to sit down fast or find something to throw up in.

"No!" Tina ordered. "If he hasn't found her yet, he will definitely find her there. She won't stand a chance," she whispered softly. She couldn't pull her eyes off of Sophie's unconscious body.

"What do you mean if he hasn't found her yet?" Ben asked. He gulped the lump lodged in his throat as his heart beat so fast, he was sure he was going to have a heart attack any second.

Tina remained silent.

"What do you know?" James snarled. His blood boiled under his skin. *How DARE she keep secrets at a time like this!*

"I know nothing!" Tina lied, still staring at Sophie's barely breathing body.

"What. Do. You. Know?!" James demanded as he yanked his bag off his back and threw it as hard as he could across the floor. Fury wasn't a strong enough word for the anger that was taking over his body.

Before Tina could respond, her eyes rolled back, and her knees buckled under her. Ben raced to catch his wife before she fully hit the ground.

"What the hell is going on?" Ben yelled, looking at James with wild eyes. However, James was too busy stumbling towards the bed to catch himself before he fell into his own dark spell. "A little help here!" Ben screamed at the ceiling. There was no reply.

James opened his eyes to find the wooden door before him. He could only see a red-colored cape encouraging him to strike like the raging bull he was. He reached out to yank the door open, but it was locked.

"Open the damn door!" he screamed into the nothingness that surrounded him.

"You need to calm down," he heard Mario's voice trying to reason with him.

"Calm down?" James shrieked. "She's in a coma with her vitals fading fast, and you want me to CALM DOWN?!" James shoved his hand through his light brown spikes on his head to prevent himself from exploding.

"The door won't open until you calm down," Jack whispered calmly in his ear. "And we need to understand what's going on."

James heard the terror and concern in Jack's voice. It stopped him dead in his tracks. Clearly, they weren't behind this. His stomach dropped as if he were plummeting down the hill of a roller coaster. Blackness lurked nearby, and nausea threated to annihilate his body.

"Breathe," Jack coached within his ears. "We can't help her if we don't work together."

Although it was difficult, James desperately gasped to get air into his empty lungs. He felt a finger brush across his forehead, steadying his runaway pulse.

"Open the door, Kid," Mario whispered. James heard the terror mixed with concern in his voice as well. Even though he still felt incredibly sick to his stomach, James reached out and opened the door. He stood in the living room of the cabin that seemed to be their go-to place to gather.

"She's not okay," James tried to say past the lump that was permanently lodged in his throat.

"We know," Jack spoke softly, placing his hand on James' shoulder.

Jack stood just a few inches taller than James, thin, and with sky-blue eyes. However, today they carried a dark grey tint like a sky expecting a violent storm. Although his hair was longer on top, like Ben's, his face would never age from the day the man with the cane murdered him.

"What happened?" James asked. He searched Jack's eyes, desperate for answers.

"We're not sure, Son," Jack said as tears filled his eyes. He quickly blinked them away.

"Algos broke through," Mario cut in. James could see by his clenched jaw he was fighting to hold back his own storm of anger.

Mario carefully leaned against the counter behind him so that he didn't punch something. He towered over Jack at 6'3" with a grey beard and mustache, and his forever look of a biker never to be messed with. His black cargo pants and boots had seen better days, but this was what he was stuck with since Clarice took his life.

If James wasn't so angry, he'd feel sorry for the men that Sophie loved. Never aging. Never moving on. Simply frozen in time, looking exactly same as the day they left Sophie's life.

"How did he break through?" James asked, turning to face Mario. *This made no sense!*

"We're not sure how he did it, but he did," Jack said as he walked over to the table and took a seat. "We need to find out, so we can stop him, though," he added. A flicker of lightning flashed across his eyes that made James's hair stand on end.

"Is it true? He's her grandfather?" James asked, taking a seat as well. He still felt like throwing up, and didn't trust his legs to keep him standing much longer.

"Jess' father," Mario muttered.

Realization set in to the entire situation. "Who would alter his own daughter?" James asked, in irritation.

"A psychopath," Mario answered bitterly.

"James, Sophie is the actual key. They knew that all the testing showed no results in Jess. However, even as a young child, Sophie was obviously 'different.' The only way he allowed Jess to walk away was to have Sophie take her place. When Jess disagreed, he sent a team to have us killed and take Sophie, but we had other plans. That's how Sophie ended up with Mario, and that's why she's been running ever since," Jack finished.

Were they kidding? "Why not just tell her?" he asked. His voice raised much louder than he had intended. "She's been looking for answers this whole time!"

"Because the mind is a finicky organ, Son. It has a mind of its own, as we've already seen. And there are rules for existing in this realm. Breaking them means we lose our access to Sophie forever.

That's not a price her mother and I are willing to pay," Jack added with emphasis.

"Plus, she shuts down when she gets overloaded," Mario reminded him. James watched sadness and frustration consume Mario's face. He hated this as much as James did. "So, she has to come to it on her own."

"Do you think that's what happened?" James asked them eagerly.

"We're not sure," Jack replied as he stared at the table before him. "We can't feel her at the moment, so wherever she is, it's not here or amongst the living."

"What the hell does that mean?" James shouted in frustration. *Why was it so hard for them to just give a straight answer?*

Mario moved over to sit at the table with them. "We can feel her when she's with you, or when she's here with us. But we can't sense her at all, which means wherever she is, it's not a place we can

10

feel her," he tried to clarify.

The room spun quickly around James. He no longer knew which end was up and placed his hand on the table in front of him to anchor himself. "Then where is she?" he gulped.

"That's what we're trying to find out," Jack said, finally raising his eyes to meet James'. "I sent her back to you, but then something happened. Algos doesn't have her, luckily, because he was still with us when we lost her."

"Does that really mean he doesn't have her, though?" James asked. The thought of Algos having access to Sophie made it impossible to get his lungs to accept oxygen.

"He broke through, but he still doesn't have access to her. We suspect he's trying to locate her as much as we are," Mario added with a little reassurance.

"Do you think she just shut down to put herself somewhere safe? Until we can figure out how to help her out?" James asked. She had done it before. Wasn't it possible she would do it again?

Jack smiled suddenly. "You know, that would be something my Peanut would do," he said, feeding on James' hope. "But we still need to figure out how Algos broke the barrier, and how to keep him out, before we try to bring her back."

"If we can bring her back," Mario muttered under his breath. Jack kicked him from under the table, but James was too busy holding on to hope, no matter how little it seemed to be.

"So, what now?" James asked eagerly.

"You need to keep her safe while she sleeps," Jack ordered. "You also have the strongest live connection with her, so just keep trying to reach her. We're going to have to work together on this. Don't be surprised that we'll be visiting you guys more often," he added in his fatherly tone.

"Can you at least make sure we're not standing?" James asked. His smile was as weak as his stomach felt.

"We'll do our best," Jack said with a smile and a wink.

Tina! "If you're talking to me, then who's talking to Tina?" James asked in a low tone.

Jack put his hand back on James' shoulder. "The girls had some things to discuss," he said reassuringly.

Mario rolled his eyes and leaned back in the chair as he crossed his arms in annoyance. James understood his irritation. Not exactly the time to be doing girl talk, but he had more important things to worry about.

"Send me back so I can keep her safe," James ordered. He had work to do.

"Good luck, my boy," Jack replied, giving his shoulder another quick squeeze before he pushed James through the door.

"Do you think she's really hiding?" Mario asked, with doubt oozing from his voice.

"We taught her how to be an expert at it, so possibly. She may need help to come back if she is, but I'm not even going to try until that asshole is locked out," Jack added. The lightning flashed in Jack's eyes, and Mario felt just how angry his friend was.

"Agreed," Mario replied with determination.

Tina opened her eyes to a wooden door. Her stomach jumped, and she put a protective hand over it.

"You're safe," she heard Jess assure her. "Please open it."

Tina took a deep breath and pushed open the door. She shielded her eyes as they adjusted to the flooding white light around her.

"Hello, Tina," Jess whispered with a smile. She sat on a couch in the middle of what looked like a log cabin warming up to a fire. She sat calmly wearing a beautiful sun dress covered in red flowers that hung nicely around her athletic curves. Her red chin length curly hair framed her face covered lightly by freckles. The fire danced in her pale blue eyes as she stared at it before her.

"Jessica," Tina replied nervously to the woman, who looked like she was a three dimensional work of art.

"I'm not here to harm you," Jess assured. "But we need to talk," she said in her motherly voice. "Come," Jess said, patting the cushion next to her as she turned to meet Tina with calm blue eyes. "Have a seat."

Tina hesitated, but made her way to the couch and took a seat.

"I don't know what's wrong with her," Tina blurted out.

"I know," Jess whispered softly. "This isn't about Sophie. This is about you." Jess directed her eyes back to the dancing fire.

Tina swallowed hard, unsure of what she already knew. Jess kept her gaze directed towards the fireplace and gave a heavy sigh.

"Motherhood is both a glorious and difficult journey," Jess started slowly.

Tina tried desperately to swallow the panic forming in her throat.

"We do what we can to keep our children safe," Jess continued softly. "Even if that means making choices, others don't understand," she added, looking Tina straight in the eyes.

"I don't know what you're talking about," Tina lied, looking into the fire.

"It will force you to choose a side, unfortunately," Jess continued, as if Tina hadn't responded. "We understand you have to choose what is best for you," she said, still staring Tina down. "We won't think less of you either way. But they deserve to know."

Tina looked at Jess as her eyes quickly filled with tears.

None of us are safe without Sophie. "We need to save Sophie," Tina said with great determination. "It will do no good to know the mistakes I've made. It will only distract them."

Jess' heart physically ached for the girl that sat before her, fighting for her daughter, and struggling with so many secrets to keep from her loved ones. She reached out and gently put her hand on Tina's thigh. "Your secrets are safe with us, but they still need to know," Jess offered.

"My life can't be saved," Tina said, looking at the floor. There was no possible forgiveness for the things she had done.

Jess tilted her head suddenly at the girl, who had already condemned herself to sacrifice. Even in her early twenties, only standing at 5'4" on a good day, Jess knew Tina was wise beyond her years and was not to be messed with. She had seen Tina's killer eyes change grey when she became scared, and turn a deeper blue when she was working on a puzzle with determination. Tina may look like an average pretty girl on the cover of magazines, but Jess knew better.

"You fight for my daughter," Jess said with authority.

"Therefore, we fight for you."

"Clarice, is your sister?" Tina asked, looking at Jess in shock as Sophie's last words came back to her.

Jess took to staring back at the fire as Tina watched her attempt to blink away the heartache in her eyes.

"You can't save everyone," Jess sighed. "But you can always try," she added with a weary smile.

Jess jerked her head quickly to stare into Tina's soul once more.

"A mother should always put her child first," Jess added firmly.

Tina understood what Jess was saying. She knew what Jess wanted her to do.

"I will tell them," Tina resigned. "Together, we will save Sophie so she can save us all. With as few casualties as possible," she added as she put her hand over Jess'. Tina felt Jess squeeze her leg slightly. Her body swelled up with comfort and love. It was a bizarre feeling, but it took away any anxiety Tina had been holding in her tiny frame.

"So, tell me about this dreamcatcher theory you have," Jess said with a knowing smile.

"I don't know if it's a theory, really," Tina sighed.

"You're the smartest person I have come across in my lifetime," Jess said, smiling with encouragement. "That says a lot since I'm still existing amongst the living," she added with a wink. "Walk me through it."

Tina grabbed the paper and pencil that appeared on the table next to her. She scribbled and describe to Jess the images that came to her last night.

"That's interesting," Jess said once Tina finished, deep in

thought. "Why do you think Sophie needs this?"

"Do you not know?" Tina asked. A heavy feeling filled her stomach.

"Know what?" Jess questioned; not sure she was ready for the answer.

"Sophie thinks the man with the cane has accessed her mind and might control her," Tina replied hesitantly.

Jess' eyes widened, her shoulders hunched forward as she wrapped her arms around herself.

"No," Jess whispered so softly, even Tina barely heard her.

"I thought you knew," Tina gasped. She felt her heart speed up. It was nearly impossible to breathe or even swallow..

"We knew Algos was pushing in," Jess breathed out. "We didn't know he could get control."

"Algos?" Tina asked in confusion, but Jess grabbed her stomach and began gasping desperately for air to get into her lungs. Tina grabbed Jess by the arms.

"Breathe!" Tina ordered her.

"We can't find her," Jess sobbed. "Her life is too low." She violently shook her head and scrambled out of Tina's arms.

"What does that mean?" Tina asked, as fear paralyzed her.

Jess backed herself up against a wall.

"Jess! What. Does. That. Mean?" Tina demanded.

"We thought she turned herself off," Jess choked out.

"Maybe she did!" Tina offered in desperation.

Jess looked at Tina, making Tina shiver to her core. It was like she could see the insanity take control over Jess, and Sophie's mother was no longer present.

16

"He's done it. Algos has done it," Jess whispered as she slid slowly down the wall. She held out her hand as a light shoved Tina through to the other side of the door.

Tina woke up gasping for air, and Ben grabbed her and pulled her into his arms.

"What's wrong?" he asked in a panic, but Tina couldn't breathe.

She looked desperately at the only person who was going to save them all. Tina grabbed Sophie's limp hand and placed it over her belly as she sobbed uncontrollably about the life that was going to be sacrificed before she ever got to hold it.

Sophie felt the life slowly leave her physical body. She felt her lungs fill up with what felt like water as she slowly drowned in nothingness. She couldn't move, no matter how hard she tried. She screamed, but nothing came out as she continued to fall deeper and deeper.

Suddenly, she hit the ground hard with a thud.

"Ugh," Sophie grunted when she landed.

She attempted to open her eyes and see where she was. An image floated before her out of focus, then she finally saw the child version of Eddie sitting on the ground, staring at her curiously.

"Do you want to play a game?" the little boy asked innocently. "Chess is my favorite...."

Sophie moaned as she tried to get her bearings. The boy sat

patiently, waiting for her to answer. "Where am I?" she asked as she held her head, waiting for it to stop spinning. The boy only gave her a shrug in response. "That's helpful," Sophie muttered as she tried to stand up. There were no doors. Only blackness, and a clear floor that she stood on but couldn't see.

"Do you want to play a game?" the little boy asked again. "Chess is my favorite."

"No, I don't want to play a game. I need to figure out where I am," Sophie snapped as she spun around to glare at him.

The boy looked like he was going to cry. Sophie sighed heavily, bowing her head, and slumping her shoulders. She tried again.

"Eddie, we need to figure out how to get out of here," she said more softly. "We can play once we get out of here," Sophie added for good measure. She turned her back to him and began slowly feeling the surrounding air to see if there was some sort of secret door she just couldn't see. Then an idea came to her, and she turned to face him again.

"Eddie, can you make a door?" Sophie asked him softly. "I think we need to make a door to get out."

The boy watched her with great curiosity. "We can't make doors here," he said, finally breaking the silence between them.

"Why not?" Sophie asked suspiciously, as she turned her back to him once more to look for a way out.

"We are not there. We're here," he said simply, as if that was to answer all of her questions

"We're not where?" Sophie asked absent-mindedly as she continued to look for an exit.

"Do you want to play a game?" the little boy asked again.

"Chess is my favorite."

"Eddie, I do not want to play a game. I know chess is your favorite, but it is not mine and we VERY much need to get out of here," she said, trying very hard to control her temper. There was no need to make the imaginary boy cry, no matter how unhelpful he was.

"You haven't changed," said a sarcastic and much older voice behind her. "I see you're even back to your natural color."

"Eddie," she whispered as she turned to face the ghost she had seen on the Vegas security video. He was short, average fit with dark brown hair who no one would notice unless they were looking. His original green eyes seemed to have faded to a permanent dark grey over the years. Sophie felt a gut punch in the stomach, knowing she was the reason they had changed.

"You're just as demanding and stuck up as I remembered," adult Eddie said with his feet up on a table and leaning back in a chair with his hands behind his head.

"Well, maybe if you would make a door so we could get out, I wouldn't have to be so demanding," Sophie retorted, crossing her arms in front of her chest and leaning on one hip.

Eddie tossed his head back and laughed. "Long time no see, Soph," he said with a weary smile.

Sophie dropped her arms. "Yeah, I know. Sorry about that," she said, suddenly consumed with guilt.

"No sweat," Eddie replied with a shrug. "I know it wasn't your fault. Just glad you finally started looking."

"Well, I didn't know I needed to," Sophie uttered, rubbing the back of her neck uncomfortably as she shuffled her feet.

"So, what are we doing here?" Eddie asked, quickly changing

the subject.

"I thought you brought me?" Sophie asked in confusion as the reality of the situation set in.

"Nah," Eddie answered. "Not that it's not nice to see you, though," he added for good measure.

"Flattery will get you everywhere, but we need to get out of here," Sophie said with her Cheshire grin. She turned her back to him to look for an exit as she carefully walked on the floor she couldn't see. She tried to feel for walls around her, but only found open air.

Then Sophie suddenly felt something else in her palm. A very tiny heartbeat. She heard Tina crying in her ear. "Oh, Tina," Sophie whispered. "Can you please make a door, Eddie? I need to get back," she said as her mind shifted to her friend and the tiny life that was apparently growing inside her belly.

"I can't," Eddie declared casually.

"What do you mean you can't?" Sophie asked distractedly, still staring at the pulse that seemed to beat against her palm despite nothing being there.

"We're not in that realm," he added a little more seriously.

"You keep saying that, but mom and dad do it all the time. It can't be that hard," she replied with a hint of frustration as she closed her hand to focus on finding an exit again.

"Soph, we're not in that realm. We're not anywhere," Eddie added with a hint of sorrow in his voice.

Sophie stopped looking for an exit. Her stomached seemed to have dropped from where it belonged as a lump grew within her throat.

"Eddie, where are we?" she whispered, not sure she wanted

to hear the answer.

"We can't get out through a door, because we're not in a realm," he spoke carefully. "We're inside your mind. You brought us here. Only you can get yourself out," he ended in a soft and sorrowful whisper.

Sophie closed her eyes as the tears fell down her cheek. Not because of where she was at. Simply because she did not know of how to get back.

<u>Two</u>

J ames woke up gasping for air.

"Finally!" Ben shouted. Nothing was more maddening than when the dead took his loved ones to have a "chat".

"Do you know what's going on?" Tina asked him eagerly as she helped him sit up to get more air into his lungs.

"No, but neither do they," James said in between gasps.

"That's what I gathered," Tina replied. Her bottom lip stuck out as she crossed her arms in front of her chest.

"So, what are we supposed to do?" Ben asked, concerned for everyone currently in the hotel room.

"Well, we think she may have hidden herself somewhere," James offered once he gathered enough air into his lungs to have them breathe on their own. "But we can't work on bringing her back until it's safe," he added with a warning.

"What does that mean?" Ben asked, on the verge of hysterics.

"Algos has broken through the realm," Tina added. "He can come and go as he pleases, but it's not by following the rules, apparently."

James narrowed his eyes at Tina before adding, "Yes, but they don't think he has her. Regardless, we're the only ones to keep her body safe while she rests, and do what we can to help on our side."

Ben slapped his hand to his forehead and shook his head before asking, "Who is Algos, and how the hell are we supposed to do that?"

"The man with the cane," James answered. "No one knows we're here for the time being," he pushed on. "And apparently Tina has a theory that we need to be working on," he said, glancing sideways at his friend.

"Me?" Tina asked, taking a step back.

"What did Jess have to say?" James challenged. Although his gut wasn't warning him, something was not adding up.

"I don't know why they think it would work," Tina said with a hint of irritation. "It's just a dumb idea."

"What's the idea?" Ben asked. He had a small, delighted smile. "And when did you come up with it?" he added.

Tina looked from her husband to her friend with the look of guilt that matched a child who had their hand in the cookie jar. She sighed heavily and sunk on to the ugly comforter on the bed that they now all sat on surrounding Sophie.

"Sophie wasn't sure, but she thought that the man with

the…Algos…was possibly getting inside her head," she said as one of her guilty confessions leaked out. "I thought she meant like just hearing him or like I hear my mother's voice correcting my posture when I catch myself slumping or something."

"And you didn't tell us?" James asked, more of an accusation than a question.

"She didn't give me anything else to go on!" Tina retorted.

"She wouldn't really talk about it, and shut down every time I brought it up! But it seemed to bother her a ton. So, I stupidly thought of making her a dream catcher to maybe give her some ease. The idea popped into my head last night while I was sleeping."

James stood up and began paced the hotel room, making exasperated sighs.

"There's plenty we talk about, Bro, that the girls don't know about, so take it down a level," Ben reminded him.

"I just don't know why she wouldn't tell me," James muttered, even though the hurt in his voice gave him away.

"She didn't even want to tell me!" Tina offered. "It was like pulling teeth! And she clearly didn't tell me everything," she mumbled.

James stopped pacing. "Oh my God, the pool…."

"What about the pool?" Ben asked, confused.

"When we were testing her abilities, she had wanted to test her ability to hold her breath underwater. But something happened. She wouldn't tell me what, exactly, but it was like she stopped holding her breath and just swallowed the water instead. Like she was trying to die or something, even though I know that's not what she was doing at all," James confessed. "I had to dive in and pull her out. She was very upset about something, but I just thought she had pushed herself too

24

far. You don't think...."

He stopped talking. James just grabbed the trash can by the bed and began throwing up. Tina rushed to James, and softly rub her hand up and down his back like his mother used to do. Ben went to grab his medical bag, but she just waved him off.

"This is no one's fault," Tina said softly, despite her own guilt betraying her voice. "She wasn't telling any of us what was going on. Probably because she wasn't sure herself. And you know her. Stubborn to confess until she has some sort of understanding and is already ten steps ahead," Tina giggled, breaking the silence.

"She is quite stubborn," James laughed half-heartedly with his friend as he sat down on the floor next to where he had set the trash can. It felt good to know he wasn't the only one completely left in the dark.

"You're one to talk," Tina said, leaning into him as she joined him on the floor.

Ben watched them with a smile. They were much easier to work with when they weren't at each other's throat. However, Sophie had come to him, too. She had come to Ben asking a lot of questions about neurology, and if it was possible to lose control of your own mind. He was pretty sure that his wife and friend often forgot how much he actually knew until someone got hurt and needed medical attention. However, it did no good mentioning it now. Sophie had sworn him to doctor patient confidentiality. That was an oath that trumped his wife or his friend. Sophie knew it, which is why she made him swear on it.

"So, what do you know about dream catchers?" Ben asked his wife, interrupting his own guilty conscious.

"The origins of the dream catcher are associated with a figure from the Ojibwe mythology known as 'the Spider Woman'. She's a mother-figure that is the protector of people, especially children," Tina started. "The dream catcher is to protect sleepers from bad dreams, nightmares, and evil spirits. The Native Americans believe that at night the air was filled with dreams, good and bad, alike."

"Great! I'll pull up Amazon," Ben said, pulling out the laptop.

Tina shook her head. "A real dream catcher is small and particularly hard to find. Most found now aren't authentic because they're not crafted by mothers or made with the right materials."

"So, where do we find a mom to make one from the right materials?" James asked.

"It's not just about finding someone to make it out of the right material. You have to activate it too," Tina added.

"I'm sorry, what?" Ben interrupted.

"We are in Bakersfield. Surely there's a Native American goods store somewhere that can at least send us in the right direction," Tina offered, ignoring her husband.

"Well, we can't all go," James said, looking over at Sophie's unconscious body.

Tina put her hand on James' shoulder. "You're the best one to protect her physically, should someone find us. Let me go. Ben can stay here in case anything changes," she offered with a reassuring smile.

Ben's breath quickened. He could feel sweat build up rapidly on his forehead. "I don't think we should separate," Ben said in a hurry.

Tina stood up and walked over to her husband before placing a gentle kiss on his lips. "For Sophie," she whispered. She took his hands in hers and squeezed them before she dropped them and went to grab her bag. "See you on the other side," she said with a wink before she slipped out the door.

"Better not," her husband whispered back. The boys both looked down at Sophie's motionless body, with no clue what to do.

Tina held her composure until she stepped outside of the back door to the hotel. Then the sob she had been holding in escaped her mouth as she threw her hand over it. She tried desperately to muffle the sound as much as possible. They would hate her even more if they knew all of her secrets. An image of her husband not even willing to touch her, and her best friend raging out of control, flashed before her eyes.

Tina needed to calm down. There were things to do. Puzzles to solve. Sophie's life to save. Yet she couldn't stop sobbing as her body convulsed. Tina forced her feet to move away from the hotel. She had to talk to someone. Someone who would understand and not hate her for her choices or mistakes.

She stopped to swing the backpack around and shook as she unzipped the bag to pull out the new burner phone. Tina took a couple of deep breaths before she dialed the number she knew by heart.

"Hello? Tina?" said a very confused female voice on the other side.

"Mrs. Moore," Tina sobbed into the phone.

"Oh, Honey. Tell me what's going on," Sally said on the other end, in her usual soothing, motherly voice.

"I need help," Tina said shakingly before she quickly lost total control.

"Breathe, Love," Sally said gently as she waited for Tina to calm down and give her the news she already knew.

Algos sat on the bench of the local college in the night's blackness. Old habits die hard, he thought as the corner of his lips drew up in a smile. He tapped his fingers against his cane patiently. The library would close soon, and his prey would be exiting. Algos closed his eyes and held his chin up to the sky as he took in a deep breath.

The stickiness of summer was in the air. He preferred the winter, even if his injured body did not. Luckily, summer was on its way out. He dropped his head as he heard a jogger approaching. Although it was always amusing to watch people react to his disfigured face, now was not the time.

Just then, the door flung open and a group of girls came out giggling.

"We can walk with you," one was saying.

"Yeah, we hate you walking alone this late at night," another whined. Her head darted around the darkness with widened eyes.

"That's completely out of the way, and ridiculous," said a curly red head that reminded him of his daughter, Jessica.

"Besides," she continued, "I'm just going to go home and crash. Studying for these finals has killed me. My brain's a complete zombie!"

"If you're sure," said another in hesitation.

"I'm sure," she said. She took the concerned girl into her arms for a giant hug. It wasn't long before she released her and pushed her in the opposite direction.

Everyone waved to each other, and the group headed in the other direction as the red-head walked toward Algos. He kept his head down so she wouldn't see his face. As she got closer, he faked a cough that wouldn't go away.

"Are you okay?" she asked with a frown.

"Yes, Dear," he said sweetly. "Just a dang tickle in my throat," he lied. "Do you have gum or candy on you by chance?" he asked in between dramatic coughs.

"I think I have mints," she said, pulling her bag in front of her and began digging through it. She was too distracted to notice how quickly he had gotten up, or that he had a syringe with a needle in his hand that he had jabbed into her neck.

Her knees buckled underneath her, and he caught her mid fall. "Shhh," Algos whispered to her. "You're going to be a fine specimen," he said with a smile.

She couldn't move. She couldn't scream. But the look of terror at the sight of him, and the realization that he wasn't the innocent old man she thought she was helping, couldn't help but spread across her face. He heard her gasp quickly at the excitement that greeted her from his own eyes.

"Yes. You will do," Algos said, like a man trying to choose a car or bottle of wine. "Here we go," he said as he hooked his cane in his belt, looked around him, and began dragging her into the woods he had made sure was behind him.

Tina looked out the window of the Civic that was her Uber, wondering how she had become so careless. She thought of what had actually happened in Vegas before they headed to Bakersfield. The horrible nausea that took over her and sent her to the bathroom more often than not before Tina could ever leave the city. It was a miracle that she even met up with the rest.

However, it would be in a bathroom stall that a woman would take pity on her and state, "The first trimester is the worst."

"I'm not pregnant," Tina said before hurling her guts into the toilet again.

"Here," the woman said, passing a pregnancy test under the door. "At least you'll know for sure." Then she was gone.

Tina had stared for what seemed like forever at the box on the floor as she quickly did the math and realized how late she actually was. Praying to be wrong, she had taken the test. Despite wanting to be a mother someday, running from a psychopath and his insane daughter didn't seem to be a great time to bring a child into the world. Then Tina looked at the stick that would change her life forever.

Consumed with a wide range of emotions, her instincts kicked in when she heard high heels enter the bathroom and nails scratch against the wall as the woman walked through the room. Something told her that this was not where she wanted to be. Tina slipped the test into the canister next to the toilet and took a deep breath before opening the door to her fate.

Clarice leaned against the counter with her arms crossed,

waiting. "Tina," she said, with the corner of her lips curled up into a wicked smile.

"Clarice," she guessed, trying to prepare herself for a battle in the women's restroom. Sophie had taught her to use what was around her when needed. Tina quickly assessed her options. There weren't a lot.

Clarice tossed her head back and laughed like a hyena. "Your day isn't today," she said, amused.

Tina put her hands on her hips defiantly and asked, "What do you want?"

"You know what I want," Clarice said, tilting her head and portraying a fake innocence.

"I can't help you," Tina said flatly and unimpressed. "So, just kill me and get it over with."

Clarice narrowed her eyes and studied her carefully.

"You're too valuable at the moment," she finally replied. "What kind of mother are you?" she added.

Tina sucked in a quick breath but remained silent.

"You wouldn't even give her to me in exchange for your unborn child?" Clarice taunted. "I would have expected more from you."

How the hell did Clarice know? Tina just found out herself! "I'm not pregnant, so you're barking up the wrong tree," Tina countered, sticking her chin into the air.

"Please, Child," Clarice sneered. "They may not know, but I've been around enough pregnant woman to know that you're a new mother," she laughed, knowing she had the upper hand.

Tina glared back at her. She couldn't sacrifice Sophie for the sake of whatever was or was not growing inside her. It could have been a false positive. These things happen all the time.

"I'm gonna guess 'no'," Clarice said, seeming to read Tina's mind. "Listen," she said with a shrug. "He'll get her in the end. He always gets what he wants. If you deliver her to me, you can go back to living your life in peace at the FBI with your loving husband and raising what I can only imagine will be a handful of a child."

Tina remained silent, not moving a muscle.

Clarice rolled her eyes dramatically before reaching into her breast pocket. Tina stepped back to get a better stance to prepare to fight. Clarice looked at her and laughed so hard she almost cried.

"You're cute," she said to Tina. "You remind me a little of myself, actually."

Tina tried to swallow the vomit that threatened to escape her throat. "I will never be like you," she growled.

"We'll see," Clarice shrugged, as she pulled out a small folded up piece of paper and put it on the counter. "I'll even give you a couple of weeks, but no more," she warned before she turned to leave the bathroom. "For what it's worth. I think you would be an exceptional mother," Clarice said over her shoulder and walked out.

Tina stood still until she was sure Clarice was actually gone before she turned back to the toilet and threw up for what seemed like the thousandth time. When she finished, Tina washed her hands and threw cold water on her face. She didn't recognize the creature that looked back at her in the mirror, sunken eyes, and a paling face that was full of misery.

She turned slowly to look at the folded up paper on the counter. After a long pause, Tina picked it up and opened it. Coordinates. Of where she was to send Sophie to her doom. Tina looked back at herself in the mirror. A life for a life. The boys would never forgive her. For putting them in more danger and giving up Sophie to have her life back.

Subconsciously, she placed her hand over her stomach and rubbed it to calm it down.

Tina kept a protective hand over her tummy as she rode in the Civic to help find a dream catcher to protect Sophie, but she didn't feel any better. Tina was being forced to sacrifice a life. War made sacrifice inevitable. The real question was which one could she live with? And which one would actually cost her everything.

Three

C larice woke up with a gasp. The last thing she remembered was her father, Jess, Jack and Sophie, all convened in some dark room that looked similar to her father's office. Jess had shot a ray of light at her again, and shoved her back through the door she had opened.

"Stupid dream," she muttered under her breath.

"You were dreaming about me again?" said a repulsive voice from the doorway leading to her room.

"What do you want, Troll?" Clarice snapped, not needing to see the face to know it was Eddie.

"The old man wants to see you in his office," Eddie smirked, but something was definitely wrong. Sweat plastered her thin curly ash brown chin-length hair to her pale skeletal face. Her blue eyes that normally contained hollowness held something much different. Something Eddie had never seen before. Fear.

She climbed out of bed and threw a sweatshirt on. She was bathed in sweat. It chilled her to the bone. "If you're going to stay for the show, you have to pay," she barked without glancing up at him.

"I know it's none of my business, but you're not looking so great, Sweetheart," Eddie said with a hint of concern in his voice. It stopped her dead in her tracks.

The only person who had ever showed care to her was her sister Jess. She didn't know what to do with his sudden hint of affection. *Do I really look that bad?*

"I'm fine," Clarice mumbled quickly, but as she stood up after putting on her shoes, her knees buckled beneath her, and she felt Eddie catch her just before she should have hit the ground. But Clarice was too busy falling into nothingness to do anything about it.

She landed on her feet like a ninja, but when she looked around, there was nothing but complete blackness. Even the floor she stood on didn't seem to exist.

"Hilarious!" Clarice shouted into the nothingness as she waited for some smart-aleck remark from her sister. Silence only greeted her.

"Okay, knock it off!" Clarice shouted with much less confidence. She spun around, looking desperately for an exit of some sort, but there was no door to be found. Suddenly, she heard her father's voice.

"What do you MEAN you can't find her?" she heard him shout.

She shivered at the coldness and ferocity in his voice.

"Be careful how you talk to me!" boomed a voice that shook the ground beneath her. Clarice stumbled a few steps, trying to get her balance. Once she did, she looked for the source of the voices she was hearing.

"I can't take over without her," her father growled.

"You can't take over until he's gone!" the voice bellowed back. "We still control this realm!"

"My apologizes," Algos muttered back under his breath.

They were far away, but Clarice saw her father standing with his cane before some giant in a cloak. Her father stood at 6'3" himself, but the cloaked figure before him was five times larger.

"What the...?" was all she got out before she felt a hand slide over her mouth.

"Shhh," a male voice whispered in her ear.

Clarice struggled immediately, but the hold on her was stronger than she had ever experienced.

"Knock it off and listen," he hissed in her ear.

Frustration was quickly brewing within her, but curiosity won the emotional battle, and Clarice stilled to hear what was taking place. She would deal with whoever held her once they were done.

"We will find her!" the cloaked giant yelled. "But you need to do your part," it warned.

"Already on it," her father snorted as he disappeared into darkness. The cloaked giant looked in Clarice's direction, but the hands that held onto her pulled her back further into the shadows. It shook its head and disappeared into the darkness in the opposite direction of her father.

"I'm going to remove my hand from your mouth, but you need to keep your voice down. I don't know how many more are out right now," he whispered softly into her ear. "And I'd rather you NOT attack me. I'm here to help," he added.

Clarice froze. *Was he in her head?* She felt him remove his hand from her mouth, and she slowly turned to see who had been holding her.

He was a few inches shorter than her. Most likely in the 5'9" area. His dirty blonde hair was wavy around his face like a surfer, and he had stubble around his mouth and chin. His emerald green eyes seemed to cut through to her soul, and he flashed her his best devilish grin.

"And who the hell are you supposed to be?" Clarice asked, already knowing the answer.

"A friend," he breathed.

"That's funny. I thought you were Corbin Dallas," Clarice retorted, throwing her hands on her bony hips.

"Can't I be both?" he shrugged with a smile before walking away from her.

She looked around her, quickly assessing her options, and reluctantly chased after him. "Where am I?" Clarice demanded as she rushed to catch up to him.

"Some would call it the dream realm. But considering the riff raff apparently coming through, it's more like Motel 6," Corbin said with another shrug and kept walking.

"Excuse me?" Clarice snapped. "I didn't come here by choice!"

"Ssshhh!" he hissed. "Yeah, I know. Which is why I had to come to your aid," Corbin added over his shoulder.

"My aid?" Clarice snorted, but at a much lower volume, as requested.

Corbin stopped, sighed heavily, and turned to face her. "Your father doesn't know what the hell he's doing. He dragged you here without realizing it. If you're smart, you won't tell him. I've seen how much family means to him." He spun on his heels and walked away again.

"I didn't know my sister had a boy toy on the side," Clarice retorted as she raced to catch back up to him, but his sudden stop made her run right into him.

"You can be a bitch out there, but I will not tolerate you disrespecting my friends in here," Corbin said as his emerald eyes changed to a deep evergreen and lightning flashed within his pupils.

Clarice stumbled back a bit, with a wicked sense of fear that she hadn't felt since the day her father murdered her mother before her very eyes.

Sensing her fear, Corbin stopped to take in a deep breath. "I'm sorry," he said more cautiously. "Sometimes I forget how much power I have in here."

"Well, that explains why my father wanted you so badly," Clarice murmured to herself.

Corbin shot his head up and searched Clarice's eyes for answers. "Do you know what he wants?" Corbin asked her. She stumbled back again. Not from fear, but from something else she didn't recognize. Or cared for.

"No, I don't," she finally whispered.

"It's not safe here for you," Corbin declared, cutting through her thoughts and sudden overwhelming emotions. "You need to go back." He slowly reached out his hand towards her face, but she jumped back immediately.

"What do you think you're doing?" she almost yelled.

Corbin froze. She didn't realize that he could feel everything she was feeling, or knew what she was thinking. He was not expecting to witness such a struggling individual based on the information Jack and Jess had provided, but things made a little more sense why Jess continued to fight for her.

"I have to put your mind to sleep for you to get back to where you belong," Corbin offered gently. "I have to touch your forehead to put it at rest so that you don't have a seizure when you go back," he added for clarity.

She hesitated with a look of conflict and uncertainty, but she eventually nodded in agreement.

"Don't tell anyone you were here," he offered with a bit of pleading in his voice. Clarice nodded again in confirmation before he gently touched her forehead and she woke up disturbingly in Eddie's arms.

"There you are," he said nervously. He knew better than to confess he knew what had happened. Only because Jack had done the same to him.

"I'm fine," Clarice mumbled in confusion. She felt Eddie pick her up and place her on her bed.

"You're going to need to sleep," Eddie ordered. "I'll deal with the old man," he added, but Clarice was already unconscious, with Corbin Dallas' face floating before her eyes as she drifted into a deep sleep.

Ben watched Sophie's comatose body like a hawk. He had ordered James to get them some dinner. It was going to be a long night. After much arguing, James had finally agreed to go. Ben finally had his chance to evaluate her like he needed to without concerned, watchful eyes over him. He ran his fingers through his long brown hair.

Being on the run didn't exactly cater to keeping the back and sides short like he preferred. Ben didn't even recognize the man that looked back in the mirror at him when he passed one. Still standing at 5'8", his muscles had definitely become more solid in their training with Sophie. But it was his hazel eyes that used to at least give the deception of brightness and innocence, that had changed to a more serious look. He knew it would happen, eventually. He just didn't realize that Sophie's burdens and keeping them safe would be the thing to change them.

Ben pushed her eyes opened and looked at them with a flashlight. The bright blue of her iris, gone. All that showed was a black pupil, severely dilated in both eyes. They twitched as he watched her fight herself, trying to break free.

"Hang in there," Ben whispered softly into her ear as he continued to get a baseline of her vitals. Her pulse and blood pressure were dangerously low, but color remained in her pale skin whenever he pinched it. Sophie seemed to be even more athletically built these days, but he would see her arm and leg muscles occasionally spasm as if she was moving despite remaining motionless on the bed before him.

Her temperature had gone back to normal, which was a relief. There wasn't much he could do with a high temperature other than keep her in a tub of ice and fight to bring it down. Ben needed a hospital to treat Sophie properly, but he also knew that wasn't an option. His wife was right. No one knew where they were, but putting her in a hospital would be handing her over as a gift. That wasn't an option.

Once Ben had made all of his notes and hid them in a safe place, he placed her hand in his and squeezed it as he laid down next to her and whispered in her ear.

"I know, as a doctor, I am not supposed to believe that you can hear me wherever you are. But as your brother, I'm going to try, anyway. Your fever broke, and your vitals are low. You're okay for the moment, but I can see you're trying to get back. I need you to understand that you can't stay like this forever. Your body will physically breakdown, and it will not end well for any of us," he said in his best doctor's voice.

"I don't know where you are, but know this...we're not giving up on you. We will do our best to keep you safe as long as possible. Because we love you. With all of our hearts. And I selfishly REALLY need you back. My wife is going crazy, and I don't know what to do without you. And you know your boy is losing his shit. So, hurry back. I love you."

Ben squeezed her hand once more and sat up quickly, grabbing a book off the end table as James came through the door with his arms full of bags.

"Anything?" James asked eagerly as he set the bags down on the table by the door.

"Just letting her know I will come drag her back if she doesn't hurry and do it herself," Ben shrugged with a smile.

"The book's upside down," James said with a frown.

"I'm trying something new," Ben shrugged. He fumbled with the book.

"Yeah? How's it going for you?" James smirked.

"I've had better days," Ben resigned, as he put the book down and got up to help his friend unload the food.

"Ti back?" James asked.

"No," Ben replied, with a hint of frustration.

"Well, I'm starving and in the mood for some mindless tv. What do you say?" James asked his friend.

"Best idea ever!" Ben shouted as he raced to grab the remote before James could get to it.

"The council is corrupted," Corbin announced as he walked into their meeting place.

"What?" Jack asked with his mouth dropping.

"Algos was talking to one of them. They're wanting to overthrow the head councilor, even though Algos will betray them all." Corbin shrugged as he sat on the couch next to a distraught Jess. He took her hand in his and squeezed it lightly as she continued to stare into the fire before her. It took them forever to calm her down after talking to Tina.

"How did you find out?" Mario asked, heading over to the

42

couch to join them.

"He pulled in Clarice by accident and we overheard them talking," Corbin said, waiting for the expected response from Jess.

"Clarice?" she said as she was pulled from her stupor. She looked eagerly into his eyes for answers.

"She's safe. I sent her back. But we heard them talking. We were right. They don't know where Sophie is. It's apparently his job to overthrow the council," Corbin said gently, not taking his eyes off Jess.

Normally, Jack would not be a fan of a man taking so much interest in his wife. However, Corbin had more powers than they had gained in a twenty year time span, and Jack knew he was just trying to get her back to them. Back to him. Corbin was not a threat. Although his intrigue with another might be a problem down the road. Jack walked over and sat next to his wife.

"You were right about Clarice," Corbin continued, giving Jess the motivation she needed. "She easily wavers. That will be beneficial," he said with assurance.

"Got the hots for the psychopath, huh?" Mario said, rolling his eyes in disgust.

"Watch it," Jack warned.

"Don't be jealous that I'm better with women than you are," Corbin snickered.

"Could you have your pissing contest later? I need to save my daughter so I can find her," Jess snapped. All the men smiled. There she was.

Corbin gave Jess' hand over to Jack and stretched back, putting his feet on the table before placing his hands behind his head. "We will have to figure out his access, but once we do, we can block it," he said with a quick nod. "They don't know I'm here, and he doesn't realize he keeps pulling Clarice to him. I will continue to follow her to get access to what we need when I'm not helping you," Corbin added with ease.

"Follow Clarice, huh?" Mario taunted, but Jess cut him off.

"Maybe I should try to reach her," she offered as she stood up.

Corbin put his feet down and studied her. "We need you for something else, and you know it," he breathed.

"I don't know that I can," Jess replied as she jumped off the couch. It was Mario that got to her first and spun her around to face him.

"Hey, Lovebug," he whispered. "You know that you're the only one able to, and we're going to be right there with you." Mario spoke in his fatherly tone that he used with Sophie. "You're the one person who can push his buttons better than anyone. So, let's get to it. What do you say?"

"I have waited a long time to really mess with him," Jess giggled as she wiped the water that threatened to escape her eyes.

"We're about to have fun. Just like the good old days," Mario whispered, winking at her.

He knew Jack wouldn't be mad, because he already won Jess' heart long ago. Mario just had to get her focused on the mission like he used to when they worked special ops together. Jess always feared that what Algos had created in her would take total control. Mario swore never to let it happen, and he kept his promise. Even into death.

They all had a part to play. Jack grounded her. Mario helped her to focus. Corbin helped calm her. And Sophie and Clarice fueled her. They all understood the role they played in this balance of good and evil. And right now, they needed Jess to tap into her evil just a smidge.

"Let's do this," Jess said with her wicked smile.

"Where's Clarice?" the old man snarled.

"Your DAUGHTER is resting. She had a fever and passed out," Eddie announced over his shoulder as he continued to stare at the computer screens that surrounded him. He needed to make sure he found Sophie before the old man did.

"Interesting," he heard the old man say with curiosity and distraction.

"Where's Clark? I need him," Eddie asked, already knowing the answer.

"You'll have to use someone else. Clark was dismissed," Algos said from the shadows.

It surprised Eddie that he wasn't barking about finding

Sophie. This wasn't good. This wasn't good at all.

"I haven't found her yet," Eddie tossed out to see what the response would be.

"What? Oh. Yes. Just keep at it," was all he got before they all heard the echo of Algos' cane move further and further away down the hall.

Nothing sent a chill further into his bones than the old man not caring if Eddie found Sophie or not.

Four

The silence was deafening. Sophie gave up looking for an exit. Mostly because she knew there wasn't one. She felt Ben squeeze her hand. She heard the words he told her, but she remained on the floor with her knees pulled in and her head resting on them.

"I have to be here for a reason," Eddie tossed out.

"What?" Sophie said, lifting her head sharply.

"You have me here for a reason, so maybe I am here to help you get out," he offered softly.

"You're not real," Sophie sighed, and went to put her head back down on her knees.

"But," Eddie declared, standing up from the table and walking towards her. "I am. I have his background. His memories. Surely, there's a reason for it," he replied, holding out his hand to her.

"You just want me to play a stupid game of chess with you," Sophie muttered, rolling her head around on her arms.

"Maybe that's it!" Eddie exclaimed in sudden excitement. "Maybe you have to play me to get out!"

"Stupidest escape route ever," Sophie retorted bitterly.

"You just don't like losing," Eddie laughed, and shoved his hand in her face.

"Well, I guess it's better than Monopoly," she said, frowning before she took his hand and let him help her up.

"Seriously. Why do you hate it so much?" Eddie asked.

"Why do you love it so much?" she countered, sticking her tongue out.

"I guess I love the mental challenge," Eddie said with a shrug. "Always trying to beat your opponent in three moves, just like your dad taught me. It forces me to see the entire picture and play out the scenarios to find the quickest route to success. You know, I wasn't good with books," Eddie added as he took his seat. "White or black?"

"Does it matter?" Sophie griped as she reluctantly took the seat across from him.

"Yes. Do you want to make the first move or sit back and deal with what I hand to you?" he added sarcastically, then he froze.

"What?" Sophie asked, slouching.

"Do you realize you have been playing a lifetime chess game?" Eddie asked in awe.

"What are you talking about?" Sophie asked. Her eyes narrowed, and she pressed her lips into a slight frown.

"Think about it, Soph," he said. "You play better than me!"

"I'm not following," she said with an exasperated sigh and shaking her head.

"Sophie, you have always played chess. Since the age of ten. It just hasn't been on a checkered board," Eddie said with enthusiasm. "Think about it!" he added, before she could cut him off again with some surrendering response.

"You're playing chess with the old man!" Eddie declared passionately. "You're always looking at the whole picture and analyzing how to stay three steps ahead. That is how you survive," he added with pride.

"Yeah, and look how well that worked," Sophie retorted.

"Yeah. You're ahead," he said, glaring down at her.

"I wouldn't call THIS being ahead," she snapped, throwing her arms out and looking around.

"But isn't it?" Eddie pushed. "No one can find you but you. You have bought yourself time to get two more steps ahead," he said, sitting back and crossing his arms in front of his chest in triumph. "So, make your move."

"What move?" she cackled.

"Move a piece stating the action plan. We'll see how it plays out, and if you win," he shrugged.

"Seriously?" Sophie asked.

"Got something better to be doing?" Eddie asked her sarcastically.

Sophie frowned at the imaginary version of her childhood friend before her. This was ridiculous. She didn't have the patience to play chess. That's why she always walked away. But he had a point.

48

Even though Sophie didn't care to play on an actual checker board, it didn't mean her parents hadn't taught her how.

"He plays all the time," Eddie answered her unspoken thoughts. "He taught your mother. She doesn't like it either. Not this version, anyway. But maybe that's the point. Maybe we have to see what he sees in order to win once you leave," Eddie offered.

Sophie sighed heavily as she reluctantly moved a piece forward.

"No. You'll lose in three moves. Try again," Eddie said without breaking concentration.

"How do you even know?" Sophie demanded. *I haven't even said anything!* She huffed loudly and rolled her eyes.

"What's that move?" he asked.

"I don't know what it's called," Sophie whined.

"No, what is your first move out of here?" Eddie asked, nodding his head toward the sky, but remaining focused on the board in front of him.

"Obviously, we need to move. We would have sat too long," Sophie said, frowning as she stared at the board with him.

He moved a piece forward. "He's located you because you were in here too long. Now, he sits and waits to take one of your team," Eddie announced, not looking at her.

Sophie glared at him, but he never looked up. "Then I go save them," she declared as she shoved another piece forward.

"He separates you and takes the rest of your team, leaving you alone," Eddie said, moving another black piece forward.

"Then I go save everyone," Sophie announced as she slammed a third white piece forward.

"Check mate," Eddie declared. "You and everyone you love is dead. Try again."

"What the hell?" Sophie yelled.

"Try again," Eddie repeated, putting the pieces back and not removing his eyes from the board.

"This is dumb!" Sophie snapped, crossing her arms in front of her in defiance.

"Is it?" Eddie asked casually. "Because I'm pretty sure you just got yourself and everyone you loved killed. So, let's try again, and see if you can win before you play with real lives. Your move," he said, not looking at her.

"This is why no one likes to play with you," she retorted. The corner of his lips curled up, but he made no response. Sophie wiggled in her chair to get more comfortable as she focused with determination to win the game. At least the one in front of her for starters.

Algos sat behind his enormous wooden desk in his red leather chair and tapped a pen mindlessly against the desk. His thoughts were distracting him more than usual today. He needed to get his act together.

"Are you ready for lunch, Sir?" asked an elderly man nearly on his death bed in an extremely worn butler's tux.

"I'm not hungry, Charles," Algos uttered.

"Sir, you cannot take over the world without eating. And you know how dream jumping wears you down," Charles reminded him.

Algos gave an exaggerated sigh and narrowed his eyes at Charles. "Fine. A sandwich will do."

"Very well," Charles said before slowly exiting the room.

Algos' mind wondered once more. More so to the day that he had rid himself of his little brother, simply out of amusement. The look of horror and confusion on Peter's face stirred excitement within as he relived pushing his three-year-old brother into the path of the speeding subway. The looks of hurt, confusion, and terror quickly spread across Peter's face before the subway train destroyed his body.

"Train is fast," Algos smirked to himself.

His father, Jim, didn't find it nearly as amusing as Algos had. His father would never look at him the same way ever again. He knew Jim had suspicions over the years. The first giveaway was the dead lab, Sam, when Algos was a toddler. He would sacrifice many animals over the years. But animals were dumb and boring after a while. So, Algos upped his game. Peter would be his first human sacrifice at age five, but definitely not his last.

Despite there being no clear evidence, or the desire to believe a five-year-old would intentionally kill his own brother, Jim would know. His tan face paled, as his hazel eyes would dilate into blackness and fear. His nervous tick of running his hands through his longer jet black hair would cause it to grey and fall out prematurely. Jim would never take his eyes off of Algos again, except when he locked Algos in his bedroom at night to keep him from attacking them in their sleep. This became a real problem, and it needed to be eliminated.

Jim and Angie whispered often behind his back. Angie was struggling with her own health issues and the mourning of her lost child to handle the psychopath that lived in her house. Jim wanted him gone. Angie didn't want to lose another son. Even if this one was murderous. She couldn't handle it, but eventually she was too sick to fight. Jim suspected it was from Algos, but the poison was undetectable, and no proof would ever be found.

One day, Angie begged Jim to take Algos out of the house for some father-son time. Jim couldn't argue with his dying wife, and took Algos for a drive. He knew better than to allow Algos around a ton of people, so a simple car ride would have to do. Jim just didn't think it would be his last.

He spent most of his time watching Algos from the review mirror. Algos stared out the window next to him and watched the trees and fields wiz by him. His birthday was coming up. Algos was turning six, and he was tired of being watched like a hawk. He had to put all of his experiments on hold except the ones on his mother, and that upset him greatly. Too much, in fact. Algos twisted the pocket knife he hid in his pocket as he stared out the window. Nothing was more gratifying than catching the prey when they least expected it. Jim never saw it coming.

When a car was finally heading their way, Algos pulled out the knife from his pocket. Jim was too busy carefully passing the Ford truck on the small road that he didn't see his son pull out the knife. All Jim knew was that he was paralyzed immediately from his neck down and drowning in his own blood.

Algos had taken the knife and jabbed it into Jim's neck, and twisted it so forcefully and quickly that Jim's spinal cord had been severed along with several of his veins and arteries. Turns out Algos had a lot more strength to him than either Jim or Angie imagined.

The car swerved into the oncoming Ford truck, taking them all off the road as they flipped into the ditch. Jim couldn't escape and neither could the driver of the truck.

Algos unbuckled himself and crawled to freedom. He smelled gas and went to investigate.

Jim choked on his own blood, and the driver of the Ford truck pleaded to be set free. Algos found a container in the back of the bed, full of gas. He picked it up with much enthusiasm, taking off the cap and pouring it over both victims.

The driver pleaded for his life. Jim prayed for the safety of his wife as he took his final breaths. Algos reached into their family Volkswagen and pulled out the emergency lighter out of the glove compartment. Algos had carefully wiped his prints from the gas can and returned it to its original place. It showed no signs of being touched.

"Bye, Daddy," Algos sneered, as he lit the lighter and tossed it into the gas puddle as he walked away. He began walking down the road. The explosion didn't make him jump. It just fueled the fire within. Today was a bonus. Two for the price of one!

Eventually, another car drove by. They stopped at the sight of such a young boy walking alone along the side of a mostly deserted road.

"Where is your family?" the elderly man had asked him.

"My daddy was in a wreck," Algos replied, pretending to be in shock. "I'm trying to get home to my mommy."

The elderly man had picked him up and put him in his Chevy truck, and drove in the wreck's direction. As the man got closer, and saw the flames before the cars, he put his hand over Algos' eyes and told him not to look. Algos had to fight his need to look and hid his smile as the elderly man's face turned from concern to horror at the site of the wreckage.

The man raced Algos back to his mother and called the police on their phone. The bodies would be too damaged to notice the knife wound, and again...no one wanted to believe that a five-year-old had taken a second and third victim. But Angie knew otherwise.

A white van would come in the middle of the night and take Algos kicking and screaming to a mental ward. Angie couldn't have any more deaths on her conscious, even if her son was the one taking them.

He was put in a strait-jacket and thrown into a padded room immediately. They would study him day in and day out, and pump him full of medication to keep him sedated. Or so they thought.

Algos got proficient at hiding the various colored pills without digesting them. Although it took longer than desired, the doctors eventually believed their medications worked, and would let him have more freedom as time slowly dragged on.

The center allowed him books and limited visitation, but his mother never came. No one came. No one cared, and that was fine with him. Algos simply read and bided his time, and played chess in the common area with an older man suffering from schizophrenia when it was approved.

The man had a lot to offer. Not only was he a skilled chess player who taught Algos everything he knew, but the voices inside his head gave brilliant suggestions to the experiments he intended on resuming once they released him. Including a theory on how to control the dead. A theory that Algos was eager to test out.

Twelve years later, Algos would go before the board and convince them he was reformed and ready to re-enter society as an upstanding citizen. He had earned his GED and some degrees in law, science, and biology. Their fake success blinded them from knowing anything different. There was just one stop he had to make before getting down to business.

The look of horror on Angie's face was priceless when she opened the door to find her murderous son before her. The rosy color of her cheeks quickly drained away at the sight of him.

"Nicolas," she barely whispered.

"Mother," Algos said with a smile and walked past her into her new home.

"What are you doing here?" Angie asked in a shaky voice.

"They let me out," Algos replied casually. "I'm a model citizen now, didn't you hear?"

"That sounds wonderful," she said, tugging at her sweater before she closed the door behind them.

"You're looking good," Algos noted over his shoulder as he found the kitchen and sat down at the table. He meant it too. Angie was healthy, in shape, with long red curly hair that cascaded down her back. She was wearing jeans and a light sweater on this crisp fall morning, but nothing could hide her athletic curves she had gained over the years. Maybe Angie knew this day would come, and she tried to prepare. She would fail all the same.

"What do you want, Nicolas?" Angie asked with a hint of irritation as she followed him to the kitchen. He could tell the shock was wearing off, and survival mode was kicking in.

"It's Algos, actually," he said with a smile. "And can't a son come and visit his mother, who he hasn't seen in twelve years?" he asked with a shrugged.

"Algos, huh?" Angie asked, not taking the bait as she walked over to finish making breakfast over the stove. "Sounds Greek."

"It is," he said with a hint of amazement in his voice.

Angie knew exactly what it meant. Pain. "And what last name are you going by these days?" she asked casually.

"Hersteller," he said, watching Angie closely.

"Interesting," was her only response. "You don't look very German, though," she articulated. Of course, her son would have picked the German word for "producer" as a last name. Angie heard him cackle, like the day he killed Sam as a toddler. Only knowing what was behind the laughter chilled her to her bone.

"Touché, Mother," Algos sneered.

Angie split the scrambled eggs and toast onto two plates and placed one before her son. "Had I known you were coming, I would have fixed a much more filling last meal," Angie said as she scooped some eggs into her mouth.

"Now, Mother. Who said I was here to kill you?" Algos asked cooly.

"A mother always knows," Angie shrugged, biting into her toast. "Although the poison has worn off," she added, casually taking another bite of eggs.

"That's a shame," Algos said, tilting his head to study her.

"You were my favorite subject," he added.

"I'm sure," she said, taking another bite of her toast. He didn't touch the food. Although it wouldn't be poisoned, he wouldn't take the chance.

"Why are you so eager to die?" he asked in fascination.

"You can't fight the inevitable," Angie replied, taking another bite. "I've already lost everything, anyway," she shrugged as she continued to eat.

"You are the first person to actually be able to accept their fate," he declared. His eyebrows raised, and his mouth hung open loosely as he studied her.

"Well, we all have a purpose. I've just come to terms with mine," Angie said, taking her last bite. The orange juice had already been sitting on the table. She reached over for her glass and began taking a gulp. That's when Algos realized his error. There were two glasses before he ever had gotten there.

She knew he was coming for her.

"NO!" he screamed, knocking the glass out of her hand, but it was too late. She already had enough in her system. She foamed at the mouth and seize before him.

His fury took hold, and he rushed to grab her by the shoulders. Algos turned her over, so the foam would escape her throat. "You will not die this way!" he shrieked, but it was too late. Angie was gone, and he didn't get to have the pleasure of being the one to do it. Algos continued to shake her violently from her shoulders and banged her limp head against the kitchen floor. "You don't get to choose!" he screamed out, but there was nothing more to be done.

Algos dropped her face first onto the floor and got up while wiping Angie's saliva and poison foam onto his jeans. Bitch. She wasn't supposed to take her own life. That was his given right! Algos angrily raided the house as quickly as possible, making it look like a home evasion. Then he walked out the front door and never looked back.

"Corbin," Algos whispered to himself at the memory of him taking his own life in the same manner. He briefly wondered if sacrificing souls were allowed in the dream realm, or if they simply went somewhere else. Algos would have to ask his oneironaut friend the next time they met. Better safe than sorry.

Five

T ina entered the antique store Sally had directed her to with a hint of hesitation. It was VERY off the grid, but Sally had assured her they would have exactly what she was looking for. A bell jingled as she opened the door to what looked like a small hut rather than a store from the outside.

"Hello?" Tina called out in a half whisper, but no one replied.

Shelves consumed the tiny space with many knickknacks, bottles with random colored liquid inside, and figurines that sent chills down Tina's spine.

"Can I help you?" asked an elderly woman from behind her. Tina jumped at the sound of her voice. "I'm sorry. I didn't mean to scare you," she quickly added.

"I'm just extra jumpy," Tina said with a weary smile.

"When are you due?" the woman asked her.

Tina's eyes widened, and she took a step back. "I'm sorry?" Tina asked.

"The baby. When are you due?" the woman asked as she moved some inventory around on the shelf behind her.

"How did you..." was all Tina got out before she got interrupted again.

"It's your aura," the woman replied simply. "It gives us all away, even when we're not showing."

Tina instinctively put a hand over her belly. "I'm not sure," she whispered.

"I would say 5-6 weeks along," the woman offered. "The heart is strong," she added with a warming smile.

Tina looked at her in amazement.

"I'm sorry, where are my manners?" the woman said, wiping her hands on her jeans and oversized t-shirt. "My name is Rebecca," she said softly. "And since you're here, I'm going to assume you need something specific," Rebecca announced as she gave Tina her hand.

"Tina," she said, taking Rebecca's hand. "And I need an authentic dream catcher."

"Your little one isn't in distress," Rebecca giggled. "But it's never a bad thing to be prepared," she added with a reassuring smile.

"It's not for the baby," Tina said, gaining her senses back. "It's for a friend."

Rebecca stopped to inspect Tina up and down thoroughly. "A dream catcher can be a powerful thing," she responded with hesitation.

"There's a powerful asshole trying to take over my friend," Tina said with determination. "We need all the help we can get."

"It may not work the way you think it might," Rebecca cautioned.

"I understand. But my friend is more like family, and I need to save my friend," Tina said with grit.

"Enough said, my friend," Rebecca replied, holding her hands up. "Family means everything. Now, let's get to saving yours."

Rebecca walked around the store collecting odds and ends before going back to get a black dream catcher.

"Black?" Tina asked.

"It's the power, elegance, and edginess that we need to get to her, and block the evil asshole from seeping in," Rebecca assured before thoroughly going through each item, how to activate the dream catcher, and the extra goodies she was giving Tina. She placed everything in a bag.

"How much do I owe you?" Tina asked her.

"Nothing," Rebecca said in all seriousness. "Your journey will not be an easy one. You need all the help you can get to beat Algos," she said, taking Tina's hands into her own.

"I didn't tell you his name," Tina said, yanking her hands back.

"You didn't have to, Warrior," Rebecca smiled. "He needs to be stopped. At all costs. Minus your little one, of course," she said with a wink. "Save Sophie. Save everyone," Rebecca added before shaking her head as if trying to clear it. Tina watched the woman's iris' change from bright blue to a hazel.

"Are you alright?" Tina asked with caution.

"Yes. Just a headache. Is this your bag?" she asked, noticing the bag on the counter.

"Yes," Tina answered, as confused as the lady before her seemed to be.

"I think I'm going to close up early. I'm not feeling well," the woman behind the counter said, placing a hand on her head.

"I hope you feel better," Tina offered, observing her. "Thanks again, Rebecca."

The woman looked back at her as if she had lost her mind.

"My name's Carol. Just come back if you need anything else." With that, the woman disappeared into the back.

"I can't even, right now," Tina said as she shook her head, grabbed the bag, and headed back to the hotel.

"What makes you so special?" asked Mario. "Besides knowing exactly how all this works," he quickly added as he stretched out on the couch in front of the fire.

"It was all just speculation until I got here, honestly," Corbin said with a shrug, and continued to read the book in his hand as he sat on the loveseat.

"Don't get me wrong," Mario started, "We're very grateful. I don't think I would ever be ready to tell that kid goodbye," he whispered.

"I know," Corbin said, putting his book down and paying more attention. "The theories were always out there about an in-between realm, which was a lot easier as a scientist to swallow than the unknown of heaven and hell."

"Do you think there's a heaven and hell?" asked Mario with curiosity.

Corbin leaned back to think about the question. "I think it's a hard thing to determine yes or no," he finally answered.

"The brain is still an unknown organ full of many surprises, but it's still studiable," he concluded. "Faith is in the beholder's eye. Science is the eye of the prover."

"You nerd guys," Mario chuckled and shook his head.

"Well, think about it," Corbin offered. "In your ops training, they taught you to manipulate someone's thinking to get to an end goal, right?"

"I think this is different," Mario laughed.

"Not really if you think about it," Corbin smiled. "It's just the bonus of manipulating in a different way. But that's why there are rules. Even the brain has its limits. Doing it the wrong way causes the host to have a seizure and possibly die. That's why you create a door. A sort of 'permission' if you will, for the host to allow you to enter. It's an acceptance on both sides. Only giving them the limited help assists them in finding what they need in the way the best suits them. No harm, no foul."

"Well, I'm glad you could get Jack and Jess here," Mario said, nodding. "Sophie needed them still."

Corbin thought about the day that Jack and Jess came to him. He told them right off the bat that he was just a student of the theory. Not a teacher of how to make it successful. That was when Jack and Jess told him of Algos, and what the madman had intended on accomplishing if he found the right person to show him how. They showed him a picture of Sophie, the daughter that would be at the greatest risk should he succeed. Corbin had apologized and told them he couldn't help. He held the door open and watched the distraught parents walk out of his office. But the thought continued to poke at him like a burning ember, giving him a sleepless night.

Someone genetically altered Sophie against her will through Jess, and now she was going to lose her parents to a psychopath with no way of fighting back at nine years old. Corbin didn't have children of his own yet, but he was positive that he couldn't live with himself, knowing what her fate was to be without his help.

It was 4 am when Corbin called Jack Harris back. "It's not a guarantee, but let's do this!" he said into the phone with eagerness. It took less than a year for the Harris' to master controlling their lucid dreams, and how to navigate once they got to the other side. Corbin monitored them while they slept, and they explained what they experienced once they woke. It would take trial and error to determine the best way to navigate once they were there.

"Did you know there was a council?" Mario asked, bringing Corbin back to the present.

"No. That was a surprise for sure," Corbin said, heading back into deep thought. "But it makes sense. No matter what 'realm' or 'plane' you are on, it would always require balance like any other ecosystem. Without balance, things collapse."

"So, why does everyone have different 'abilities' here?" asked Mario.

"Each person has a unique genetic makeup, much like fingerprints," Corbin explained. "Their skills, talents, and energy are all unique. Those things never leave us. They just take a unique form, much like ourselves," he added with pride.

"Then what all can you do?" Mario asked eagerly.

"We're going to find out, my friend," Corbin said with a mischievous smile.

Sophie moved another piece forward, but before she could even speak, Eddie answered, "No, and you know it."

"I didn't even say anything!" Sophie protested.

"You didn't have to," Eddie said with a frown. "We've been doing this for a while now, and you're only making safe moves. Safe won't save anyone at this point."

"Well, I can't exactly walk in alone, now can I?" she retorted.

"Can't you?" he asked her with a hint of excitement.

"You're mad," Sophie said, shaking her head feverishly.

A wicked female laughter broke their banter like a glass shattering onto the floor.

Sophie's eyes widened as she tried to swallow the lump suddenly lodged in her throat. "What the hell is that?" Sophie hissed.

"I don't know, but it doesn't sound good," Eddie responded with a hint of fear in his voice.

"S.O.P.H.I.E..." the voice sang. It sounded oddly familiar, but Sophie couldn't place it. All she knew was that it wasn't Clarice.

"Eddie," Sophie breathed, "if we're in my mind, then who the heck is that?"

"You tell me," he replied, with the terror in his voice betraying him.

Sophie twisted in the chair to see what was hiding in the shadows behind her. She gasped immediately. Across from where they were playing chess was a single metal folding chair. On it sat Sophie, herself, in a blood red ops uniform and her old jet black hair color. She sat posed with her legs crossed and her hands clasped on her knee. When she looked Sophie in her eyes, there was no color. Simply black dilated pupils, and a grin that sent shivers down Sophie's spine. She cocked her head to inspect Sophie as she slowly stood up from the chair.

"Don't," Eddie pleaded as he grabbed her hand.

"Chess is such a child's game," cooed the other Sophie. "How about we play a different game?" she taunted.

"Sophie. Don't," Eddie ordered.

"What did you have in mind?" Sophie asked calmly, as she tried to assess what exactly she was dealing with.

"The best kind," the other Sophie said sweetly. "A battle to the death."

Sophie fought to keep the bile out of her throat and the panic attack that threatened to consume her.

"And what are you supposed to be?" Sophie asked her, trying to distract them both until she got grounded.

The evil twin tossed her head back and cackled like a hyena. After what seemed like a lifetime, she finally replied, "Why, you, of course." She paused dramatically before continuing. "Without inhibitions, just like granddaddy likes us. I'm you, when everything is stripped away, and he has control like destiny dictates."

The darkness closed in. Everything around Sophie spun around her faster than a merry-go-round, when they all heard a male voice boom, "No!"

The ground shook. The chess pieces fell to the floor, and Eddie grabbed onto the table before him. Sophie's evil twin grabbed the chair she had been sitting on, and original Sophie fell out of her chair and stumbled back, trying desperately to find her footing.

A massive wooden door opened to the left of her, and a cloaked figure grabbed her by the wrist and dragged her towards the door. Sophie's twin was furious, but unable to follow. Sophie couldn't take her eyes off of the version of her that was controlled by the man with the cane.

When the door slammed in front of her, there was still a small window to watch what was happening on the other side. The evil twin screamed at the top of her lungs, and the door vibrated from the power she exhaled. Eddie just broke up into puzzle pieces and floated into the darkness, leaving her evil twin to fume with anger on the other side of the door.

"Where are we?" the cloaked figure demanded.

"My mind," Sophie whispered, as she watched a very pissed off version of herself pace outside the door like an animal waiting out its prey.

"No, where are we now?" he demanded as he tightened his grip on her wrist.

Sophie looked down just in time to see a skeletal hand turn to flesh. When he continued to squeeze her wrist, she forced her eyes to look around.

"A library?" she answered in more of a question.

"I need to know where we are. Exactly," he insisted.

"Your guess is as good as mine," Sophie retorted, yanking her wrist away before he broke it.

The cloaked figure let out a heavy sigh. "Please look around and tell me where we are," he offered more gently.

Sophie glared at the figure and rubbed her sore wrist before looking around. Man, was everyone bossy inside her head. She would have to work on that, she thought, giving herself a mental note. Just then, a royal blue book appeared in her hand. It read *Mental Notes.* She dropped it instantly.

"You have got to be kidding me," she mumbled.

"Where are we, Sophie?" the cloaked figure asked impatiently.

"Because I remember everything I hear, see, touch, whatever, I always divided them in my head," Sophie muttered. "Apparently, this is my library of everything I have ever come across."

"Interesting," he replied in awe.

"And who are you supposed to be?" she asked the cloaked figure as he took inventory of every knowledge Sophie had ever absorbed.

"I'm the lead council of Death," he replied, distracted as he continued to take inventory of their surroundings.

"I'm sorry, what?" Sophie asked, completely confused.

He picked up a sherbet orange book and began flipping through the pages. "I control the dream realm your parents live in," he said casually as he took in whatever the orange book was offering.

"Great! You can take us back there! I really need to get back," Sophie said as hope filled her heart again.

"Not exactly," he responded with no follow up.

Sophie walked over and yanked the book out of his hand.

"What do you mean, 'not exactly'?" she demanded.

The cloaked figure let out another dramatic sigh before walking over to pick out a different book. "The only reason I'm here is because I have more power than the others, and you drew me in," he said, picking out a red book to investigate its contents.

Sophie grew angry. He was neither forthcoming nor helpful. "Well, how did I do it, so we can reverse it?" she asked through a clenched jaw.

The cloaked figure paused from reading the book and looked up at the ceiling in thought. "I'm not really sure," was his only answer.

"Well, you're extremely helpful," Sophie growled under her breath.

He smirked and went back to reading the book. Sophie walked back over to the door and stared at the deranged version of herself waiting on the other side.

"I guess we have to go out then," she said to herself more than him.

"No!" he yelled and caused the ground beneath her to shake.

"Knock it off!" she yelled back as she grabbed the door for balance.

"Sorry," he said more softly after a beat. "We can't go out that way."

"Why not?" Sophie demanded, with her hands on her hips and her back to the door.

"You're not supposed to collide," he shrugged and went back to reading the red book.

Sophie grabbed the first book within reach and threw it at the cloaked figure, who ducked immediately and missed the attack. He tilted his head to study her.

"Why?" he asked in confusion.

"Because I need to get out of here and you're of NO USE!" she yelled back, making the walls quiver around them.

"Sophie, calm down," he begged. "Your emotions effect our survival in here. Just take a breath," he pleaded.

Sophie took a deep, controlled breath before glaring at the black figure before her. "Please stop being so annoying," she mumbled.

"I don't mean to be," he offered in a softer tone.

Sophie felt guilty for her outburst. "I'm sure. I'm sorry. I'm just really having a rough day," she sighed. "It's not every day you find out your blood comes from a psychopath,"

Sophie moaned.

"He's not your only blood," he grumbled.

"Yeah, I know. My parents are exceptional, but it's still a lot to digest," Sophie said as she looked back out the window at the psychopathic version of herself that continued to pace like a ravenous animal outside.

"No, I mean, the reason I got pulled in here is that he's not your only blood," the cloaked figure repeated.

"What?" Sophie said, as she turned to look at him.

The cloaked figure exhaled loudly before removing his hood. The man before her looked like what she imagined her dad would look like if he ever aged. "He's not your only grandfather," he said cautiously.

Sophie's brain couldn't take any more surprises, and she felt him catch her before she hit the ground, but she was too busy shutting down into a deep sleep to stop herself from falling.

Six

Clarice opened her eyes slowly. She was half relieved to see the ceiling of her room. What the heck was going on? She slowly sat up and put her bare feet on the cold cement floor. Her warm body welcomed the chill of the cool floor. Flashes of Corbin appeared before her eyes.

"Go away," she mumbled.

The request was granted, and her eyes focused once more. She slowly looked around the room and noticed the cup of tea on her desk. Clarice tilted her head in speculation.

When she stood up, her legs wobbled beneath her. Clarice stumbled to the desk and quickly took a seat in the cold metal folding chair. Next to the tea was a note.

"Drink this. It should help. No. It's not poisoned." -Your Favorite Troll

What was Eddie up to? And why was he being so nice suddenly? She leaned down and sniffing the brown liquid, but most poisons didn't contain a scent. Clarice knew from personal experience.

"Drink it," she heard Corbin's voice inside her head.

"Yeah, cause that's going to convince me," she snapped to no one.

"Drink it," she heard him say more sternly.

"I will not let you kill me," Clarice retorted.

"I'm not your father," she heard him declare back to her.

She grimaced, but knew he was right. After much hesitation, Clarice put the cup to her lips and drank. She felt better instantly.

"See," she heard him say.

"Don't get cocky," Clarice growled. "And go away." Although she wasn't sure she really meant it.

"See you around, Slick," she heard him say.

The silence was deafening and unwanted. Clarice continued to drink the tea and tried to force her head to focus when her heart seemed oddly cluttered.

James sat next to the bed in a chair, holding Sophie's hand like he had done so many times since they had met. "Come find me," he whispered to her, squeezing her hand.

Ben watched silently from the other side of the room. He wasn't concerned that his friend was begging the love of his life to come back. Ben was concerned that James didn't even flinch when Ben's phone rang. He stared at it, unsure of what to do.

"You should probably answer it," James said over his shoulder, never taking his eyes off of Sophie.

Ben frowned, but grabbed the phone and hit the answer button.

"Is it true?" he heard Roger's distressed voice on the other side.

"Dr. Moore?" Ben asked, confused.

"Is she unconscious?" Roger asked.

"Yes, Sir," Ben confirmed.

"Her vitals?" Roger asked.

Ben hesitated. "Very low," he whispered. "But that's all I can monitor without equipment," he replied guiltily.

"Where are you?" Roger demanded.

"Bakersfield, CA," Ben replied.

"I'm going to send you coordinates. I need you to take her there," Roger insisted.

"She's solid as a rock. I'm not sure moving her is the best option," Ben replied, concerned.

"You're sitting ducks in a hotel, Son. We've got to move her. We don't have a choice. I will send you coordinates. Just get her there. I'll be joining you shortly," he ordered.

"If more of us are together, it will just give him a faster way of finding us," Ben argued. "Finding her."

"We'll be off the grid. This is more important," was Roger's final demand before he hung up the phone.

74

Ben stared at the phone in his hand as if it was going to self-destruct any second.

"Dad?" James asked, semi-sarcastically.

"Yeah," Ben answered, confused.

"Ben, what does he want?" James asked sternly, bringing Ben's attention back to his friend.

"We have to move her," he replied with desperate concern.

"No," James replied defiantly.

"Bro, we don't have a choice," Ben whispered. "We can't take her to the hospital, and we need to keep her safe. That's what you're supposed to do, right? Keep her safe?" he added for good measure.

James looked at his friend and the woman that he loved. "What if we hurt her?" he whispered softly.

"Moving her will not hurt her physically, or mentally. But staying here may cost her both," Ben answered in his doctor's voice. "We just need to figure out how."

James removed one of his hands from holding Sophie's, pulling out his wallet in his back pocket. He pulled out the solid black business card with only a phone number typed in silver on it. He tossed it to Ben and went back to hold on to Sophie with both hands.

"It's time to call some friends," James declared, staring at Sophie.

"Who's number is this?" Ben asked with apprehension.

"The only other person alive that loves her as much as I do," James replied, never taking his eyes off of Sophie.

Ben picked up the black business card and stared at the only writing on the card with great hesitation.

"Call it," James ordered over his shoulder.

Ben sighed and dialed the number.

"Hello?" he heard a very confused man answer on the other end. The voice sounded familiar, but Ben couldn't place it.

"Hello," Ben said with less conviction. "I'm calling about Sophie," he said in more of a question than a comment.

"Where is she?" the man demanded on the other side.

"We're in Bakersfield, CA. But we need to move her, and we need help," Ben replied.

"What's wrong with her?" the man asked in terror.

"She's unconscious and not waking up," Ben said uncomfortably, giving a stranger so much information.

"Her vitals?" he commanded.

"Low," Ben replied, feeling a little better that he might be talking to a medical professional.

"We'll be there tonight," the man announced before hanging up.

"We?" Ben asked to the dial tone. He took the phone away from his ear. "James?" he asked his friend. "Who's coming?"

"The calvary," was James' only reply.

Tina grabbed her phone when she felt it vibrate in her pocket.

You're going to move her. We'll be there soon. -Sally

With her head swimming in confusion, Tina put the phone back in her pocket and held onto the bag in her lap as she watched the scenery pass her by from the bus window. Tina kept replaying Rebecca's words over and over in her head as she tried to solve the puzzle. Rebecca wasn't the woman that stood behind the counter at the end of their conversation, which only concerned Tina even more.

She was quite used to things not being "normal" since Sophie entered their lives. However, it gave her little comfort knowing there was yet another player in the game. One that seemed to have great "abilities" to reach the living, and the one person they could ask who this Rebecca might be was unconscious. Tina started to despise the thing she loved most...puzzles.

She grew overwhelmingly tired and laid her head back to "rest her eyes". She didn't expect what was to come next.

Sophie opened her eyes, but found herself in blackness again. No library. No cloaked figure. She was just lying on the ground that didn't seem to exist.

"Hello?" she heard Tina's voice call out.

"Tina?" Sophie called back.

"Sophie?" she heard her friend cry out with some relief as she suddenly appeared before her.

"Tina!" Sophie cried out and ran towards her friend, but slammed into an invisible wall and stumbled back.

"Sophie!" Tina cried out, but was greeted by the same invisible wall once she got close to her. "Where are we?" she asked in sudden panic.

"I don't know," Sophie said, rubbing her head from the collision.

"Sophie, we need you to wake up," Tina said with great urgency.

"I know. I'm trying," Sophie replied. Her voice was sharp and animalistic.

"Are you okay?" Tina asked her. Something wasn't right.

Sophie broke out in a hysterical laughter.

"Sophie?" Tina asked, swallowing the lump in her throat. Something was very wrong. When her eyes focused, she quickly realized that Sophie didn't look like Sophie at all. She had her original short black bob and was wearing a red leather suit.

"Well, you're half right," the girl before her cackled.

"Who are you?" Tina commanded.

"I'm still her. Just the better version of her," the girl snarled.

"Something tells me otherwise," Tina said, suddenly glaring at the girl before her.

The Sophie copycat tilted her head and studied Tina like a wild animal stalking her prey. "Aren't you the interesting one?" she purred.

"What the hell do you want?" Tina demanded.

"Oh, I'll get what I want. But apparently not this way," the girl said, waving her hand in the air. Tina woke up with a gasp.

"Are you kidding me?" she yelled out loud. Everyone on the bus turned to stare at her.

Once the bus came to a stop, Tina quickly got off and ran the rest of the way back to the hotel.

"Sophie!" she heard her name being called by a semi-familiar voice.

"Come find me," she heard James's voice whisper in her head.

"James," she murmured back, but when she opened her eyes, she found herself in the library of her memories, and an older version of her father staring at her with great concern.

"Sophie," he whispered out his relief.

Sophie put a hand to her swimming head as she tried to sit up. "What happened?" she asked in confusion.

"You passed out," he said, helping her sit up on the couch that turned up.

"Well, it's been a long day," Sophie mumbled in protest.

There was a long, awkward pause. The man got up and went to browse the books to give her some space. Sophie watched him in a mixture of frustration and confusion.

"So you're my dad's dad?" she asked, finally breaking the ice.

"Yes," he said, looking at her, impressed.

"You look just like him," she confirmed, knowing his question. "What am I supposed to call you?" Sophie asked slowly.

"My name is John," he said with hesitation.

"How long have you been, well, here?" Sophie asked.

"I'm not sure. Time is different in your mind than in my world," he replied.

"No, I mean, how long have you been dead?" Sophie asked, clarifying. He was very literal.

"Oh. Jack was in college, I think," John replied, deep in thought. "Time works differently in my realm," he said with a shrug.

Sophie tilted her head to study John. "Do you talk to him?" Sophie asked.

"No," John answered firmly. "It's against the rules."

Sophie shook her head. "What?" she asked.

"I'm head of the council. We don't interact with those among us. There would be no order," he said simply.

"So, you've been in the same realm and never spoken in over ten years?" Sophie asked as fury built up.

"Has it been that long?" John asked with interest.

"Yes!" Sophie blurted out.

"Huh," was the only response she got.

"You're infuriating," Sophie mumbled.

"Am I?" he asked in surprise.

"Yes!" she replied.

"I don't mean to be," John commented with a hint of sorrow. "I guess they have disconnected me for too long," he said as he looked up, deep in thought.

"Let me guess, you were some sort of doctor?" Sophie asked sarcastically.

"A scientist," John announced with pride.

"Like dad?" Sophie asked.

"He was a scientist?" John asked in surprise.

"Yes," Sophie replied, suddenly realizing that John had been out of the picture longer than Sophie even knew. "He was a great one, too," she added with pride.

"Fascinating," John said with a smile.

Sophie paused and took a deep breath. "How did you die?" she asked finally.

John looked around as if trying to pull his own memories from the surrounding books. "I was driving," he drawled. "He was playing at a concert. Trumpet, I think."

"Were you in an accident?" Sophie asked, suddenly realizing that she knew nothing about her grandparents. Any of them.

"I stepped on the brakes," John continued, deep in thought. "But they didn't work."

Sophie's eyes widened as she tried to catch her breath. "Like they were cut?" she asked.

"Possibly," John replied slowly. "I think the car slid off to the side. Into a tree."

"How awful!" Sophie exclaimed.

John dropped the book he was holding and grabbed onto the bookcase next to him. Sophie jumped up to be by his side.

"A man came by," John whispered so softly she barely heard him. "But he wouldn't help me." Sophie's stomach dropped, guessing she already knew the rest of this story.

"He poured gasoline over the car and set it on fire. I couldn't get out," John said, looking at Sophie in panic. "My legs were broken, and he left me to burn."

"Algos," Sophie growled.

"Yes," John whispered. "I didn't remember until now." Water filled his eyes and it flooded him with emotions he hadn't felt in years.

"I'm sorry," Sophie whispered with guilt.

"Sophie, we need to get out of here," John said in distress.

"I know," she said, looking around for an exit.

"No," he said, turning to her and clinging to her. "Time is not the same here. And the longer we stay, the more you get lost. You will get trapped here. Forever! We both will!" John cried out in horror.

Sophie's heart jumped to her throat. "Forever?" she asked in a whisper.

"Yes," he confirmed.

"How do we get out of here?" she asked with sudden determination.

"Only you know the answer," John said, looking at her with sorrow.

"But I don't!" Sophie shouted in frustration. The walls shook, and some books fell from the shelves.

"Calm down!" John ordered. "Remember, your emotions control this environment. If you keep losing it, you'll crush us both and we'll die in here."

Sophie stopped to take a deep breath, when a thought suddenly came to mind.

"Aren't you already dead?" Sophie asked before she broke into a giggle. She did not know what had come over her, but she couldn't stop it. John shortly followed in her giggle fest.

"Technically," John answered with a smile.

"So, how do I figure out how to get out of here?" Sophie asked more seriously.

"Well, we're here for a reason. Maybe the answer lies in here?" John suggested.

"Then let's get to work," Sophie said with great determination She walked up to a bookcase and began scanning its contents. "John," she added softly. He looked up from the book he was holding. "I think you're my favorite grandfather," Sophie said over her shoulder with her Cheshire grin.

"Good to know," he chuckled, thankful to know she was finally remembering the light she held along with the dark before he went back to studying the book in his hand. *Mario.* He had a lot to learn about his granddaughter before he would forget her all over again, but she didn't need to know it.

"Are you ready?" Jack asked his wife.

"I was born ready," Jess said with her determined smile. She closed her eyes and took a deep breath in and out before she went searching for Algo's unconsciousness.

She lucked out. He was actually sleeping, which would make this easier. Jess created the door before her. She knew he wouldn't enter. She would have to break the rule to open it herself. Jess took another deep breath before reaching out and opening the door before her.

Algos was sitting at his desk, looking over some paperwork. He didn't hear her enter. He didn't sense her coming.

"Hello, Daddy," Jess said with no emotion. He would not see the adult version of her. Only the teenage version she wanted him to see.

"The prodigal child returns," Algos sneered as he looked up.

"Not exactly," Jess said, strolling in his direction.

"Then what do you want?" Algos snapped.

"I want you to let me go," Jess whispered.

"Let you go?" Algos replied, throwing his head back in a cheeky laugh.

"Please, Daddy. I'm tired," Jess said sadly, as she played the part.

"I didn't raise you to be weak," Algos growled.

"Even the mighty have to rest," she begged him. "You promised!"

"I lied," he said with a shrug.

"You never lie to me," Jess said, using the trigger words. She watched him pause and lay the papers down before him. "You always said I earned the right to be your favorite. Have I not earned the right to rest?"

He looked at her with great curiosity.

"Why would you leave me?" Algos asked, curious about the answer.

She knew she had him.

"Every child needs to spread their wings," Jess replied with a hint of sorrow.

"Clarice never leaves," he countered.

Jess fought hard to control her anger, that was boiling deep within.

"We're not talking about her, we're talking about me," she disputed.

Algos sat back in his chair and crossed his arms as he stared her up and down. "You're too valuable to give up," he replied with simplicity.

"Isn't a daughter always too valuable to her father?" Jess asked curiously.

"Nice try," he sneered and went back to looking at the papers before him.

"Why can't you love us like a normal father?" she huffed like the teenage version she knew he was seeing.

"I'm not a normal father," Algos replied coldly.

"I'm well aware," she growled. "Which is why I don't like you very much," Jess said, before turning on her heels and storming back through the door she had created.

He watched her leave and, oddly, felt nothing. Why was he so different? She was special to him, but not in a way she understood. Why couldn't he pretend to at least try to give her what she wanted. He shook the irritation from his head and went back to studying the papers before him.

Jess opened her eyes and found her husband eagerly studying her. "Are you okay?" he asked softly.

"Let the games begin," she said with a triumphant smile.

Seven

T ina burst through the hotel door and doubled over to catch her breath as she slammed it shut behind her. Ben rushed to her side. "You okay?" he asked her impatiently, waiting for her to catch her breath.

"We need to get out of here," Tina said, even though she already knew it didn't matter where they went. The war wasn't on their playing field.

"We're working on it," Ben told her assuredly, as he took her bag and led her to a chair. "You were gone for a long time," he said in concern. Tina hadn't realized how dark it had gotten outside.

"It took a while to find the right store," she replied honestly. Tina looked over at James, before turning back to her husband and mouthing, "We need to talk".

Right on cue, there was a light knock on the door. Everyone turned to stare at it. Another, more forceful, knock came. No one moved.

"Open the door," demanded the voice that Ben recognized from his earlier phone call.

Ben let go of his wife to go open the door.

"Don't," Tina hissed, but he ignored her.

Ben opened the door to find a tall slender woman with grey hair past her waist pulled back in a ponytail, wearing jeans and a t-shirt with a large skull on the front of it. Next to her was standing a gigantic man with a grey beard and mustache, with gold earrings and a bandana with thinning long grey wavy hair. His black leather jacket was tight, but was a cover for the matching black t-shirt with a large skull. It was Donna and Cecil, the leaders of Mario's old biker gang.

"Where is she?" Donna demanded, as she pushed past Ben. She stopped at the sight of James holding on for dear life to the unmoving Sophie.

"Oh, Kid," whispered Cecil as he, too, pushed past Ben.

"Was this from the testing?" she demanded as she glared at everyone in the tiny hotel room.

"No," whispered James. "Algos," was all he could get out.

"No," gasped Cecil.

"He doesn't have her," Tina clarified. "He tried, but Jack pushed her back to us. She woke up to tell us who he was, and then turned into this," she said, nodding in her friend's direction.

"We need to get her out of here," Donna whispered.

"Do you have the location?" Cecil asked Ben.

"Yes," Ben replied in unease.

"Relax, Stud. We already had the heads up," he said, putting a heavy hand on Ben's shoulder. "Let me see the phone."

"Who told you?" Tina asked in curiosity.

"You're not the only ones the dead visit," Donna said with a weary smile. "We've been planning for this since she was little. We just didn't think it would be under these circumstances," Donna said, looking solemnly over at Sophie.

"Can you help her?" Tina asked.

"We can keep her safe," Donna replied. "This battle is hers to fight," she added in frustration.

"Grab your stuff. We're getting out of here," Cecil ordered. He walked over to where James held onto Sophie's hand. "I need you to let go," he whispered as he placed his hand on James's shoulder. "Just until we get her into the van," he added, knowing what the young man was struggling with.

James looked at Cecil with a blank stare, but nodded. Cecil bent down and picked up Sophie's body into his arms. A tear escaped his eye as he felt how weakened she had become. Cecil gave a not-so-subtle cough to clear his throat before going over to the window. Donna opened it, and Cecil carefully carried Sophie outside and down the fire escape. James went to follow, but Donna stopped him.

"You need to go out the front and check out," she said in her motherly voice. "It needs to look like everything is normal," Donna added.

James looked out the window and watched as Cecil took the utmost care to put Sophie into the black van as Daryl, the biggest biker in the crew with a shirt too tight to cover his bulging tattooed muscles, supervised and kept watch. With his long jet black hair and beard to match, it would be hard to mistake him for someone to mess with. Only the crew had met him before and already knew he was the world's biggest teddy bear when needed, and smarter than anyone would guess.

James looked at Donna with hallow eyes and nodded before grabbing his stuff and heading for the door. "Meet you in the alley in 10," he replied as he headed downstairs to walk around the block and double back without being followed.

"I'll go check out," Tina said. She kissed Ben and left him with Donna as she made her way to the front desk. She grabbed her most recent collection of supplies from the table before she left.

"Her vitals?" Donna asked, as she watched from the window.

"Low," Ben whispered in sorrow. "But her muscles flinch, so I know she's moving around. Wherever she is."

"We got the equipment Roger requested. He will meet us there," Donna informed him over her shoulder. "Do you know how to monitor her brain?" she asked, suddenly looking at him.

"Yes, Ma'am," he replied in his best doctor's voice.

"Good," Donna said, giving him a weak smile. "Something tells me the battle is going to have to be won there first."

"Do you think she's stuck in her own mind?" Ben asked her, looking for answers.

"I think she has a lot to settle before she'll find her way back to us," Donna replied regretfully, as she turned back to watch the van. "But we'll keep her safe in the meantime."

"We're running out of time," Ben whispered, eager to let someone else know the truth.

"I know," Donna sighed. "But if anyone can do it, it's our Sophie."

"I hope you're right," Ben whispered as he grabbed his things and walked out the door.

"Me, too," Donna whispered. "Me, too."

She took a few minutes to make sure no prints or evidence of their presence remained, or any clues that might point to where they were going. Her girl needed all the help she could get. And Donna was going to give her everything she had. Even her life, if it came to it.

Clarice stormed into the lab like hell on wheels. "Where is she?" she demanded.

"We're still looking, Ma'am," announced a new eager red-headed, freckled girl. She reminded Clarice of Jess, but it would not deter her from her mission.

"She was last seen in Albuquerque," Eddie replied dryly over his shoulder as he continued to scan the computer screens on the wall ahead of him.

Clarice already had an ace up her sleeve. Something only she knew about, but she still had to the play the part until Sophie was hand delivered as promised. "Taking you awfully long, isn't it, Pet?" she sneered.

Eddie rolled his eyes and ignored her. He was already regretting being nice to her and getting her some tea to help with the aftereffects of her recent "journey". Eddie knew there was still good in

Clarice. It just had been long ago diminished by Algos. A shame. When Clarice put her mind to something, it was definitely taken care of. A skill that came in handy during war.

"I don't see you helping," he simply retorted back.

"My job isn't to locate her," Clarice said in a warning tone before turning on her heels and heading to the training room. If Eddie didn't do his job soon, she would have to step in. But in the meantime, she could sharpen her skills as she waited.

Clarice wrapped her hands and prepared to attack the bag when her eyelids fell heavily over her eyes, and she staggered to the wall to slide down it before she fell flat on her face.

When she opened her eyes again, there was a large wooden door in front of her.

"Bug off! I have things to do!" she screamed out to no one.

"Open it," she heard Jess warn her.

There were really only two people who could make Clarice do anything. Unfortunately for Clarice, Jess was one of them. She sighed heavily before reaching out to open the door.

Light flooded her eyes instantly, and Clarice covered them quickly to take some of the sting from the brightness away.

"Hey, Clare Bear," said Jess as she stepped into the light and provided Clarice with the shade she needed to allow her eyes to adjust.

"Don't call me that," growled Clarice. Jess just smiled her ornery smile. The smile that told Clarice she wouldn't be stopping any time soon. "What do you want?" Clarice demanded.

"Nothing," Jess replied with a shrug. She reached out in front of her and grabbed Clarice by the hand as she pulled her further into the room.

"Yeah, right," Clarice mumbled. Jess' hair was pulled back into a ponytail. A sign that she was in "play mode". She was in her usual jean shorts, t-shirt, and tennis shoes. Just as Clarice had always remembered.

"I'm not in the mood for your games," Clarice declared loudly.

"I don't want to play games, Sis," Jess replied as she walked over and sat on the swing set that appeared out of nowhere. Clarice watched her carefully, but also with curiosity. Where was this going?

"Do you think she knew?" Jess asked softly, as she swung back and forth slightly on the swing.

Clarice hesitated. "Who?" she asked, finally taking the bait.

"Mom," Jess answered, with sorrow in her voice.

"Know what?" Clarice asked, taken aback.

"What he was," Jess clarified. "What he did to us."

Clarice felt something on the inside. She didn't know what exactly, but she didn't like it. She was in danger when she let her guard down. Clarice learned at an early age that in order to survive, she needed to feel nothing, just like her father. However, Clarice rarely felt nothing at all like he did.

She sighed heavily and walked over to sit down next to her sister. "They fought a ton right before...." Clarice offered, unable to finish the sentence.

"I don't remember very much," Jess confessed.

"I remember enough," Clarice mumbled as she matched Jess' rhythm on the swing. "She wanted him to be better," Clarice said, more to herself.

"I know you saw it happen," Jess said as she continued to swing, not looking her sister in the eye.

92

"She wasn't his first. She wouldn't be the last," Clarice shrugged. "But she did what she could, I guess, considering," she added, not looking Jess in the eye.

"I'm sorry I couldn't save you," Jess whispered as they continued to swing in time.

"I don't think I'm meant to be saved," Clarice replied flatly.

"She died fighting for us. For you," Jess tried to remind her.

"Yeah, and look where it got her," Clarice retorted bitterly. "Where it got us? He took out Andrew without a flinch. Our own brother, just gone. All because he cried too much when he was sick at three-years-old. You really think her life meant anything to him?" she screeched as she shook her head.

"Andrew," Jess whispered the forgotten name.

"Do you not remember what happened to your stupid dog?" Clarice retorted.

"Mickey," Jess murmured.

"Although I agree with that one. That dog wouldn't shut up," Clarice replied, rolling her eyes.

"He was barking because someone was too close to the house!" Jess yelled in defense. "He trained him to protect us, then got pissed when he did and kicked him to death!" Anger grew within Jess as her eyes turned gold from the emotional fury that brewed within. She looked at Clarice, mad as hell.

"Yeah, well, getting mad about it now doesn't do much good, does it?" Clarice asked. Partially because it was true, and partially because the look on Jess' face brought her great discomfort.

"Why stay?" Jess asked, as she blinked her fury away.

"I lost the chance," Clarice mumbled, as she continued to swing and went back to looking into the darkness before her.

Jess stopped swinging. She knew her sister was good deep down. It might be immensely buried, but it was there. "When?" Jess asked, in shock.

"Doesn't matter," Clarice said, jumping off the swing. "Are we done? Because I have things to do," she said, not showing any emotion other than irritation.

"Like go after my daughter?" Jess asked.

"Relax," Clarice said with a frown. "We haven't found her, yet." She knew that's what Jess needed to hear. Clarice just wasn't sure why she felt she needed to give it to her.

"I know," Jess said, looking down at the ground.

Clarice tilted her head to study her sister. "You don't know where she is, do you?" she asked in sudden interest.

"What will you do when you find her?" Jess asked, quickly changing the subject.

"Give her to dad. Maybe buy my freedom," Clarice said with a shrug.

"You'll never be free," Jess said, staring down her sister with a frown.

"I don't mind paying this price," Clarice said with a wicked smile and a wink.

"He'll destroy her and everything else," Jess growled, trying to hold back her fury.

"It's not my concern," Clarice said casually as she tossed her hair back and walked away.

"Isn't it?" Jess warned. "What if she was yours?"

"She's not," Clarice yelled over her shoulder as she put space between her sister and herself as she looked for the door. "Let me out," Clarice demanded.

"She's got as much of you as she does me in her," Jess pleaded. "Doesn't that make her worth saving?"

"Nope," Clarice shouted over her shoulder as she continued to look for an exit. "Let me out," she added with more force.

"Go," Jess called after her. "But remember, you carry the same blood. Mother fought for us. She fought for YOU. Shouldn't you return the favor?"

With a wave of her hand, Jess gave Clarice the exit she needed. "Blood means nothing in this family. You, of all people, should know that," Clarice retorted before she yanked open the door and woke up gasping for air.

She looked wildly around the room, but found herself alone in the training room where she had started. Blood meant nothing to anyone in this family besides Jess. And she was gone. Their mother made stupid choices and fought with a man who didn't care if she lived or died. Jess would be the only one he ever cared for, even a little.

Jess. The daughter who argued and didn't obey or stay loyal. The daughter who got herself murdered because she wanted a life outside of his plans. The daughter who found love, and gave birth to a creature that would give him everything he ever wanted. If he could catch her and screw her up like he did them. That feeling stirred within her again, and she yelled out her frustration.

Algos sat in his big leather chair behind his wooden desk, distracted. Yes, he told the disgruntled council members he would take out their leader and they would rule together, but even death appeared to be manipulative. Algos had no intention of ruling with anyone else other than himself. They would come to learn that soon enough. However, for his plan to be in full effect, he needed to find his granddaughter. ASAP.

Funny. Usually the family was nothing but a disappointment for him. From his own parents, to his wife, to his children. Who knew that it would be his granddaughter that would finally fulfill his prophecy. Algos just had to find her. Eddie was searching for her physical body, but he suspected it would be the mental side of Sophie that he would need to locate first, which meant he had to find out where she was hiding in the stupid dream realm.

"Charles!" Algos yelled, deep in thought.

His trusty servant came out from the shadows that he seemed to hide in regularly. "Yes, Sir?" Charles answered.

"Send a message to Bates. I need him to do me another favor," Algos barked his demand.

"Very well, Sir," Charles answered with a bow before shuffling back into the shadows.

Algos bent over and began scribbling notes feverishly in front of him, when a vision of his dead wife flashed before his eyes. He froze immediately. Then he saw her again. It was the vision of the first time they met.

Despite having several degrees already, thanks to the asylum, Algos still liked to peruse the local college campus. Mostly because there were test subjects eager to make a few extra bucks to get them through their expensive college years. That's when he saw her. Interesting, he thought to himself as he glided over to his next prey.

"Go away, I'm not interested," she said, without taking her bright blue eyes off the book.

He stopped in his tracks. This was not the usual response he got when he came up to women. They were usually eager to eat up his charm. Well, at least until he had them tied to a metal table and watched the life exit their eyes.

"Who said I had anything to offer?" Algos asked, intrigued.

"You all do, and I'm not interested. I don't care what you have to offer, I prefer my book. Please and thank you," she replied.

Algos sat down anyway. He studied her as much as the book she held. "What's that about?" he asked, nodding towards the book.

"You can find it in the library. Go check it out and find out," she retorted as she continued to read.

"Nah. I'd rather hear it from you," Algos replied in his best charming voice.

She rolled her eyes and sighed deeply before putting the book down to look at the irritation that wouldn't go away.

"Fine. What do you have to offer, so I can turn you down and get back to my book?" she asked bitterly.

"I like thrillers, and I don't remember seeing that on the list," Algos answered with a shrug and smile.

"Again, it's in the library. Go read it for yourself," she snapped and went back to reading.

"Okay," he announced before getting up and heading straight for the library that was right across from her seat. She took a second to peek over the top of her book, shook her head, and went back to reading. Within minutes, he came out and sat next to her again. This time, he pulled out the same book and began with page one.

She tried to hide her shock, but her smile of acceptance with his persistence gave her away. They sat in silence for a couple hours, with the girl only occasionally looking up to see how obvious it was that he wasn't going anywhere.

In the third hour, she laughed and put her book down. "What do you want?" she asked him again.

For the first time in his life, he wasn't sure. "I don't know," Algos replied honestly.

"Well, it's late. How about we get some dinner and talk about how far you've gotten?" she replied with a smile.

It didn't give him butterflies. It didn't make his stomach jump. But something stirred within him. He just wasn't sure what exactly. Algos had felt nothing like this before. In fact, he had felt nothing at all as far as he could remember.

"Okay," he replied with a shrug as he followed her to the cafeteria.

They talked for several hours. She was actually quite fascinating. A psych major with a flare for excellently written books. She argued theories with him and challenged everything he offered. "I'm not scared of you, you know," she declared bravely.

"Why not?" Algos asked in fascination.

"You're just not that scary," she said with a shrug.

"You don't know me," Algos said with a wicked smile.

"Yeah, I do," she smiled wickedly back.

And that was the start of the most bizarre relationship he would ever have with another person. Now that he thought about it, he might not have been the master manipulator he thought he was. But Algos couldn't give her what she wanted. He wasn't capable even though he tried.

He killed people in the late hours and spent the rest of his time with her when she wasn't in class. When she graduated, Algos asked her to marry him. He didn't know what love was, but he assumed this was it. She had eagerly accepted. They moved in and, unexpectedly, Clarice came. Then Andrew. Then Jess.

He continued to kill. He just made sure it wasn't in his hometown. Traveling gave him a break from trying to be what he could never be. A father. Clarice followed him everywhere he went. Andrew cried entirely too much, and Jess was too little to do anything with just yet. But Andrew reminded him of Peter, and that was something that Algos didn't care for. At least Clarice remained silent and just watched closely from afar.

Andrew was a different story. He wanted to be held. He needed attention 24/7. Father to son didn't seem to allow Algos to manipulate as easily as brother to brother had. Algos didn't like it. And when he wouldn't coddle Andrew like he demanded, Andrew just cried. Constantly.

Then Andrew got sick, and his wife was so ridiculously concerned. Andrew became more clingy and his wife was becoming less stable. So, Algos went into his bedroom one night and stuck the needle right behind his ear. A poke too small to detect.

Despite having a powerful urge to just snap his neck and be done with it, it was more important to test the undetectable poison Algos had been playing with for years. It was his own personal blend. Something he was very proud of. This dose wouldn't cause the body to deteriorate before his eyes. Algos knew his wife would still need a body to bury. So, this would have to do for now. He didn't notice Clarice in the hallway. He didn't notice she saw everything.

However, killing Andrew just put his wife in more of a tailspin. She demanded that he spend more time with the children he had left. Nine-year-old Clarice, and three-year-old Jess. Luckily for them, the girls were more tolerable, but he didn't like being told what to do. She knew that, and she did it anyway. It was her own damn fault.

One night after work, Algos came home to her lecturing about being a "better father" to those who remained. But it was not the right day to be doing this dance. Algos had lost three test subjects prematurely, and he didn't want to hear it.

So, he took her life with his bare hands. She should have just let him be. She should have just tended to the children herself and left him alone to his work. She might have lasted. At least a little longer.

Clarice had walked in on him, but to his surprise, she didn't cause him grief. She just watched. Like she always did. He disposed of the body, and the girls never spoke of her again.

Without her mother, Jess clung to Clarice, and Clarice was too eager to take her on. Algos had to intervene. Why not train them both to bring in subjects and clean up the messes for him? And why not have a little fun along the way?

Algos had them train to be the best assassins before they grew old enough to retaliate. He eagerly showed favor to Jess just to spite Clarice, but Jess had many hidden talents and was quite gifted at whatever he asked her to do. Algos tried to enhance those skills, but that experiment failed.

He didn't calculate how strong her spirit was, though. Or the effect of finding Jack would have on them both. Algos knew he couldn't take out Jack directly. Not yet. Not without losing Jess. So, he took Jack's father away instead. His mother was already gone from cancer long ago. He smiled as the memory played out before his eyes. Poor sap didn't see what was coming.

It ended up making their bond stronger, which Algos was not pleased about, to say the least. Jess continued to work less and less for him, but his hold was still strong enough to always bring her back. The kids got married, but Algos still was winning in the end. Until Jess got pregnant. Then everything changed.

She was acting out and demanding to be set completely free. He was honest and told her, "no". It wasn't an answer she was willing to accept. Jess offered to fight for her full release. Algos had underestimated her spirit yet again and was permanently broken in the process. It slowed him down a little, but it didn't stop him. The cane was proving to have its uses.

Jess walked out, but Algos wasn't satisfied. He didn't care that she had earned her way to freedom. He wasn't ready to give it to her just yet. Algos tried to lure Jess back, but she wouldn't come. She had a daughter to protect, and that daughter was proving to be even more special than Jess.

To test his theory, he had Clarice try to drown the child in the pool, but Jess cut in and put the testing to a stop. She would later come after him and take his handsome face that he had grown accustom to luring his prey in with. Algos was done playing games. If Jess wanted to be free so badly, he would let her. And put Sophie in her place.

Algos knew Jess would put up a fight. He once again underestimated how much. He put a team together, distracted Clarice, and watched his own daughter and husband put up the fight of their lives. A fight that cost them theirs. When Algos attempted to collect the child, she was nowhere to be found. A hunt that had been going on for over ten years. Algos was tiring of this game and found a way to win once and for all. All he had to do was find Sophie.

Eight

"I need to tell you something," Tina whispered to Ben as they rode in the back of a fully tinted van with Donna, Cecil, Daryl, James, and Sophie's still body.

"What's up, Smarty?" asked Daryl.

Tina gave him a weary smile. Daryl was a huge typical biker on the outside, but a very intelligent biochemist who helped them "test" Sophie back in Albuquerque. Tina knew her nickname was out of respect.

"So, a couple of things," Tina started slowly. "First of all, I think I met a new player."

"Seriously?" Ben yelled. Tina put her hand on his thigh and kissed him on the cheek softly.

"This one is on our side, I think," she informed them reassuringly. "Anyone remember the name Rebecca?" Tina asked.

Everyone paused for a second before confirming that no one knew the name.

"She helped me find the dream catcher," Tina informed them as she replayed the scene at the store.

"So, she's dead?" Donna asked with concern.

"My guess is yes, but I've never seen them control people like that before. Although, that was what Sophie was concerned about. That the man with...Algos, was trying to do to her," Tina reminded them.

"That can't be good," Daryl said, deep in thought.

"What's the other thing?" James asked her, still holding Sophie's hand and not taking his eyes off of her.

"Someone brought me into the dream realm on the bus," Tina said, squeezing Ben's thigh. "There wasn't a door, and it was very different. It was pitch black, but there was a clear barrier wall between us," Tina continued.

"Us?" Ben said in a panicked whisper.

"Woman," Tina announced. "Sophie, but not Sophie. She had on a red outfit and the black bob she had when we met her. I'm not sure if it was Algos or not," Tina added in a hurry. "Someone who didn't know that Sophie had red hair, now."

"What the hell?" Ben yelled.

"The clear wall made it impossible for them to access me," she continued on. "That angered them. They said they would try to get what they wanted another way. I bring it up, because if they can access 'hosts' in their sleep and make them do things, we need to be careful,"

Tina ended with authority.

"How many of those dream catchers do you have?" Donna asked wearily.

"Just the one," Tina replied softly. "But Rebecca said it would keep anyone in the house or area safe."

"Let's hope she's right," Cecil said over his shoulder as he continued to drive toward the coordinates.

"We need to let them know," James said absent-mindedly, staring at Sophie.

"They kinda just come to us," Ben reminded his friend.

"Well, that's going to have to change," James replied bluntly.

Just then, Donna's head grew heavy, and she slumped over onto Daryl. Everyone watched helplessly.

"Hello?" Donna called out. Her voice shook as much as she did.

"Hello, old friend," she heard Mario's voice call to her.

Donna's eyes narrowed as she tried to focus on the surrounding darkness. "Yeah, and what's something only we would know?" Donna yelled.

There was a pause of silence.

"I was the one that broke Cecil's tailpipe, but you took the blame because you said my behind would be whipped enough in my lifetime," Mario said with a warm chuckle as they presented a door before her.

Donna opened it and found the usual suspects sitting around

the table in the cabin that was the replica of the one in Colorado.

"Hey," Donna said with a weary smile.

Jess nodded for her to join them and waved her hand to produce a steaming cup of tea before her.

"You alright?" Mario asked, looking her up and down. Something wasn't right.

"We're not sure," Donna replied. She retold the story she had just heard Tina share.

"Do you know a Rebecca?" Jack asked his wife.

"Not that I know of," Jess answered honestly.

"I'm all for having allies, but I prefer to know where they come from," Corbin added the obvious.

"I'll take it if it means saving Sophie," Donna added. Jess put her hand over Donna's.

"Thank you for always keeping my daughter safe," Jess replied in her mother-to-mother tone. Donna nodded knowingly.

"Who do you think the other one is?" Mario asked in frustration.

"I don't know, but they weren't here," Corbin confirmed. "I feel everyone here."

"Then who and where is Rebecca?" Jack asked, deep in thought.

"We will need to work on it from our end," Jess confirmed. "Roger is on his way," she informed Donna. "How does she look?"

"She's definitely weak," Donna admitted. "She's pale, and her vitals are low. But you can see muscle spasms like she's moving around," she added with interest. "Wherever Sophie is, she's still moving."

"Fascinating," Corbin whispered out loud.

"We need to figure out how to keep Algos out before we try to bring her back," Jack informed Donna.

"I understand," she replied firmly.

"Be safe," Jack added softly.

"Always," Donna replied with a sly grin and a wink. "The kids want to know the best way to contact you if we learn something," she added quickly.

"We're not as in tune when we hunt, but close your eyes and call us. We can still hear you when you need us," Corbin added in his doctor's voice. "If there's no door, try to wake up," he added more firmly. "It won't be us."

Donna nodded in acknowledgement and stood up to leave.

"Thank you, old friend," Mario said, giving her a hug and gently brushing his finger across her forehead.

She woke up in a gasp to find herself wrapped in Cecil's arms. "Why aren't you driving?" she asked, confused.

"Because I don't stand on the sidelines while the dead play with my wife," he retorted in frustration.

She put her hand on his cheek softly. "Mario says, 'hi'," she smiled at him. Donna felt the van still moving and knew Daryl had taken her husband's place. She gave the latest instructions and informed them that Roger would meet them soon.

"I don't like this," Cecil said, still holding onto his wife and shaking his head.

"No one does, but it's a battle we were chosen to fight. And for that girl, I would move mountains," Donna said softly as she stared at Sophie's unresponsive body. She pushed herself out of her husband's reluctant arms and bent down to Sophie's ear. "And if you don't hurry and make your way back, I will come get you. And neither of us wants that," Donna said in her warning mom's voice. The corner of Sophie's mouth curled up in a slight smile. "That's my girl," Donna said, patting her on the thigh and leaned back into her husband's arms to rest during their long journey.

Sophie heard Donna's motherly warning. She heard everything her loved ones whispered in her ear, or had her feel. Including James' hands that held hers so tightly. "Come find me," he had told her.

"I'm trying," Sophie mumbled in frustration.

"What?" John asked.

"Nothing," she answered with a heavy sigh. "Why do I feel so tired in here?"

"Not sure," John said, suddenly studying her more than the blue book he held. "Maybe your body needs more rest since we're in your mind," he offered, full of doubt. This was not his expertise, but he knew one thing. The longer they stayed, the less likely they could leave. Forever.

Sophie looked down at the yellow book in her hand that read *Edward* on it. "I think I need a nap," she confessed honestly.

"Only a short one," John announced. "We don't know how much time we're losing in here. It could be faster than we can handle," he admitted honestly.

"I understand," Sophie replied as her eyes grow too heavy to hold open, and she went to curl up on the couch. She grabbed the throw on the back of it and pulled it up under her chin. She just needed a second to rest.

"Hello?" she heard Eddie's voice calling in her ears.

"Eddie?" Sophie called back into the darkness before her. So much for getting any rest. "Eddie, where are you?" she called out.

"No clue," he replied nervously. "There's no door."

"No door?" Sophie whispered. Was this the actual Eddie and not the one floating around in her head? Sophie turned around and found a different version of Eddie before her. An older version. "Are you...?" she asked, unable to finish the question.

"Wow. You look real. I'm guessing this is just a dream, but I'll take it. Nice to see you, Soph," Eddie said with a weak smile.

"Hey," she whispered, grabbing her arms in front of her uncomfortably. "Listen, Eddie. I'm sorry. I didn't..." she started.

"I know," Eddie replied, widening his smile. "I'm not mad," he added for good measure. "I know there's no door, but in case you are real, where are you?" he asked cautiously.

"I'm not sure," she lied. Friend or not, he'd been with Algos for years. Sophie wasn't sure which side he actually stood on.

"I wonder why we're here?" Eddie asked, looking around.

The image of the yellow book with his name on it flashed before her eyes. "Interesting," she said to herself.

"What?" Eddie asked, turning back to face her.

Just then, a gigantic steel door shot up behind Sophie.

"Great," she said in irritation.

"What does a steel door mean?" Eddie asked slowly.

"Nothing good," Sophie replied over her shoulder as she stared at the oversized steel door before her. "I really just needed a nap!" she called out to no one.

"Are you supposed to go through that thing?" Eddie asked nervously.

"Usually," she said with a frown.

Eddie walked up to stand beside her. "Well, let's do this," he said with determination, staring at the door.

"I'm not sure you're supposed to go," Sophie said, looking at him nervously.

"Well, I'm here, so we might as well find out," he replied, looking back at her with his boyish grin.

Sophie looked back at the door and sighed heavily before she reached out to open it, only it flung open without touching the knob. "Well, that's new," she laughed nervously.

Eddie put his hand on her shoulder. She felt his warmth and his nervous energy. "Let's do this," he repeated with a nod. "But just in case, you can go first."

"Gee, thanks," Sophie said with a sarcastic laugh.

She took the lead, but as they got closer to the door, the world on the other side was not only abandoned, but on fire. It was night, and like the apocalypse movies she had seen with James, Tina, and Ben.

"This looks promising," she said cynically.

Eddie's eyes widened as he took in the scene before him. "You're telling me," he muttered.

"Here goes nothing," Sophie declared with a shrug.

It was deathly silent, minus the occasional explosion. No sign of life. Simply destruction. They both walked down the middle of the street. The buildings all had broken windows, spray paint of hatred and evil was on every building, or at least the rubble of what were buildings. Abandoned and destroyed vehicles cluttered the street.

"Great place," Eddie said sarcastically.

"I'm not sure this is all of it," Sophie said with sadness.

Fires burned around them in the distance.

"What do you think happened here?" he asked.

"No clue," Sophie answered honestly. "Nothing good," she added.

She saw a female figure stalking the roof tops and watching them. Sophie stuck out her arm to stop Eddie. "We're not alone," she whispered.

"Oh, goody," Eddie said, looking around nervously.

"Just stay close," Sophie ordered.

"Like I was going to go anywhere else," Eddie replied uneasily.

Another female figure was swinging from building to building in the shadows on the other side of them.

"You don't happen to have any weapons on you, do you?" she asked quietly.

"Left it in my other suit," Eddie replied cynically.

"Great," she mumbled.

"I've got you," Eddie offered with hope. "You're the best weapon I've ever seen," he added.

"Depends on how many," Sophie said as her eyes calculated all the pairs that seemed to watch them.

"And how many are we talking about?" he whispered back.

"Too many for comfort," she sighed.

"Awesome," he replied, moving closer to her.

"Just keep moving," Sophie ordered.

They continued to walk in the middle of the street. They were being watched from the shadows. She continued to watch out of the corners of her eyes as they crept down the street. What was the point of this vision? Or was it more than just a vision? Panic set in, and her stomach dropped, filling her throat with bile that she tried hard to swallow down.

The structure of the surrounding buildings was damaged, and war had clearly taken place prior to them arriving. The real question was, what was the life that hid in the shadows? And more importantly, which side were they on?

"This is a war zone," Eddie whispered in her ear.

"This WAS a war zone," Sophie hissed back.

"Sophie," he whispered in great concern.

"What?" she retorted over her shoulder.

"You," was his only reply.

When Sophie looked down, she saw what he did. Her veins were glowing a bright neon reddish orange. It looked like lava was coursing through her veins.

"What the heck?" she gasped, as she stopped to look at her hands and arms light up not only herself, but the entire street before her.

"We need to get out of here," Eddie pleaded in her ear.

"Right," she breathed. Sophie tried to focus on the path in front of her. It had to be leading them somewhere. They continued to make their way forward.

Suddenly, a giant set of stone steps appeared at the end of the road with no building behind it.

"That's odd," Eddie said. He was trying to stay close to Sophie, but the light and heat her veins continued to produce made it difficult to do so. However, that might be the point, so he was going to fight it as much as possible.

"Going up?" she asked over her shoulder.

"Apparently," he said, noticing that Sophie was getting hotter and brighter the closer they got. "Maybe we can get a better view of where we are," he offered.

They slowly started climbing the large, slightly crumbled, stone staircase. After what seemed like an eternity, they finally reached the top. They looked around them. Nothing but destruction was as far as the eye could see.

"Sophie," Eddie hissed nervously.

Sophie turned to face the direction from where they had come and saw what Eddie did.

"Is that?" Eddie muttered.

"Yes," she gasped, as her mouth dropped open. Her eyes widened, and she froze. Her body was shaking despite the immense amount of heat that surrounded her and burned within. In front of them was an army. An army of Sophies. They wore red combat outfits, with black bobs, and held nothing but hallow and fully dilated eyes. Sophie shone brighter, and their eyes turned red in response.

"What does this mean?" Eddie asked, nervously.

"He's making an army," Sophie uttered. "He's cloning me," she said in hysteria. She turned immediately to Eddie and grabbed him by the arms. "We have to stop him!" she begged and shook him, trying to wake him up.

Unexpectedly, he was yanked from her hands and pulled all the way back through the door. Sophie started hyperventilating as she turned to look at the army of herself before her. They gave Sophie her own wicked smile back and bowed to one knee as if she was their leader. Their queen.

"NO!" Sophie screamed back at them.

She felt male hands around her, shaking her awake. "Sophie!" John called to her.

"I'm okay," she managed to get out as she held up her hand to stop him from shaking her.

"What happened?" he asked her urgently.

"I need to get out of here," she gasped, trying to catch her breath.

"We already knew that. What happened while you were sleeping?" he demanded.

"Algos is trying to make an army of me," Sophie breathed out. "He wants me to lead them."

"Has he already started?" John asked her hastily.

"I don't know. I just...saw them," she said with a shutter.

"I don't think you should sleep anymore," John said with great concern.

"I haven't slept yet!" Sophie snapped. "And I seem to learn a little more when I do, but I don't feel much like closing my eyes at the moment," she replied honestly.

He swept her into his arms like her father used to after a bad dream and rocked with her. John felt Sophie giggle in his arms and pulled her back to see her face.

"What's so funny?" he asked, concerned.

"I know where dad gets it from," she giggled and went back to allowing him to hold her.

John held onto his granddaughter, deep in thought. Despite having been taken from his son too early, it appeared they had more in common than he had realized. John wondered if he would go back to forgetting them all when he returned. He was aware of the importance of getting back, but he selfishly enjoyed getting to be a part of a family again. They chose John for the job against his will. Or was this always supposed to have happened? He tried to focus on caring for his granddaughter, but too many things weren't adding up for his comfort. And his gut never steered him wrong. Alive or dead.

"What has you so deep in thought?" Jess asked her husband.

"My father," Jack answered with a frown.

"John? What's got you thinking about him?" she asked curiously, as she sat down next to her husband on the couch in front of the fireplace.

"I don't know," Jack answered grimly, looking at his wife.

"I haven't thought of him since we've been here, and lately he's all I see. You know everything has a meaning in here, but I can't, for the life of me, figure out what this is supposed to mean," Jack stated honestly.

"Is it a particular memory, or just in general?" Jess asked, trying to help.

"It's all over the map," he replied in frustration. "From being a kid and buying me my first chemistry set, to the day he was supposed to come to our concert and never made it."

"Are you just on higher alert with Algos?" she offered. "Thinking of all family?"

"He's not alive, and we haven't seen him in here," Jack answered, logically. "There would be no need to save someone already gone through."

"This place is massive. He might be here, and we just haven't crossed paths with him yet," Jess hypothesized.

"We've been here too long not to have crossed him by now," Jack said with a chuckle. He loved it when his wife tried to help him solve his puzzles.

"Well," Jess said, deep in thought. "We know where your mother is. We know where my lovely father is. I don't remember my mother, so even if I have crossed her, I doubt I would know it," Jess replied matter-of-factly. "It's true we have been here for a while, but I agree. Nothing happens in here without reason. However, we need to focus on Algos first. If your father is here with us, he must be protected as well."

"I know," Jack said as he leaned over to kiss her on the top of her head. "But it's being awfully persistent. There might be an answer in there somewhere," he added.

"I agree," Jess replied. "But you're the smartest person I know, and we need your help with Algos," she scolded. "I know you will find both, though," Jess said with a smile and a wink. "So, we will work on it as a side project just in case." She leaned over and kissed her husband on the cheek, and laid her head on his shoulder. They watched the fire crackle before them and thought about solutions to both dilemmas and shared ideas back and forth.

They didn't hear him. They didn't sense him, but Corbin watched from afar. Jack was right. Nothing happened in here without reason. If he was seeing John, it meant he was in trouble or had an answer to a clue. That meant Corbin must locate him. Pronto.

<u>Nine</u>

E ddie woke up in a gasp. It took him awhile to get his
body to calm down. Although it was nice to see Sophie,
the event scared him to his very core. Seeing an entire army of her and
watching their eyes glow in response to her with what he could only
describe as "lava veins".

It wouldn't shock him one bit that the old man would want to
carbon copy the greatest weapon on earth. Clearly, what Eddie had
witnessed was going to be what the world would turn into if Algos
accomplished his goal.

Eddie needed help, but who? Clarice couldn't be trusted, and
the dead could only help so much. However, they needed to know
what was going on all the same. He closed his eyes tightly and

whispered, "Jack. I need you."

Daryl carried Sophie's unconscious body into the Goldfield Hotel. From the outside, the vast brick building stood four stories tall, with dusty windows that looked like they hadn't been touched in decades. With the reputation of being a haunted hotel, 247 miles southeast of Carson City, NV, and a population of less than 300 people, it was the perfect place to keep Sophie safe until she woke up.

Ben was concerned taking her into such a disastrous location until they got inside. The outside was a facade compared to the remodeled inside. Everything had been modernized, including a gaming room, a large family kitchen, and a room that was a doctor's dream. Hospital equipment filled half the floor, minus the doctors, nurses, and being on record for being a patient. Ben started hooking Sophie up to the monitors for her heart and brain.

"Your dad was very specific," Cecil said as he patted James on the shoulder. "There's x-ray machines and more in another room."

"He always is," James replied with a weary smile. He noticed the Lazy Boy recliner and extra bed close by. "Always," he said again. His father knew him oh so well.

"Let's get that thing activated," Donna ordered Tina. She nodded towards her bag of goodies. Tina went to work with Donna's help. Ben was busy checking Sophie's vitals. In the next room was a ton of biker men and women relaxing, watching tv, playing games, and reading.

"A lot of people," James observed.

"A very important person to keep safe," Cecil replied with a wink and smile. "We don't mess around, Stud. And it's not our first rodeo. We may not be able to help with the mental mumbo jumbo, but we will fight to the death to keep her safe physically."

His eyes widened. "Everyone?" James asked in surprise.

"Everyone," Cecil confirmed.

James looked over at Sophie. Once Ben finished, he walked over and took the chair next to her. He pulled her hands into his and squeezed them tightly. There was no change in her, which could be both good and bad. Either way, it appeared moving Sophie didn't seem to hurt her. Ben had been right. James' eyes grew heavy suddenly, and before he could say anything, his head fell back and James was out cold.

The wooden door awaited him.

"Well, at least you waited until I was already sitting down," James mumbled, before he reached out and opened the door. He was not expecting the sight that greeted him.

"We have a problem," Mario said quickly as he pushed James into a chair to sit next to a stranger. However, he wasn't a stranger. James guessed it was current Eddie.

"A bigger problem than we already have?" James asked, not taking his eyes off of Eddie.

"Eddie saw Sophie," Jack replied in relief.

"You?" James asked bitterly.

"Yeah," Eddie said defensively. "No, I don't know how, but I did," he added quickly.

"How is she?" Jess cut in, looking at James desperately for an answer.

"She's safe and resting," James announced with a weary smile.

"But it didn't harm her?" she asked eagerly.

"Not at all," James confirmed.

"Where is she?" Eddie demanded.

"None of your damn business!" James snapped.

"James," Jack interjected.

"He works with the enemy. I'm not telling him a damn thing! And neither should you!" James yelled with venom in his voice.

"I'm on your side, Dude," Eddie snapped back.

"Are you?" James accused.

"Enough!" Jess yelled, shaking the room around them. Everyone silenced immediately. "Tell James what you guys saw," she added with a warning.

Eddie replayed the dream he had of Sophie.

"So, where was this?" James ordered.

"I don't know," Eddie replied honestly. "Why don't you ask her?"

"Why you and not me?" James barked more than asked.

"I don't know!" Eddie snapped back. He was secretly enjoying that Sophie chose HIM over this guy. He didn't understand what she saw in him, anyway. He wasn't worthy of her.

"We need to focus," Jack warned them both.

"We're all on the same team. Team Sophie," Mario

reminded them both.

"For how long?" James accused more than questioned.

"Eddie needs help to find out if Algos started the cloning or not," Jess said in her motherly tone, and taking James's hands into hers. "We need Tina."

"Absolutely not!" James yelled. He tried to pull his hands away, but Jess tightened her grip.

"I know you love them both, but we need to stop this. For everyone's sake. Especially theirs," Jess emphasized.

"She's already working on a project," he reminded her.

"I am well aware," Jess said with a weary smile.

"Why not just ask her?" James asked, suddenly realizing there was a reason they came to him and not Tina directly.

"Because we need to all work together. There's a lot going on, and it's going to take the entire family to succeed," Jess answered calmly.

Something was up, and that wasn't it. Why did they want him to know Sophie reached out to Eddie and not him? Was this just to throw in his face that he wasn't her first?

"You were and you know it," Jack warned under his breath.

James looked up in alarm. Could they all hear his thoughts?

"No," Jack confirmed with a smile and a wink. Everyone else just looked around like they were trying to figure out what was going on.

"Why don't you just ask Sophie what we saw?" Eddie insisted, but everyone ignored him. That meant only one thing. Wherever Sophie was, she wasn't able to answer questions. At least not at the moment. The thought made Eddie sick to his stomach. "She's not okay, is she?" Eddie whispered, looking to Jack for answers.

"We need to focus on Algos," was Jack's only reply.

Eddie was silent and stared at the table for what seemed like an eternity. "Listen," he whispered, not looking up. "I don't know why I saw her, but I did. And what we saw was nothing but destruction and death. She told me we need to stop this, and I agree. I just can't do it alone."

Eddie looked up and caught James' stare.

"I need help, because I'm monitored a ton. Especially right now. So, I can't dig as much as I normally would without being detected. However, I've seen what Tina can do. If we work together, I will last a little longer, and give you everything I find out before he takes my life."

James suddenly felt a ping of guilt. They took the guy against his will to fight against a childhood friend. James could understand why he had to play both sides in order to survive. Eddie's bold declaration made it sound like he would choose Sophie's side until the end. However, James also knew first-hand, facing death in the eye made you do things you didn't expect, plan, or mean to. Most crumbled under the pressure, and this was not a battle to be putting fate into the hands of someone that couldn't be relied on consistently.

"I have to get back," James said, looking at Mario for an escape.

"I get it," Mario said with a smile and went to put his finger across his forehead to send him back.

"Have faith," Jess announced right before he did.

James woke up gasping for air.

"What's the word?" Ben asked wearily.

"They need your wife," James said, as he worked on catching his breath.

"For what?" Ben demanded.

"Does it matter?" Tina said, climbing down from the ladder next to Sophie's bed. She had just hung up the dream catcher carefully over Sophie's sleeping body.

"It does to me!" Ben protested.

Tina sighed heavily. "It shouldn't. We need Sophie to save the world, and I really need it saved. I don't know about you," she replied.

"They want you to work with Eddie. Apparently, Algos plans on cloning Sophie," James announced in frustration.

"I'm sorry, what?" Ben said, as he almost gave himself whiplash. "This just keeps getting better and better!"

Tina narrowed her eyes and frowned. "Why not just ask me?" she asked.

"That's what I said," James said, glad that his friend saw what he saw.

"Well, this is getting interesting," she replied with a smile of determination. The same one she always got when a puzzle showed up, and insisted that it couldn't be solved.

"I don't like it," Ben muttered.

"Neither do I," James confirmed. "Let's be on our A game, boys and girls."

"Agreed," Tina said excitedly.

"Of course you would be excited," Ben said sourly to his wife.

"When one door closes," Tina said sweetly, kissing him on the cheek and skipping off.

"That girl will be the death of me," Ben sighed.

"Let's hope she's the only one," James laughed, and looked down at Sophie. He leaned down and whispered in her ear softly, "Why him and not me?"

Sophie heard the hurt in his voice and started looking desperately for her book on James. She wasn't sure how she got to Eddie, but if she did it once, surely she could do it again? But someone else had the book, and it wasn't who she was expecting.

Rebecca flipped through the red book titled *James.*

"What is that?" demanded the cloaked figure that loomed over her.

"I'm not sure," she answered with great curiosity as she thumbed through Sophie's memories of James.

"Will it help?" the figure asked in great desperation.

"Something tells me, yes," Rebecca replied, deep in thought. The boy was Sophie's strongest living connection. If anything was going to bring her back, it would be him.

"How, exactly?" the seven foot figure ordered more than requested.

"Let me see," replied Rebecca with a sinister smile. They needed Sophie, and James appeared to be the answer. She just had to figure out the best way to get him to help them.

Sophie started fingering every single book in her library. His name had escaped her, but she was sure that she would know it when she came across it.

"Sophie?" John asked in concern.

"Someone keeps talking to me," she replied over her shoulder. "I know him. I just can't remember his name. I need to find the book," she said, distracted.

Panic filled John's stomach. They had already been here too long. If she couldn't remember James' name, that was a sign she was losing her memory. Oddly, John couldn't locate the red book he had already studied from front to back, either. That couldn't be a good sign. Something wasn't right, and they weren't getting anywhere in here.

They both heard Sophie's evil twin cackling wickedly on the other side of the door. "When are you going to come play with me?" she taunted. Sophie walked over to the window and shuddered at the face that stared back at her. It was herself, only with dilated black eyes that seemed to have a red iris instead of a normal color.

"Get away from the door," John ordered.

"Come, come, Sophie. Time is running out," she cooed on the other side. She tilted her head from side to side like a woman possessed.

Sophie backed away from the door and went back to fingering through her own memories. She heard the other Sophie slam her hand against the door. The entire room shook with her fury. Sophie didn't turn around. She wouldn't give her the satisfaction of knowing how much her alter ego disturbed her.

There were two things Sophie was looking for. How to get out, and how to survive the darkness that ran through her blood. She took a slight second to look over her shoulder, but no one was at the window. Sophie needed to find out what would make her turn into that thing on the other side of the door, if she had any hope of stopping herself from becoming the creature that waited to kill the good in her on the other side of the door.

"What if I can't find the answer in here?" Sophie whispered to John.

He stopped studying the purple book titled *Tina* and looked up at her blankly. "The answer is always there for us to find," he offered with little emotion. "We just have to be open to accepting it when it presents itself. Here," he said, giving her the book he held. "She sounds very smart. Maybe there's something in here."

Sophie looked down at the book. *Tina.* The name sounded familiar. She just couldn't put a face to the name. She walked over to the plush chair and began reading. Her eyes grew heavy as she read about the FBI technical specialist that she called sister by chapter 3.

"So, how does this work exactly?" Donna asked Tina, nodding in the direction of the dream catcher.

"In theory, the dream catcher protects the child, or in this case Sophie, from bad dreams and thoughts. The good dreams float down the feathers and beads onto the sleeping person, and the bad dreams get caught in the web. It's believed that in morning light, when the sun touches the dream catchers, the bad dreams disappear," Tina shrugged. "Dumb, I know," she said, shaking her head. "But I figure we need all the help we can get," Tina sighed as she walked over to the chair to take a seat. The baby shouldn't be making her this tired yet.

"You alright?" Donna asked in a low whisper to not panic the boys.

"Just need a nap, I guess," Tina shrugged. She curled up into the chair, and Donna placed a throw over her.

"You've been doing an awful lot of running, Dear," Donna offered. "Catch some shut eye. I've got her this shift."

Tina let the weight of her eyes take over and sank deeper into the chair. However, when she opened her eyes, she found herself surrounded by pure darkness.

"Great," Tina mumbled in annoyance to herself. This is how the evil looking Sophie showed herself to Tina last time.

"Hello?" she heard Sophie's voice.

"I'm not buying it this time!" Tina yelled out, with her hands on her hips in defiance. "I'm not playing your games!"

Sophie appeared before her and started walking towards her. She watched Tina and studied her from head to toe. It reminded Tina of the first time they met. "Are you Tina?" Sophie asked cautiously.

"You know I am," Tina replied in suspicion.

"We know each other, right?" Sophie asked her.

"Clearly," Tina answered in irritation. Where was this going?

"I'm sorry," Sophie said, honestly. "I don't know how this works."

Tina squinted and studied the girl before her with clearer eyes. Minus the current hair color, this Sophie was like the one she met the first time in the Moore's kitchen with her best friend. Tina was tricked last time, though. She needed to tread lightly, just in case.

Sophie looked down at her hand suddenly. She felt the tiny

heart beating in her palm. She looked at Tina with great excitement. "Congratulations," Sophie said with a smile.

Tina took a couple of steps back and put a hand over her stomach.

Sophie put up her hands and took a slow step back. "I don't mean you harm. I was just reading about how we met, and I'm thrilled for you. Honestly," she said, sincerely.

Tina tilted her head as she studied the girl before her. "Why don't you remember me?" she asked suspiciously.

"I don't know," Sophie said with a frown. "I think the longer I stay stuck, the more I lose."

"And where are you, exactly?" Tina asked, with a hint of hope.

"Stupidly, inside my head," Sophie replied in frustration.

"But I don't know how to get out. Do you know?" she asked Tina in desperation.

Tina's heart sank and a lump quickly formed in her throat. "I'm afraid I don't," she whispered back. "But I can see what I can find out," she offered quickly, taking a couple of steps toward her friend. This wasn't good. This wasn't good at all.

Sophie didn't notice. She was too busy pacing back and forth where she stood. "I need to get out," she said, more to herself. "I think people need me."

"Yes," Tina said softly as she continued moving towards her. "I am one of them," she said with a weary smile.

Sophie looked up at her. Water filled her eyes. "I'm trying," she whispered.

"I know," Tina assured. She knew she shouldn't trust the vision in front of her, but something told her she had the right Sophie this time. And this Sophie needed Tina to help her get back. "Do you know what a dream catcher is?" she offered.

"That web looking thingy with feathers and beads that Indians used to keep their children safe from bad dreams?"

Sophie said in confusion.

"Yes," Tina said with a giggle. "You have one over you while you sleep. Hopefully, you won't be having any more bad dreams," she offered her friend.

"Really?" Sophie asked, impressed. "That means a lot," she whispered. "The last one wasn't very good." Sophie shuttered at the vision that played before her.

"Maybe it will help you be able to find the answers you need," Tina said, reaching her hand towards Sophie's shoulder.

Instinctively, Sophie took a step back to be out of reach. Tina dropped her hand with hurt and disappointment mixed together. Sophie watched the pain pass over the girl's face.

"I'm sorry," Sophie said softly, as she took a step closer to Tina. She took her arms and threw them around Tina, and gave her a hug. Tina accepted her warmly. After a bit, Sophie pulled back. "Do you know the boy who talks to me?"

Tina tried to hide the fear that was suddenly flowing through her body. "James?" she asked, slowly.

Sophie looked at the sky before nodding. "That sounds familiar."

"He loves you very much," Tina told Sophie in her motherly voice.

"Can you let him know? I will try to remember and find him. He keeps asking me, but I am not finding the answers I need to get out

130

quickly," Sophie replied with a frown.

"You know," Tina offered. "Some people say that when we're trapped within ourselves, sometimes that means we need to find peace from within in order to move on."

"Really?" Sophie asked her.

"Lord knows I've taken every *Cosmo* quiz ever written," Tina laughed. "That seems to be a common theme. I know, personally, when I'm all out of sorts, usually Ben comes to my rescue to calm me and I can get back to the task at hand."

"Ben," Sophie repeated. "Your husband, right?"

"Yes," Tina said with a smile. "Your doctor," she said with a wink.

"You must be the power couple then," Sophie offered with a smile.

"Not as powerful as you and James," Tina said, bumping her shoulder slightly into Sophie's.

"I have someone, too?" Sophie asked in shock.

"You do," Tina confirmed. "And we're always here when you need us."

Sophie smiled her Cheshire grin that Tina loved the most. "I like the sound of that," she said, sheepishly.

"So, what's it like where you are?" Tina asked, trying to understand what was going on.

"We're hiding in a library. Apparently, I catalog my memories into books. Yours was purple," Sophie said with a shrug.

"Excellent color," Tina said. "But who do you mean by 'we'?" she asked, trying not to be alarmed.

"He's…" was all Sophie got out. She oddly couldn't recall his name, or anything else for that matter. "I can't think right now, but he's safe," she assured, sensing Tina's fear. "He's trying to help me get out," Sophie added.

"Eddie?" Tina asked.

"No, but I did see him. That's how I learned I can sometimes talk to people if I'm holding their book. But I can't find his book," Sophie said with a hint of frustration. "It's an enormous library," she added for clarification. "I will keep looking," she said with determination.

Tina smiled at Sophie wearily.

"You need your rest," Sophie said, suddenly. "You both do," she added, nodding towards Tina's stomach.

Tina put a hand on her stomach and smiled. Then a thought came to her. "No one else knows yet," she warned.

"Your secret is safe with me," Sophie said with a wink. "If I don't forget it to begin with," she giggled nervously.

"How did you know?" Tina asked her suspiciously.

"I feel the pulse in my hand. Like someone put my hand on your stomach," Sophie said, lost in thought as she stared down at her palm.

Tina couldn't hold in her excitement. "I did!" However, her excitement was quickly replaced with worry. "So, you feel everything that happens to you out there?" she asked in concern.

"I can hear people, too," Sophie supplied. "I just can't figure out how to get from here to there," she added in irritation.

"Well, if anyone can figure it out, it's you," Tina said quickly, changing the subject. "I believe in you, and I'm always here for you."

"I knew I liked you," Sophie said with her Cheshire grin. "Now, rest," she whispered before she walked away.

"Sophie!" Tina called out, but the darkness quickly turned into a bright blue sky as a cloud picked her up and carried her off to sleep.

Ten

Eddie paced his dungeon of a room as he racked his brain for the best way to work on this problem. The old man had never crossed Sophie's path. Everyone that had tried to take Sophie out had been killed, and the cleaning crew was always sent to destroy the bodies, so there was no evidence that they had ever existed. No one got close enough to Sophie to take her DNA, and she was careful never to leave anything behind. Did he collect it with no one noticing? The pit of his stomach rumbled with fear and nearly brought him to his knees.

Was that why the old man didn't care if they located Sophie? Did he already have what he needed? The room spun out of control and he ran to the sorry excuse for a bathroom to hurl out his guts.

"Calm down, Son," he heard Jack whisper in his ears. "We don't know anything yet. But we need to find out."

"On it," Eddie replied to no one.

"On what?" Clarice snapped, breaking his thoughts. "Other than the floor?" she added in disgust.

"Go away," Eddie snarled at her.

"Love to, but we have a certain someone to track down," Clarice said bluntly. "I need you to have found her. Yesterday," she added in irritation.

"Is that your father's orders?" he asked, trying not to sound hopeful.

"That's always my orders," Clarice warned. "And I actually follow mine, so I'm going to need you to get back to it, buddy boy."

"Give me a second," Eddie breathed out as he tried to get his stomach to settle.

Clarice studied him intently and found him to be legitimately sick. Despite how she felt about the troll, she said in a low tone, "I hear peppermint tea is good for soothing the stomach." She twirled on her heels and left before she felt anything else.

Eddie looked up in confusion and watched her leave. That girl was seriously bipolar and needed medication. He turned and placed his cheek against the cool metal lid of the toilet he was still clinging to. An image of little Sophie flashed before his eyes.

Sophie. The girl that saved his life from Tucker in the cafeteria so many years ago. Although she never showed as much appreciation for him as he had for her, she still took the time to get him out of a pickle, should he ever find himself in one. Even at a young age, Sophie took his breath away, gave him butterflies in his stomach, and made it impossible to think of anything or anyone else besides her. It wasn't just because she was a girl who was nice to him. There was something about her that just made you want to be around her all the time.

Sophie didn't have any friends outside of Eddie, and she had only taken him on, per her father's request. However, she grew to enjoy his company somewhat. Sophie sought Eddie out and shared little by little of her secrets, wishes, and desires, and Eddie was eager to hear them. He's not sure when exactly he decided he was going to give Sophie the world, but Eddie did a long time ago. However, fate had other plans, and they left Eddie alone to suffer from one unpleasant situation to another.

He used to resent Sophie. Resent her for never coming to save him like she had so many times before. Once Eddie realized it was only because Sophie wasn't able to for so many years, the resentment quickly faded into forgiveness. Then again, he could never stay mad at the woman he loved.

Eddie froze immediately. He never realized that all the heightened emotions he carried for the girl down the street was actually love, but things were becoming more clear as he sat back and rested his head against the cement wall behind him.

All those lost years together, and now Sophie had found another. Is that why the Harris' forced him to meet with James in his dreams? To know that Eddie didn't have a chance? Was he doomed to be in the "friend zone" and watch her be in love with someone else?

Eddie had watched her for years! He had been the one to fight to keep her safe LONG before this James guy entered the picture. And Sophie only loved him back because she didn't know there were other options. Maybe if Eddie let her know she could choose another, Sophie wouldn't settle for the first one she had crossed paths with? Because James wasn't the first. Not really.

Sophie. Something was wrong with Sophie, and Eddie needed to save her. He had seen the same vision Sophie had, and he needed to stop it. Yet, James appeared to have Sophie in his possession, and she wasn't able to answer his questions. Was she in a coma somehow? First, Eddie needed to find out if the evil army they saw together existed. Second, he needed to not die in finding out so that he could save her and tell her how he felt.

Eddie used the toilet to help pull himself off the floor. He had work to do. The nausea was gone. Only fire, determination, and desire remained. He changed his clothes and headed to the lab to find his girl and figure out how to keep her safe.

Bates heard the cane pound against the pavement long before he saw Algos. He tried hard to keep his composure. It was never a good thing when Algos offered to meet you in public. Even Bates knew his time was running out. It was just a matter of when.

Algos could sense Bates' fear long before he approached him. Bates, to him, was a modern-day version of Gollum from *Lord of the Rings.* He considered money and his life to be his "precious", which is why he was so easy to manipulate.

"Bates," Algos nodded, as he sat down next to the withering away creature that sat on the bench under a dying tree in the middle of the cemetery.

"Algos," Bates replied without making eye contact.

"I need Dr. Jeffers, again," Algos stated bluntly.

"But, Sir, he disappeared as instructed," Bates said in confusion, but smart enough not to look directly at Algos.

"Can you find him or not?" Algos barked while keeping his eyes forward. A couple visiting a nearby grave looked up in shock and hurried along on their way back to the car.

"Of course, Sir," Bates lied.

"You know the price if you fail," Algos growled his warning.

"Let's focus on the price if I don't fail," Bates countered, as he shifted uncomfortably on the bench.

"Fifty million," Algos said with no emotion.

Bates choked on the air he had been breathing. "That's an awfully generous location fee, Sir," he said as he grew giddy, thinking about how he was going to spend his fee.

"It's of great urgency," Algos carried on. "Life and death," he snarled.

"Of course, Sir. I will get right to it," Bates replied with a bow, and quickly headed as far away from Algos as possible.

Algos leaned back on the bench and took in the surrounding sights. Death. He's greatest love. Soon to be blurred beyond recognition. Once Algos found Sophie, he would be invincible. Just like he was destined to be. A smile crept across his lips as Algos counted how many of the buried bodies in the cemetery he had helped put there. The large number pleased him.

Corbin was pacing around the cabin floor, driving Mario nuts.

"You're going to wear the floor down to dirt," he told Corbin, with a hint of irritation.

"Huh? Oh, sorry," Corbin said, when he looked up to find Mario sitting at the table making some notes.

"What's on your mind, Doc?" Mario asked him.

"There's just a couple of things bothering me," Corbin replied honestly, staring at the floor, deep in thought.

"Just a couple?" Mario asked sarcastically.

Corbin looked back up at him and frowned.

"Do tell," Mario offered. The only problems he was ever used to listening to were Sophie's. He had taken on the roll against his will. Otherwise, Mario was the kind of man that kept to himself and dealt with problems as they came. However, he could read people effectively. And Corbin had things he had to sort out. Mario would be the sounding board, allowing Corbin to focus on his own tasks once they were done talking out his problem.

"Well, for starters," Corbin replied, "I'm curious about how Sophie reached Eddie. It didn't appear to effect him poorly, but if she's able to do it not being in here, that means two things."

"And those would be?" Mario asked, with sudden curiosity.

"Sophie could cause more harm than good without realizing it," Corbin answered.

"And the second?" Mario asked, unsure if he really wanted the answer.

"Our Sophie is a hell of a lot more powerful than anyone expected. Without her being aware, that makes her even more dangerous. If Algos finds her, none of us will survive," Corbin finished, looking at Mario with great concern.

It took Mario a second to digest the information he was just given. "Well, we just have to keep him out, and find her first. We always do," he said with a shrug, and went back to making some notes.

"No, you don't understand," Corbin said, taking the seat across from Mario, and putting his hand over Mario's writing hand to get his attention. "The vision Eddie described will be true for out there and in here," he breathed. "No one will be able to save her from herself."

"Don't be ridiculous," Mario said, pulling his hand out from under Corbin's. "Sophie would never hurt us. I know she won't," he said defiantly.

"Do you for sure?" Corbin asked, quietly.

"Yes! I do!" shouted Mario, as he stood up and put some space between them.

Corbin put his hands up. "Hey, I believe you. But if she gets lost in herself, a choice will need to be made for everyone's safety."

"Don't," Mario warned over his shoulder.

"You know I'm right," Corbin said as he stared down at the table in front of him.

"Why don't you put your energy into focusing on doing what we need you to do in order to survive," Mario warned, with venom oozing from his voice.

"I just wanted to tell you, because it might be you and me that decide," Corbin said as he slowly stood up and began pacing the floor again.

Mario hung his head down in resignation. He knew Corbin was right. Mario didn't like it one bit, but he was. He gave a deep sigh as he held onto the counter while his heart shattered into tiny pieces over his goddaughter. "I will do it, if it comes to that," Mario replied quietly.

Corbin stopped and looked at the man, destroying himself at the thought of not saving the daughter he had helped raised and kept safe. "I know," Corbin said matter-of-factly. "So, what do we know so far?"

"We confirmed that Jeffers guy helped Algos get in," Mario reported as he turned around and leaned against the counter he had been holding onto. "My guess is Dr. Jeffers didn't know what he was dealing with. If Algos knew there were rules, he was not one to care. Jeffers disappeared shortly afterwards at the instruction of Algos."

"It appears less than half of the council is corrupted," Corbin added. "Based on what I have collected, it's just a few that have been swayed into following Algos. He didn't bother to get everyone. Just enough to get freedom to come and go as he pleases."

"You said every time he comes, if he's thinking of someone, they get pulled in, like Clarice, right?" Mario asked.

"Yes, but he only did it once, so far. Apparently, Algos doesn't think about anyone much, including her," Corbin answered, with sorrow in his voice.

"That is not a bear you want to poke," Mario warned.

"What?" Corbin asked in confusion, staring at Mario.

"Not only is she a hot mess, but you'll have to deal with Jess. And you've seen what she can do," Mario advised, as he walked to the table and sat down again.

"I don't know what you're talking about," Corbin retorted, shaking his head.

"Uh huh," Mario said, as he frowned with doubt.

Corbin rolled his eyes and went to sit at the table with him.

"Sophie's safe for now, but I worry about the effects of her being trapped so long," Corbin offered honestly.

"What do you mean?" Mario asked panicked.

"That's the thing," Corbin said. "I don't know without being with her."

"Let's not worry about what we don't know, and focus on what we do know," answered Jack, as he came to sit at the table with the other men. "What have you found out?" he asked Corbin once he sat down.

"Your dad doesn't appear to be here," Corbin confirmed. "I've looked everywhere."

"What does that mean?" asked Mario.

"He most likely moved on a long time ago," said Corbin with a shrug.

"Then why the constant flood of memories?" Jack asked him with curiosity. "We both know something never means nothing in here."

"You will not like the answer," Corbin warned.

"Out with it, Doc!" Mario shouted at him.

"The only explanation is that he is a part of the puzzle, or he's in danger. And if he's not here...." Corbin said, dropping off.

Jack nodded in understanding. Mario looked from Corbin to his friend.

"So, if he's a part of the puzzle, maybe we should focus on that part," Mario offered.

It had taken Mario a long time not to hate Jack for taking the woman he loved, but over the years, Jack had become the brother Mario never had. He couldn't stand seeing Jack suffer. He had already lost enough, as is.

"What do you remember, exactly?" Corbin asked Jack.

"I mean, there are a lot of things," Jack said, leaning back to think. "John bought me my first chemistry set," he answered with a shrug. "He'd always let me help with his experiments. In fact, after John died in the car wreck, I switched from band to scientist to honor him. There wasn't anything he didn't have an answer for," Jack responded with a smile as he watched the memories play like a movie before him.

"Man, could we use him, now," Mario said, shaking his head. "It would be nice to have someone with answers."

"We do," said Corbin, as his face lit up.

"Who?" Jack asked, looking at him with confusion.

"You!" Corbin answered with so much enthusiasm, he spilled Mario's open beer bottle over his papers.

"Hey, Man!" Mario yelled, as he quickly pulled his papers away.

"Sorry," Corbin said quickly, before turning to Jack.

"I don't understand," said Jack in confusion.

"We've been going the wrong way," Corbin announced. When both men looked at him as if he had lost his mind, Corbin tried to clarify. "We've been going forward instead of backwards!"

"Doc, I'm gonna need more than that," Mario said in frustration as he tried to save his own notes.

"Jack, you're the only one that knows both men completely. Instead of guessing Algos' next move, we need to go backwards and study the moves from the past," Corbin said, as lit up like boy opening presents on Christmas morning.

"Like chess," Jack said, smiling, realizing just what Corbin was needing him to do.

"We don't have time for games," Mario said, confused, as he watched Jack jump up and grab the chess board that appeared on the table by the couch.

"But we're already playing, my friend," Jack said with glee as he set the board down before him and Corbin. "We just haven't been playing like the masters we are," Jack added with his own Cheshire grin.

"I suck at chess," Mario said, shaking his head. "I'm just thankful Sophie never wanted to play."

"Mario, you're better than anyone. You just play with a different board," Jack said, looking up and putting his hand on Mario's shoulder. "Watch!"

"We're aware of everything that has happened since you got here, so let's go from the day before you arrived," Corbin said with eagerness.

Jack thought long and hard. "I had made the necklace for Sophie," he said, moving a pawn forward. "We knew Algos was going to use the satellite to cause 'natural disasters' around the world and profit off of it."

Corbin moved his own pawn forward. "Algos most likely made the plan to kill you both, and take Sophie when he realized you weren't going to play ball."

"No," Mario said, shaking his head. "I mean, yes, he wants the satellite, but Sophie was on his radar to take long before Jack stopped playing nice," he added, taking a sudden interest in the game.

"Okay," Corbin said, pulling his pawn back. He thought for a second, then moved it back into play. "Jack was the last excuse he

144

needed to take them both out and take Sophie."

Jack moved another piece forward. "I had already set up all the funding, and left the instructions for Mario while Jess arranged all the teaching to take place once we were gone."

Mario shifted in his seat uncomfortably. He didn't like this game. Then he felt Jack's hand on his shoulder.

"We need to do this to win, my friend," Jack assured him.

Corbin was studying his next move. Mario sighed in resignment. He took a piece from Corbin's side and moved it forward. "I had intel that Algos was gathering teams around the world for an assassination. He offered each party twenty million for success," Mario added gloomily.

Jack smiled and nodded at him. The men continued the chess game. Moving pieces forward and backwards as they each provided information from what they knew had happened all the way to what they knew of Jess' childhood.

"That's it," Mario whispered.

"That's it, indeed," Jack confirmed.

"This is where we need to start from," Corbin said as he studied the board, pleased with the result.

"Let's get to work," Jack said, as he stood up and went to talk to his wife.

Tina woke up and stretched her aching bones from sitting in the chair for so long. It was late, according to the moon that shined through the tinted windows.

"Hey, sleepy head," James whispered as he knelt down in front of her.

"Where's Ben?" Tina asked, quietly.

"Cecil forced a beer down him and put him to bed," James snickered.

"Sounds about right," Tina giggled. She looked over at Sophie's sleeping body. "How is she?" she asked sadly.

"Her vitals remain steady, but no change," James answered, looking over at her. "I just don't know what to do for her."

"I'm not sure we can do anything for her," Tina said gloomily. "I think this is a battle she has to fight herself. But keep talking to her and touching her," she added. "She can feel and hear you."

James looked at her in sudden alarm. "You saw her, didn't you?" he asked. The bitterness came through without him realizing it.

"I did," Tina said, putting her hand on his knee.

"I just don't understand. Why everyone but me?" James asked with obvious hurt oozing from every pore of his body.

"Something's wrong," Tina confirmed. "Sophie barely knew me. She said something about reading a memory book with my name on it, but she still didn't know who I actually was."

"What does that mean?" James asked as he stood up in panic.

"Ssshhh!" Tina hissed as she stood up, too. "I think the longer Sophie's trapped, the more memories go missing. Starting with the most current ones," she answered with a frown. "But she said she hears you and feels you holding her hand," Tina added quickly. "Sophie even said she will come find you once she figures out how to get out."

James shook his head. "Why was I the first to go?" he mumbled in frustration.

"I don't think you were," Tina said in her investigator's voice. She walked over to her friend and looked up at the dream catcher. Maybe Rebecca wasn't on their side after all.

"What do you mean?" James hissed, as he followed her over to Sophie.

Tina continued to study the dream catcher. There wasn't anything Rebecca had given her that could do them harm. Tina had made sure of it. "What if you're purposely being blocked?" Tina declared slowly. "Like the dream catcher blocks bad dreams, what if something or someone was blocking you?"

"Why block me?" James asked, staring at the dream catcher with her.

"Because you would be the one person to help bring her back," Tina offered, still staring at the black ring above Sophie.

"We need to take that thing down," James asserted. He turned to get the ladder, but Tina grabbed his arm to stop him.

"We're not sure that's what's causing it," Tina articulated, still staring at the dream catcher above Sophie.

"Well, we don't know that it's helping either," demanded James.

"I think it might be," Tina said, deep in thought.

"I don't understand," James pleaded.

Tina turned to face him. "I didn't tell you everything," she confessed. She told him about her encounter with the other version of Sophie. "This was the real Sophie this time," Tina declared once she finished. "I think the dream catcher is keeping whatever that other thing was at bay. It had said it was going to get whatever it wanted. One way or another. I think we need the dream catcher to not allow it to use us against Sophie," Tina revealed.

James looked from his friend to the woman he loved more than anything on this planet. "So, how do I help her if they won't let me access her?" he begged.

"We just have to find a work around," Tina said, with a smile and shrug.

"And where do we find one of those?" James exasperated, turning to Tina.

"Oh, Honey. I've got moves you haven't ever seen before," Tina said with a wicked grin as she sauntered past him and went to find her laptop.

James looked at Sophie's unresponsive body. He walked over and took the chair next to her. "I know I always tell you to 'come find me', but I'm realizing that maybe it's my turn to come find you. I just have to figure out how. Once I do, I will come to you. And we'll leave together, like we always do," he said, squeezing her hand and kissing her on her forehead. "They can try as hard as they want. I'm not leaving you. Ever."

Sophie woke up and felt her cheeks wet. She heard what he had said. She may not remember him fully, but she sensed he was a man of his word. For that, she was thankful.

"Are you alright?" John asked cautiously.

"I'm forgetting," Sophie said, looking at him with sorrow.

"I know," John said, glancing at the floor in discomfort. "We just need to find out how to get out of here."

Sophie looked out the window on the door. Even from the couch, she could see her evil counterpart sitting in the metal folding chair with her elbows resting on her knees, and barely holding her head up. But her glowing red eyes locked with Sophie's blue ones, and panic and nausea filled Sophie's stomach. She heard Tina's words whisper softly in her ears.

Some people say that when we're trapped within ourselves, sometimes that means we need to find peace from within in order to move on.

Sophie wasn't sure what she had to do exactly, but she was sure that it had something to do with the version of herself on the other side of the door. She just prayed she would be the one leaving, and not the girl who's eyes glowed red and was dying of thirst for blood.

Eleven

D r. William Jeffers paced nervously in the dump of a hotel room he had been hiding in since last week. "Keep moving," Bates had told him, and so he did. He stopped to look in the mirror that he had already passed a thousand times and ran a hand nervously through his already thinned grey hair. The wrinkles around his eyes had definitely increased, and his hazel eyes were full of fear.

William should have listened to his gut when Bates first entered his office. He had told Bates that he didn't know about this "dream realm" they kept bringing up. No one did! No one knew what actually happened once it was time for you to meet your maker, except for those that already had. William was not looking forward to joining that list, either.

150

The man who went by the name of Algos scared him to death. He didn't care that William didn't have the answers he sought, but he had no problem threatening his life if he didn't tell him something. So, regretfully, William offered Dr. Corbin Dallas. Algos simply said he wasn't an option. That was when William heard of Corbin's untimely death.

William had a family! However, Algos could have cared less. So, he told Algos everything he knew about this so-called "dream realm" over the years of studying it with Corbin. Corbin had been much more fascinated by the subject. William just looked at it as a hobby of sorts and only studied what others had already shared. He hadn't messed with trying to cross over himself.

At 76 years of age, William was too old to be playing the game of living on the run. Luckily, his wife was already gone, but their children and grandchildren remained. However, for their own safety, William was forced to fall off the face of the earth without notice. Without giving them one last kiss goodbye. William hated Algos and Bates, both, for taking that away from him. He looked at the bag that he had hastily packed so many months ago, grabbed it, and put his hat on his head to leave the hotel room.

When he opened the door, he nearly fell onto his back as he stumbled as quickly away from the figure before him. Algos smiled in amusement at his reaction.

"Dr. Jeffers," Algos said, dryly.

"I have done nothing. I have told no one," William stammered out as he tried to get his heart to stop beating so rapidly before he had a heart attack.

"I am well aware," Algos said, entering the room. "Take a seat.

We have some things to discuss."

"You said you were done with me," William said nervously as he backed into the worn out chair behind him.

"Things have come up," Algos shrugged as he took a seat on the very uncomfortable and cheap queen sized bed.

"I don't know anything else," William begged.

"Let me be the judge of that," Algos said with a wicked smile. "Now, Dr. Jeffers, what do you suppose happens to one if they are killed in the dream realm? Would they just be dead for good? Or would they be more like an obnoxious cat that would have nine lives and keep returning?"

"Beats the heck out of me!" William shouted in desperation. "Without being there, I can't guarantee anything!"

"Very valid point," Algos stated as his eyes glimmered with excitement at a new idea. "How would one go about locating someone within? Hypothetically, of course," he added as he stared down at the trembling doctor before him.

"Again, I have no clue!" William exasperated. "I only studied what others expressed. I never looked into it myself. I have already told you this!"

"Yes, you have, Doctor," Algos said as he tilted his head to study the doctor. Excitement rose as he absorbed Dr. Jeffers' fear pulsed out from his body like shock waves. "Just one more thing," Algos said in a tone that left poor William on the verge of having a heart attack right then and there.

Algos sat in the hotel room for several hours admiring his handiwork as Dr. Jeffers' body swung by a rope back and forth from the sprinkler system. It looked like a suicide. Of course, they would both know otherwise.

Algos knew the only way to get the answers he needed was to have a guinea pig on the other side to play with. He would track down Dr. Jeffers and get the answers he needed from the other side. Algos guessed that most people would have felt a little guilty taking a life for this kind of bidding, but Algos wasn't most people.

He enjoyed watching the life leave Dr. Jeffers' eyes. It gave him the same thrill it had always done. A thought suddenly crossed his mind, and Algos secretly hoped he never lost the thrill of a kill. There would be nothing left to enjoy. Then where would he be?

Algos grabbed his cane and wiped the handle of the door off after closing it. No one would second guess this poor man staying in such a sad location had taken his own life. The note sealed the deal, and Algos made sure there was no evidence of foul play. Now, to get back to the task at hand. He would have to locate Dr. Jeffers before the others did.

Clarice paced the lab. "It can't be THAT hard to find her!" she barked at the techs scrambling around her.

"The only trace was the bus from Vegas to Bakersfield, Ma'am," stammered Clark's female replacement.

Clarice glared at the girl, who provided her with no answers.

"Eddie!" she yelled over her shoulder. "What was the point in you joining us if you can't find her? Isn't this your expertise!"

Eddie rolled his eyes. "They were in a crappy hotel, in a crappy area that had crappy surveillance in the area. I can only work with what I'm given," he retorted.

"Are you even trying?" Clarice growled back.

"Hey. I enjoy breathing," was his only response. They were both well aware of what happened when someone failed the old man.

"There's no direction or anything?" Clarice snapped.

"Nope," the red-head replied. Clarice glared at her again. She really despised red-heads. She stomped over to stand next to Eddie with her arms crossed, glaring at the tech that shivered before her under Clarice's stare.

"Are you not the least bit curious why he doesn't care if we find her or not?" Eddie asked under his breath, distracting her.

"What?" Clarice replied, not taking her eyes off the red-head.

"He hasn't been down here in days. He hasn't asked. He hasn't ordered. He doesn't care if we find her," Eddie whispered, observing her out of the corner of his eye.

Clarice froze. "That's because he knows I'm handling it," she finally said defiantly, but the doubt seeped into her sentence, giving her away. "Find her!" Clarice shouted, before turning on her heels and storming back to her room.

Got her, Eddie thought to himself. He casually leaned on the main switchboard, and all computers went dark. "Damn it! he yelled. He felt everyone panic around him.

"How do we fix this?" stammered the red-head, clearly fearing for her life.

154

"Get me that flashlight and metal box over there," Eddie ordered, nodding to the corner. She rushed over to grab it and eagerly handed it to him. "Give me a second," he said, as he went to climb under the table.

"Let me help," she said, following his actions.

"You can help by giving me some space," Eddie commanded with authority. "Get back to your station. We should be up in just a few minutes." She hesitated, but finally left him alone to mess with the wiring.

Now was his chance. Eddie took the short black cable out of the box that he had put in there long ago. He just had to hide it well enough to not be noticed, or he wouldn't live to help Sophie anymore.

After a few minutes, all the monitors came back to life. Eddie heard the ripple effect of everyone letting out the breath they had been holding since it went out.

"Are we good?" she asked readily.

"Yes, but a little advice," Eddie answered as he got off the floor. "Unless you want to end up like Clark, I'd say this 'glitch' doesn't leave this room," he said loud enough for everyone to hear.

"Who's Clark?" the red-head asked, confused.

"Exactly," Eddie warned and stared her down a bit before getting back to work.

The red-head hesitated, but swallowed the lump that was apparently stuck in her throat and went back to work. Poor kid. She had no idea who she's really working for, but Eddie had bigger things to worry about. Like getting Tina access to the mainframe undetected to see if Sophie's fears were correct. More importantly, if Algos already started cloning Sophie or not.

He excused himself to go to the bathroom. Eddie checked every stall to make sure he was alone, and then he went to the last stall and pulled the burner phone that was inside the toilet tank in a plastic bag. The smallest he could get his hands on.

"You're in," Eddie texted to Tina.

"TY" was the only response he got before putting it back, flushed the toilet, and going out to wash his hands and get back to work.

Clarice was originally heading to the training room, but the weak feeling that consumed her told her she needed to sit down, and fast.

She raced to her room and slammed the door shut, locking it. Clarice stumbled to her bed and barely got her body on it before falling into darkness.

She fell for what felt like an eternity before landing like a cat on the black ground that seemed to be invisible to the eye. Her father's voice was in the distance. She had learned her lesson not to call out to him, but simply followed the sound.

Clarice saw the seven foot cloaked figure standing before her father, but she couldn't clearly hear what they were saying. How was she supposed to take cover when there was nothing around her? Clarice had to do something. She couldn't hear a thing.

She took in a breath and crept slowly and as quietly as possible. Suddenly, she felt a hand cover her mouth and another slide

156

softly around her waist before pulling her behind a wall that suddenly appeared.

"Welcome back," she heard Corbin whisper in her ear before removing his hand from her mouth.

"Don't flatter yourself. I didn't have a choice," Clarice hissed over her shoulder while not taking her eyes off of her father.

"Where is he?" Algos demanded.

"We have separated him. He's in holding, but I can't keep him there for long," the male voice stated loudly.

"Fine. Just give him to me," Algos ordered.

"I do not take orders from you!" yelled the cloaked figure. The ground shook underneath them, and Clarice lost her footing and fell back into Corbin. He caught her quickly and put her back on her feet. Her heart beat faster, but she ignored it. She felt his smile behind her, regardless.

"It's merely for both our protection," Algos backtracked. "He will help me find your leader, so I can take care of him. Do you not want him dethroned?" Algos taunted the cloaked figure before him, unaffected by its size.

The cloaked figure tilted his head to study Algos for a second before responding, "I will retrieve him."

"Who did your father kill?" Corbin whispered softly into Clarice's ear.

"Hell if I know," Clarice hissed back.

"You don't know?" Corbin asked suspiciously.

"I don't track his every move. I haven't even seen him in days," Clarice muttered, unsure of her need to tell him the truth.

"Do not move!" the cloaked figured ordered before being

surrounded by black fog and disappearing.

"Guess we're about to find out," Corbin said with gloom.

Before he finished his sentence, the cloaked figure reappeared, holding a man by his collar. The man wore a worn khaki suit and hung his head low. There didn't appear to be any life left in him until he looked up and saw Algos.

"No!" he cried out and fought to break the cloaked figure's hold on him with no success.

"Who is that?" Clarice asked curiously.

"I don't know," Corbin lied calmly.

He did know. It was Dr. William Jeffers. The only other person who played in the oreironaut world with Corbin, although William was more of a bystander. He just studied it from afar for a hobby. Corbin unconsciously tightened his grip around Clarice's waist as he tried to control his anger.

Of course, Algos would go after William when he didn't get access to Corbin. Guilt consumed him. Even Clarice felt it in her stomach.

"What is his purpose?" the cloaked figure demanded.

"I need to test a theory," Algos said as he looked at Dr. Jeffers like he was the dessert they had deprived him of as a kid.

"I have told you everything I know!" William shouted. "You have already killed me!"

Corbin tightened his grip even more on Clarice. She put her hand softly over his. "You're going to crush my ribs if you keep tightening your grip," she said half sarcastically.

"Sorry," Corbin said, loosening his grip but not letting go, and Clarice didn't fight him about it.

"Hey, Doc," Algos said with a sickening, wicked grin.

"Long time no see."

"You just KILLED ME!" screamed William. "Please let me go!" he begged. However, his pleading fell on deaf ears.

"Did you find out how to locate others?" Algo asked, ignoring him.

"What?" Williams asked in confusion. "No!"

"That's very disappointing, Dr. Jeffers," Algos said, but his smile remained. "Put him down," he ordered the cloaked figure.

"He appears of no use," the figure said in confusion.

"I'm not done," Algos laughed. "Please, put him down."

Clarice was in shock. She couldn't remember a time that her father had ever used the word "please" in her entire life. "Something's not right," she whispered.

"What do you mean?" Corbin asked as he watched the figure put his friend down.

"He's going to kill him," Clarice answered honestly.

"He can't," Corbin said, shaking his head in denial. "Not here."

"Now, I don't have time to play, I'm afraid. Time is of the essence," Algos said as he quickly wrapped his cane around William's neck and pulled him into his own body.

Clarice had seen her father kill thousands of times, but there was something different about this one. She gasped and threw her hand over her mouth as Corbin pulled her closer and they both watched in shock as William's body flailed around until it finally went still. Algos released his grip and watched the body slide down to the ground and remain limp.

"Hmm," Algos said. "I would have expected more of a climax," he said in disappointment.

"You may not kill in here!" the figure screeched.

"I just did," Algos said with a shrug as he tilted his head to study his prey. "So, what now?"

"Nothing!" the figure said in anger. "If you die here, you're gone forever!"

"That's what I needed to know," Algos said, before turning on his heels to walk away. He stopped in mid-stride and turned back around. "What happens to the body?" he asked in curiosity.

Just then, a shadow swirled above the body before forming an oversized skeletal hand that picked up the body and crushed it into dust. Clarice turned to Corbin and hid her face. She was not ready to accept what she had just seen. Corbin took her into his arms and held her tight as he tried to control his own emotions.

Once the shadow merged back into the ground, Algos replied, "Interesting." Then he spun his cane twice before walking off.

"That's not good," Corbin whispered. "Clarice," he said as he pulled her away from him. "Tell no one what you saw," he said with authority.

"I don't even know what I saw," Clarice said, still in shock. Jess' face flashed before her eyes. "Jess," she whispered.

Corbin took her chin in his hand and lifted her eyes to meet his. "I need you to be careful. I will protect Jess as long as I can, but I can't protect you," he said honestly.

"She will be gone for good," Clarice said, still in shock.

Corbin took her by the shoulders and shook her. "Clarice," he said firmly. "I need you to focus," he ordered.

"This is what he wants?" she said, looking at him for answers.

"And more, I'm afraid," Corbin said with sorrow. "I need to find Jess. When you wake up, tell no one. Do you understand?" he asked.

Clarice didn't respond.

"Clarice!" hissed Corbin.

She finally focused on the figure before her. "I understand," she said with a nod.

"One day, you'll have to decide which side you're really on," Corbin whispered softly before brushing his finger over her forehead and sending her into a deep sleep. He knew he should have just wiped her memory, but maybe if she did, remember. Maybe. Just maybe.

Clarice didn't wake up. She remained in a dreamless sleep. Well, almost dreamless. Minus the sight of Algos killing Jess in the darkness, where she would have no hope of surviving like she had last time. Although Clarice's eyes never opened, silent tears ran down her cheeks as she slept.

Corbin's voice echoed in her head.

"You'll have to decide which side you're really on."

It would be the voice that would haunt her until the end.

It was the middle of the night, and everyone at the Goldfield Hotel was forced into a deep sleep without their knowledge. They would not see the black dream catcher lighting up the room as it worked its magic. They would not see that it protected them from more than Algos, including the evil that brewed within the unconscious body that laid in the hospital bed next to James. Except for one.

Rebecca kept her distance in the game room as she watched the dream catcher help stop whatever was trying to be released. She watched as blue gems that looked like diamonds slid down the feathers like rain and found their way to each sleeping forehead. Whatever was attacking Sophie was strong. Stronger than Algos, and stronger than even Rebecca.

This could be a serious problem. Everything Rebecca had been working on in the last couple of decades could be undone if she didn't figure out how to harness the power that threatened to destroy her plans.

Twelve

Sophie stared at a wooden table as she read through book after book with various names. Simon, Giselle, Ben, Mario, Greg, Molly, Hellen, but the one name she knew she needed to find seemed to be missing.

"How fast do you read?" John ask in fascination as he held onto a red book titled *Jessica Harris.*

"About twenty thousand words a minute," Sophie said with a shrug. "Why?" she asked, suddenly remembering that she's not like most people.

"It's just really fascinating to watch," John chuckled. "Any luck?"

Sophie looked back down at the book before her with a frown.

It was a light blue book titled *Dr. Elaine Cox.* "Not really," she answered in frustration. "It helps me remember stuff, but I'm not finding anything that suggests how to get out of here," she said, leaning back and crossing her arms.

Tina's words came back to her.

"Some people say that when we're trapped within ourselves, sometimes that means we need to find peace from within in order to move on."

"John?" Sophie asked as she turned to face him directly. "How did you find me exactly?"

"Well," he said, taking a second to think. "It felt like my blood was boiling inside of me, and panic filled my body," he replied matter-of-fact. "I knew I needed to find the source to restore balance. So, I closed my eyes and allowed my spirit to be pulled to the power that called to it."

"I called you?" Sophie asked in confusion.

"Not exactly," John replied and sat down in a chair next to her. "As head of the council, I have the most power. I am in charge of keeping balance, so I feel more than the others. You were just more potent because we're related."

Just then, something hit the window of the door and it shattered. "You can't stay in there forever," Sophie's twin taunted from the other side.

"Ignore it," John ordered.

"Kinda hard to," Sophie said, still staring at the window. "She's so angry," she whispered. "What do you think she is? Really?"

164

"She's you," John said with a shrug. When he saw the horror in Sophie's eyes, he realized he needed to be better at explaining things to others. He was very out of practice.

"She's a part of you," he clarified, but he saw it brought no peace.

"Great," Sophie mumbled.

John reached out and put his hand over hers. "She's not the only part," he reminded her. Her veins lit up in an icy blue hue in response to feeling his power against her skin. "Interesting," he said as he watched her body respond to his power.

"I'm not a science project," she protested as she yanked her hand away and crossed her arms disgustedly.

"Sorry. I just haven't been able to touch anyone in a really long time," he said sadly. Guilt consumed Sophie.

"I'm sorry," she whispered. "It's just apparently several people turned me into a freak just for the heck of it," Sophie said in anger as she looked back down at the book in front of her.

"I read that one," John said. "Elaine did nothing but try to help."

"I wasn't talking about her," Sophie clarified.

"You know why you're so fascinating to me?" John asked suddenly as he sat back to study her.

"I'm the by-product of your child?" she said with a laugh.

John let out a laugh. "Well, that, but you are the most gifted person I have ever come across." Sophie rolled her eyes, and he leaned in to make his point. "You're more powerful than I am," he said in a whisper. "And you're still alive," he added.

Sophie froze as she took in what he had said. "Mom always said I was given 'gifts' and never to view them as a 'curse' when I was little," she whispered.

"No one knows better than a mother," John said with a smile. "I knew I liked that girl from the first day I met her," he laughed.

"How did you meet her?" Sophie asked, suddenly eager to hear more of her mother's story.

"Oh, Jack was such a nervous wreck," John said as he smiled, lost in the memory playing before him that Sophie couldn't see. "Kept telling me to not be so 'nerdy', like I knew what that was supposed to mean! But Jack brought Jessica over to have dinner with the two of us. She asked a ton of questions about my inventions. Jack was so embarrassed, but Jessica just giggled and asked me a million more questions. I don't know if she was just humoring me, but she definitely proved how important Jack and his family were to her. Even if it was just a 'nerdy dad'."

"I don't remember that side much," Sophie replied with doubt.

"It was there. She was just too busy protecting her cub," John reminded her. "I knew that night that Jack was going to marry that girl, and I couldn't have been more thankful."

Sophie looked sadly at the table before her. "Do you really feel like that?" she asked quietly.

"Absolutely!" John said with a gigantic smile.

"Her father killed you. He killed your son," Sophie said, staring at him in disbelief.

"Her father. Not her," John emphasized.

"His blood runs in her veins. They run in mine!" Sophie protested.

"So does mine," he said with a wink.

Sophie looked back at the window. "Apparently, not enough,"

she mumbled.

"Why are you so sure?" he asked her.

"Because she exists," Sophie said, looking back at him in misery.

"Yes," John confirmed. "And so do you," he added. "Sophie, you have to understand. To have balance, there must always be bad and good. Yes, you have some less than desirable parts of your family tree, but there's so much more good than evil on it."

"I have a psychopath for a grandfather!" Sophie exclaimed.

"And a lead council of death. Accident or default did not choose me. Look at your own parents. They were exceptionally powerful. Your mother has more of his blood in her than you do, and look at all the good she still produces."

The scene of her mother fighting Algos and the enjoyment of the kill that her mother had in her eyes made her shudder.

"Enough," John ordered. "She went to fight him for you.

A psychopath doesn't fight for anything other than themselves. Do not judge your mother on one instance. Here," he said, shoving her book towards Sophie. "Read it again," he demanded.

"I already did," Sophie whined.

"Read it again, Smarty Pants," he commanded.

"Fine," Sophie said in resignation and picked up the red book.

"Read it slowly," John emphasized. "You clearly missed a lot the first time," he said with a frown.

Sophie rolled her eyes and started reading the memories that were her mother, but her evil twin threw something else at the window on the door that made her look up again.

John waved his hand, and a small wooden door covered the

window instantly. "Read," he insisted, nodding at the red book.

Sophie sighed dramatically and read once more.

Rebecca watched James from afar. She had borrowed a biker body to study him. It seemed impossible to believe that the limp body that laid on the bed connected to all sorts of machines was what everyone was fighting over. She sat on the couch, occasionally sneaking a peak at the scene before her.

She smiled to see the dream catcher hanging above Sophie's body. "Good girl," she whispered to herself.

Rebecca knew she was more powerful than most expected, but if she got caught breaking the rules of the realm, then all of her hard work would be for nothing.

She couldn't access Sophie. She had already tried. There was a force more powerful than even her that was keeping the girl untouchable. Rebecca would have to find another way. She watched James sit ever so patiently, holding Sophie's hand in his. She was too far away to hear what he was telling Sophie, and it would be too obvious if she got too close.

It didn't matter. Rebecca was a master at patience. She had to be. You can't get what you want without a little patience. She knew that time was running out, but if she was going to get what she wanted, she would have to figure out how to use James to her benefit. Puzzles were her expertise. This was good, but Rebecca was better. They wouldn't know what happened until it was too late.

Ben leaned over to his wife. "So, how do we know if the dream catcher is helping or hurting?" he asked.

"We don't," Tina whispered back. "Not without asking Sophie if there's been a change, and well…" she dropped off.

"What if we could ask her?" James said, sitting up in the chair next to Sophie.

"I don't think they can help," Tina said, knowing that look.

"It doesn't hurt to ask," James said, and before there could be any more discussion, he closed his eyes and whispered, "Corbin."

When he opened his eyes, he saw the wooden door before him.

"Open it," he heard Corbin instruct him. James eagerly opened it. Only, instead of the cabin he usually found himself in, it was some sort of office surrounded by books and piles of papers that consumed the entire room. "Sorry for the mess," Corbin said with his nose in a book. "What's up?"

"I know you have to work on keeping Algos out," James started, "but is there a way for me to reach Sophie while she sleeps?"

Corbin looked up in thought. "I guess it would depend on where exactly she's hiding."

"We're pretty sure it's inside her own mind," James confirmed.

"That, unfortunately, doesn't narrow it down," Corbin said with a frown. "Entering the wrong place could get you lost forever."

"I have to try!" James shouted.

Corbin stopped and put his book down. "How is the dream catcher working?" he asked.

"We do not know. That's why if we could find her and ask her," James said in frustration. "Tina said she's forgetting," he added.

"Forgetting, how?" Corbin asked in his doctor voice.

"It took Sophie awhile to remember her," James reported. "But she remembered Eddie immediately," he mumbled.

"So, she's losing her most recent memories first?" Corbin asked to clarify.

"Maybe," James shrugged. "She doesn't remember me at all," he added sorrowfully.

"Doesn't remember you?" Corbin repeated.

"Repeating everything isn't exactly helpful," James growled.

"That makes no sense," Corbin said, trying to clarify.

"Tina said there might be something blocking her from remembering me."

"Now, that makes sense," Corbin said, looking frantically for something.

"Do you think it's Algos?" James asked with concern.

"Definitely not," Corbin confirmed. "He's still scrambling to find her."

"How do you know?" James asked in doubt.

"He's trying to get some members of the council to find her for him," Corbin replied as he continued to tear up his make-shift office.

"So, who would block me from being contacted?" James asked in more anger than curiosity. "What are you looking for?" he asked, irritated.

"Ah ha!" Corbin said, holding up a very thick dusty book and blew the dust off of it. He began flipping through it frantically until he found the section he needed. "Our brains are extremely finicky and complex," he said as he read the section he needed.

"So you keep saying," James said, annoyed. "That's helpful, how?"

"I once studied that when the brain is fractured, it could send false signals," Corbin replied.

"English, Doc," James growled as he was losing his patience.

"Basically, someone thought you might pull Sophie back to freedom. It's possible that they have a way of sending her false signals that are blocking the people that can help her from coming to her," Corbin replied with a frown.

"Tina got through," James reminded him.

"They might not realize that Tina is as helpful as she actually is," Corbin declared.

"So, how do we stop them?" James asked.

"We will figure it out," Corbin said, putting his hand on James' shoulder, but James pulled away.

"When?" he shouted.

"We have more important things at the moment," Corbin said in a low voice.

"What's more important than Sophie?" James yelled.

"Lower your voice," Corbin warned. His eyes glowed icy blue in a way that silenced James, forcing him to swallow his anger. "I just watched Algos kill someone who was already dead, and when that happens, there's no coming back," Corbin whispered with caution.

"What does that mean?" James whispered frightened.

"It means if Algos gets a hold of me, Jack, Jess, Mario, or anyone and we die in here, that's it. I saw it with my own eyes," Corbin replied.

James' face went white. "That's not good. That's not good at all."

"No. It's not," Corbin said softly. "We need to stop Algos from entering this realm. Once that's done, we can save Sophie."

"But what if it takes too long?" James asked.

Corbin didn't reply. Not because he didn't want to. He honestly didn't know. "One battle at a time," he sighed.

"I understand," James said with a nod. "You can send me back."

"Are you okay?" Corbin asked him with suspicion.

"You have your hands full," James said as convincingly as possible. "We will just have to keep her safe and help you as much as possible from our end."

Corbin knew that look. Jack had the same one. James would not wait. He was going to do everything to save the woman he loved. "Very well," Corbin said with resign. "Good luck," he said with a smile and brushed his finger over James' forehead, and James woke up with a gasp.

"Well," Ben asked.

"We're on our own," James said with a frown as he tried to catch his breath.

"That's comforting," Ben said sarcastically.

"They've got their hands full," James announced.

"Full, how? Exactly?" Tina asked suspiciously.

Rebecca looked up from the couch with interest.

"Apparently, Algos has figured out that he can kill in the realm and eliminate people for good," James announced in frustration.

"What?!" Tina and Ben gasped in unison.

It took all the strength Rebecca had to stay in the body she was currently hiding in.

"Yeah, Corbin says if Algos kills any of them, there's no coming back. Period. Corbin watched it first-hand," James said softly, but it didn't escape Rebecca's ears. This changes everything.

"Ben, is there a way to connect James to Sophie with the equipment we have here?" Tina asked in sudden eagerness. "Maybe we can help push him through to her, and bypass whatever is currently blocking him. I think I can design a program to help us navigate. Brain waves are much like computer language. If we could tap into the right wave, we might get them connected."

"I love the thought, but that's a dangerous game. The brain is fragile. There's no guarantee James could reach Sophie, and no way to guarantee they would both leave," Ben affirmed with a frown.

"Get me to her," James said defiantly. "We can find our way out."

"What do you mean you're blocked?" The girl that Rebecca was using as a host asked. Everyone turned to look at her. "Like, is it a mental thing, or do we need to go beat up someone?" she added for good measure.

"We honestly don't know," Tina said with caution.

The girl on the couch shook her head as she looked around in confusion.

"You okay?" Daryl asked her as he studied her.

"Just had a weird dream," the girl said, shaking her head in puzzlement. It was a dream, right?

Rebecca had left her host and went back to the realm to rethink her strategy. This changed the playing field for sure, but could she still do what she needed to? She looked over her shoulder to make sure she wasn't being followed and then headed for her secret spot, where she could strategize and come up with a new plan. As soon as possible.

"Did you know?" Jess asked her husband.

"Know what?" Jack asked, not looking up from his current project.

"That James would be the one?" Jess asked, observing him.

Jack stopped fiddling with some wiring to look back at his wife. "You know I didn't," he replied, hurt by the implication.

"All this time, we tried to keep her from people," Jess whispered to herself.

"We tried to keep her safe," Jack corrected her. "Thank God for fate," he added with a chuckle.

"Do you think he can really bring her back if she ever loses control?" she whispered, barely able to get the words out.

Jack dropped everything to stand up and go to his wife. He pulled her into his arms. "I bring you back, don't I?" he whispered as he kissed her gently on the top of her head.

"You know you do," she laughed lightly. "But they're more, aren't they?" she asked, already knowing the answer.

Jack sighed, knowing what his wife needed to hear. "There's a reason they met when they did. There's a reason he felt protective of her right away. There's always a reason. We just didn't know how much it mattered until we got in this realm. Now, we know better," he

174

whispered.

"He will die for her, won't he?" Jess asked.

"Let's hope it doesn't come to that," Jack replied.

"He's her chosen protector," Jess said with a slight smile.

"Every key needs one," Jack assured, although something told him that this was going to be much bigger than either of them were. Jess and Jack both had power greater than most in the realm. Corbin was on a completely different scale from both of them combined. All these years in the realm only taught them one thing. It would forever change, and not always for the better. Change was coming. They could both feel it. And against their desires, Sophie had already become a part of it. No one knew how, but when that much evil flows in your blood with that much power, no one is safe.

Jack secretly prayed while he swayed with his wife in his arms. He prayed James was actually the chosen one that they were all guessing he was. If not, death was just as much at stake as the living was.

Thirteen

She read her mother's book, but she already knew something John didn't. Sophie knew how powerful the other version of herself actually was. She had taken plenty of lives over the years. When she had faced Clarice, she had lost complete control and the worst part was how much she loved how it made her feel.

John was right. There was still good in her, but something told Sophie that it might not be enough. What Algos did to her mother remained dormant, but was even more powerful in Sophie. Her mother's desire to kill like her own psychopathic father flowed in her veins like it did Sophie. Only Sophie had the power to never come back from it. That scared Sophie the most.

She lightly ran her finger over the yellow book titled *Ben*

176

Miller. "I miss you, Brother," Sophie whispered softly. Her eyes grew very heavy. She folded her arms on the table in front of her and laid her head down. Just a quick little nap….

"Hello?" she heard his voice calling to her.

"Ben!" Sophie called out and ran to his voice.

"Sophie?" he asked in confusion.

"You're a sight for sore eyes," Sophie said with a smile as she ran and threw her arms around his neck.

"Is this really you?" Ben asked with caution.

"Yes," she said, pulling back with a laugh.

"Tina said you were forgetting," Ben said cautiously.

"I've been reading up," Sophie said with a smile. "It's helping me remember a little more."

"How can we help you?" Ben asked eagerly.

"I don't know," she confessed. "I have been through almost all the books, and I don't see an answer anywhere," Sophie declared in frustration.

"Why am I here?" he asked in sudden apprehension.

"You were the last book I read," Sophie shrugged.

"But why not, James?" Ben asked, shaking his head.

"Who?" Sophie asked with a frown.

"James," Ben said, looking at her with great concern.

Sophie looked blankly back at him and shook her head. "I don't know who that is?" she said slowly. "Should I?"

"Please hang in there, Hun. I will get to you," they heard James whisper to her.

"That," Ben said, pointing to the black sky above them. "You don't know who that is?" he asked, studying her.

"Oh, he talks to me all the time," Sophie said. "He seems really nice," she said with a smile.

Ben stopped breathing. Tina was right. For whatever reason, James was being blocked from Sophie. Then a thought came to him.

"Sophie," Ben asked her in his doctor's voice. "Have you noticed any kind of difference in your surroundings?"

"What do you mean?" Sophie inquired.

"I'm not sure," Ben said. "Have things seemed to have gotten better or worse in any way?"

Sophie took a second to think. "I haven't had any more visions," she replied honestly. Her evil twin was getting more mad, she thought to herself. "Why?"

"We weren't sure if the dream catcher was helping or hurting," Ben said, studying her. "Are you sure it seems to make things better? Because if not, we need to take it down," he said firmly.

Maybe that's why she was getting angrier? "I think it helps," Sophie said honestly.

Ben took her hands in his. "How do we help you get out of here?"

Sophie hung her head low. "I don't know, honestly. But we used to talk about mind powers. Do you think I really have any?" she asked, looking into his eyes with anxiousness.

"I wouldn't put it past you," Ben said with a smile. "Why?"

"I think I'm going to have to fight my way out," she said, deep in thought.

"Fight, how?" he asked panicked.

"I'm not sure," she lied. "How am I doing?"

"Honestly, I'm surprised your body hasn't started shutting

down yet, but it will the longer you're here. We need to get you out."

"Trust me, I'm trying," she said with determination. Then a thought came to her mind. "Was Tina okay? After seeing me in here?"

"As far as I could tell," Ben answered. "Why?"

Sophie thought of the life that grew inside her friend. "I don't know how this works, and I just wanted to make sure I wasn't harming anyone," she said honestly. "I can't sleep very long. I need you to wake up first."

"Sleep?" he asked.

"Yes. Apparently, if we're both asleep, we have a better chance of reaching each other," she said, looking over her shoulder. Someone else was there. She sensed it.

"Oh, and Ben?" Sophie asked.

"Yeah?"

"Tell him to keep talking to me," she requested in a low whisper.

"I couldn't stop him even if I wanted to," Ben replied with a smile. Sophie gave a small smile in response before screaming, "WAKE UP!" Ben was suddenly pulled back into the darkness.

"Sophie?" the girl asked in a timid tone.

"Giselle?" Sophie answered back.

A girl with platinum blonde hair pulled back in a ponytail that went past her waist and looked like she might break if someone even looked at her wrong walked fearfully in Sophie's direction.

"Aren't you dead?" Sophie asked with caution.

She watched Giselle's eyes light up in recognition. "Gee, thanks for the reminder," she said with a laugh. "Where are we?"

"Not sure exactly," Sophie lied. She couldn't trust herself right now.

Giselle looked around before looking back at Sophie. "I think I'm supposed to tell you something," she said with a frown.

"Oh, yeah?" Sophie asked, putting her hands on her hips. "What's that?"

Giselle frowned as she tried to rack her brain. They were very specific about what she was supposed to say. "I'm trying to remember," she said as she thought back to the specific words she was supposed to use.

Something gave Sophie an uneasy feeling about this version of her so-called friend from her past.

"Do you remember Paris?" Giselle asked her, buying herself some time.

"I do," Sophie said, studying the figure before her, thankful she had refreshed herself with Giselle's book.

"I wanted to tell you it wasn't your fault," Giselle said, getting off track.

Sophie froze and stared at her.

"It wasn't your fault," Giselle repeated. "But thanks for giving Simon what he deserved," she said with a thankful smile.

Sophie's heart went to the girl before her, but something still wasn't right. "I'm sorry I couldn't save you," Sophie whispered, but kept her guard up all the same.

"I know," Giselle said, nodding in confirmation. "He was a real a-hole, wasn't he?" she said with a weary smile.

"That he was," Sophie said, returning the smile, "Was that what you wanted to tell me?"

"No," Giselle said slowly. "Oh yeah! I'm supposed to tell you not to trust those that cross your path. No one is who they say they are," she said with a triumphant nod.

"Does that include you?" Sophie asked in doubt.

"No, Silly!" Giselle laughed. "But some are here to harm you. You need to be careful."

"I always am," Sophie said, crossing her arms in front of her.

"You were always better than me," Giselle said with a weak smile, looking down at the invisible ground below her.

"Who told you to warn me?" Sophie asked.

"What?" Giselle asked, looking up. "Oh, I can't say," she said nervously. "There are rules."

"You just told me not to trust anyone, and now you can't tell me who told you to tell me?" Sophie questioned.

"Oh, yeah. That's a good point," Giselle said, trying to think.

"Giselle, are you in trouble?" Sophie asked, with a hint of apprehension in her voice.

Giselle looked up at her friend. If she said too much, there would be a colossal price to pay. She wasn't sure she could afford it. But wasn't she sent for a reason?

"Sophie, we ALL are in trouble if you don't wake up soon," Giselle said. If she didn't tell her friend the truth, it wouldn't matter. "I need you to understand that there are people in here trying to make sure you never wake up. And if that happens, then no one will survive. The dead or the living," she whispered as she looked over her shoulder nervously. "Trust no one," Giselle added, pleading.

Sophie thought of John and felt sick. Had she been working with the enemy all along? "Thank you," Sophie said in a whisper. "I will remember the advice."

"Sophie," Giselle said timidly. "We're rooting for you. You're not alone."

"Who's we?" Sophie asked, desperate to get more information.

"Oh, you know. The usual crew," Giselle said with a wink and smile.

Usual crew? Who was that? But before she could ask any more questions, Giselle was gone.

Sophie woke up with one less ally and a head swimming of confusion.

"Did you tell her?" one of the female cloaked figures demanded.

"Yes, I did," Giselle said with a confident nod.

"Did you tell her anything else?" demanded another.

"No. I did not. I know the rules," Giselle lied with determination. She was a terrible liar, but for her sake, she hoped they bought it.

They looked her up and down before finally demanding, "Leave us!"

Giselle didn't hesitate to take herself out of the council's den.

"She told her more," one announced.

"Nothing that the girl didn't need to hear," Rebecca said, walking into the room. Only three council members were in the room.

"Time is running out," a cloaked figure shrieked.

"I'm well aware," Rebecca announced. "But we'll wake her up one way or another."

"I'm sorry we're late!" Roger yelled as he entered the room where Sophie slept. He stopped cold at the site of her unconscious body. He quickly swallowed the lump in his throat.

"Oh, Love!" Sally exclaimed as she rushed to grab Sophie's other hand that wasn't already being held by James.

"Hey, Mom," he said with a weary smile.

"Jamie Moore, when was the last time you ate or slept?" Sally demanded. He shuddered at the name.

"Kinda busy, Mom," he replied with a groan.

"And what if someone came in here right now? How would you keep her safe if you're not taking care of yourself?" she lectured.

Roger had composed himself and threw himself into "doctor mode". "Vitals?" he asked Ben.

"Low, but she has very active brain scans, and every once in a while," Ben said, just as Sophie's muscles flinched. "That happens," Ben finished. "Our girl is fighting for sure to get out."

"Let's see if we can't help her," Roger said, pulling out a small black briefcase.

"What is that?" James demanded, watching his father pull out some syringes.

"Have I ever put your life in danger?" Roger said, filling the syringe.

"No, but..." James said in protest.

"Have I ever put Sophie's life in danger?" Roger asked, cutting off his son.

"No, but…" James tried again.

"Am I not the best infectious disease doctor in the world?" Roger asked him with eminent authority.

"Roger Moore, your ego helps no one," Sally interjected.

"It's not ego, Mama, if it's true. Son?" he said, turning to James.

"No," James muttered in response.

"Okay, then," Roger said, turning back to Sophie. "It's taking her longer to come back to us, so we need to pump up her system to make sure it doesn't start collapsing before she makes it back."

"What are you giving her?" Tina asked, coming closer to watch.

"Some immune boosters that we developed should anything ever happen to her," Roger said in deep concentration as he gave her six different injections. "We're lucky her brain is still so active. That's our saving grace. Once the brain slows, there won't be anything else we can do," Roger whispered.

James looked at his father in horror.

Sally put one hand over James'. "It doesn't mean we will not fight one hell of a fight until then," she said, squeezing his hand.

"Benjamin, get me up to speed," Roger demanded once he finished.

Tina and Ben told the Moore's everything that they had learned. The dream catcher seemed to help, but something was blocking James from Sophie's memory. Everyone was under the assumption it was because Sophie would do anything to get back to James and vice versa, and clearly someone with the power to separate them knew this, too. They just didn't know who.

Sally listened, but never stopped squeezing Sophie's limp hand in hers as she studied her son. She had a lot to do to get him back to

184

fighting mode, but as a mother, it was a job only she could do. Sally would get her son back to where he needed to be, both mentally and physically. If Jack and Jess were right, the fight was long from being over. Some battles had already been lost and won, but the war was far from finished.

She reluctantly let go of Sophie's hand. "I'll be back, Love," she whispered into her ear before marching to the other side of the bed. "Get in the kitchen," she ordered James, and pointed in the direction he needed to go.

"I'm really not hungry, Mom," James said with a dramatic sigh.

"I wasn't asking," Sally said, crossing her arms.

"Mom, not now," James said, rolling his eyes.

"Jamie, I am your mother and you will do what you're told," she warned him. When he didn't move, she went to her last resort. She grabbed him by the ear and dragged him yelling the whole way.

"Remind me not to get on her bad side," Ben whispered to Tina.

"I wouldn't," Roger confirmed. "Now, tell me the rest."

Tina looked at Ben and back at Roger. Had Sally given away her secret?

"We can't fight the war without all the information. So, tell me the rest," he said more firmly.

"Sir," Ben started.

Roger held up his hand. "I know you keep things from him, so he stays on his needed path. It's not my first rodeo with you three, so I need to know what you've found out without telling my son," he said in his fatherly voice.

They both sighed heavily before spilling the small information they were both able to collect without James. Like, Sophie seemed to pull them in when they were both sleeping, but Sophie said she couldn't stay asleep too long. Neither knew what that meant. Tina explained the "other Sophie" she crossed paths with, and anything else they could think of. Roger listened intently, nodding in confirmation as he took the information in.

They also told him about Sophie's vision of being cloned. Tina informed Roger that Eddie had gotten her access, but so far nothing showed Algos had actually started the "program". Roger's face grew pale with the news.

"We can't let that happen," he said in a whisper.

"You're not telling anyone who doesn't agree with you," Tina replied. "But it's a maze of data, and I have to make sure I don't incriminate Eddie," she added. "It's his life if he gets caught helping us, and I'm pretty sure Sophie would never forgive me," she said with a frown.

"There are other ways of getting that kind of information," Roger said with a weary smile. "Let me dig around and see what I can find out to help."

"Be careful who you ask," Ben warned. "There're new players, and we're not sure who all we can trust."

Roger looked around to the room where the non-patrolling bikers rested and recharged with mindless tv. "Are we safe here?" he asked in a whisper.

"Mario and Jack vouched for every single one. We're good here," Tina confirmed.

"Good," Roger said, relaxing. "Got that encrypted laptop still?" he asked Tina.

"Of course," she said with a smile of pride.

186

"I'm going to need to borrow it for a bit," he said.

"Grabbing it now!" she said, jumping up to go get it.

"Tell me the truth," Roger said, looking at Ben.

"I don't know how much time Sophie has left. She's held up longer than most, but even her genetics will not help save her if she doesn't wake up soon," he replied in his doctor's voice. "Something's not adding up," Ben added.

"What's that?" Roger asked him.

"We're assuming that someone's blocking James from Sophie, but if Sophie's trapped in her own mind, what if it's Sophie blocking herself because she doesn't want to wake up?" he mumbled.

"Why do you think that?" Roger asked him.

"Would you if you knew where your bloodline ran through?" Ben asked with a frown.

"Then we have to make sure she knows that's not the only bloodline she has. And you and I both know environment has a huge role," he said with a grin.

"The girl spent a lifetime on the run!" Ben hissed back.

"That's not the environment I was referring to," he said calmly, putting his hand on Ben's shoulder.

"She remembered me rather well," Ben confessed. "But Tina, not as much."

"What do you remember about your rounds in the mental wards?" Roger whispered to him.

"I remember not wanting to go back," Ben said with a shudder.

"Come on, Son. Put your doctor hat back on," Roger said with a smile. "The patients themselves."

"Well, there's an alarming amount of people that struggle with a chemical imbalance that can send false signals and emotions, often causing them to act out inappropriately," Ben said in thought.

"So, what if Sophie's just 'unbalanced'," Roger offered. "We know she shuts down when her brain gets overloaded. Finding out the man that killed your parents and chased you your whole life would definitely overload one's brain."

"Agreed," Ben said.

"So, what if when she restarted, she was 'unbalanced' and her brain started fighting with her, giving her false information? Think of how much PTSD takes place with soldiers that return from battle. Sophie has been a soldier since she was ten years old. Well, technically before with training," Roger added. "And she can't see what's false and what's real because she's lost confidence in what reality provides."

"How do we help her win the war with herself if she's not physically awake?" Ben asked, deep in thought.

"We're going to have to be innovative," Roger said with a nod. "Can you work on that?" he asked Ben. "I'm going to help Tina with her cloning project," Roger said, standing up and patting Ben on the back.

"I can try," he said with a shrug.

"We're past the trying stage, Bejamin. It's do or die," Roger told him with authority.

"Yes, Sir," Ben nodded, and went to make a list of books he would need someone to get from the library.

"Eat," Sally demanded.

"Mom," James protested.

"I don't have to be a doctor to see you're not taking care of yourself. Eat," she said with warning.

James shoved the pasta she had placed before him with great resign.

Once she was satisfied with the amount he had consumed, Sally sat down across from her son. "Tell me what you know," she said more softly.

"We already have," James mumbled in between bites.

"I am well aware. Now, tell me what YOU know," Sally insisted.

"I know I'm really pissed off," he said, frustrated.

Sally smiled and tried to stifle her laugh. There he was. "Yeah, and what are you going to do about it?" she prodded.

He looked at her like she had lost her mind. "Mom, I have tried everything! And I seem to be the ONE person who she can't reach. I feel utterly helpless and ANGRY!" he shouted. "What am I supposed to do?"

"You're supposed to take care of yourself for starters," Sally nagged. "Then, you stop feeling sorry for yourself and fight for your loved ones," she finished, crossing her arms and staring down at him.

Sally was average height, slender, and her blonde hair had become more grey from the stress of being on the run, but even James knew not to cross her.

"She talked to Eddie," James said, unable to hide the pain in his voice.

Sally sighed, knowing exactly what was hurting her son. She reached over and put her hand over his. "Listen, Jamie," she breathed. "When a girl falls in love with her soulmate, it doesn't matter who else she talks to. Her heart will forever only belong to one." James looked up at her with water filling his eyes. "Trust me. Your father made it very difficult at times throughout the years, but even he learned that there would forever be only one for me, even in the afterlife. I have seen how she looks and talks with you. A childhood best friend has nothing on you, nor will he ever."

James looked down at the table in silence. "I don't know what I'm supposed to do to help her. All I ever do is stare at her lifeless body and pray she comes back to me," he said in a half sob.

"Then maybe you should start thinking about how you can get to her instead," she said with a smile. "Love is only strong when both people are fighting." Sally squeezed his hand. "Now," she said, patting his shoulder as she stood up, "What do you want for dessert?"

Fourteen

C larice woke up and immediately felt nauseous. She grabbed the trash can by her bed and vomited.

"What is wrong with you?" she heard Eddie ask from the doorway. Didn't she lock the door before laying down? She asked herself.

"Nothing," she growled as she wiped the vomit from her mouth.

"Are you pregnant or something?" Eddie snickered.

"Not funny," she barked back at him.

"Sorry, I just haven't seen you so sick before," he said with a shrug.

"What do you want?" Clarice asked as she laid back down. The room was spinning around her, and she was ready to get off the ride.

"I'd thought you'd want to know that someone caught a license plate to a van that probably had Sophie and her crew hiding in it. We're tracking it now," Eddie said with a shrug. He's already warned them and knew his team would never find the van.

"That's not finding her," Clarice moaned as she tried to get the motion sickness to stop.

"It's not not finding her either," Eddie said with a frown as he watched her in misery. "What's going on?"

"Why do you care?" she yelled out as she grabbed her head. It suddenly felt like it was being crammed in a trash compactor.

"I'm getting the doctor," he said and turned to run down the hall.

"No!" she yelled after him, but he was already gone.

What was going on with her? What had Corbin done to her?

"Something's wrong. I can feel it!" Jess said in desperation.

"I know. I feel it too," Corbin said with a frown.

"What's wrong?" Jess asked in panic.

"There's a price for being pulled in like she's been. It seems like she's paying for it," Corbin said as he shuffled through the books in his makeshift office.

"We need to fix it," Jess said as anger brewed within.

"I don't know that we can," he told her honestly.

"We can't let her just die!" Jess exclaimed.

He looked up at her. "We're not going to," he said calmly. "Let me review some things and I will see what I can do. I promise."

"Well, I can't just sit here!" Jess declared before storming off. She was going to take care of her father. Once and for all.

"What's wrong with her?" Algos asked dryly.

"I really don't know, Sir," the elderly doctor stated. "I will have to keep her here and run more tests."

Algos sighed with irritation. "Be sure that she returns sooner than later," he warned.

"Of course," the doctor replied. He wasn't sure what tests he could run, but it didn't hurt to start with an MRI and some bloodwork for a baseline. Algos walked back to his office.

Clarice knew better than to mess with his experiments, but she was definitely ill. This would not be helpful to his plans. He needed her to do the leg work for him. After all, he had spent her whole life breaking her. Grooming her. Turning her into the loyal killer he needed at a moment's notice. Although her emotions still were an issue from time to time, she was easy to manipulate when needed.

He sat in his oversized chair and leaned back. His eyes felt heavy, so he closed them and took a breath. When he opened them, a younger version of Jess sat in a chair across from him. She was calm, with her arms across her chest, and staring at him with no emotions giving her away.

"Well, hello," Algos said, with a wicked grin creeping across his lips.

"Hello, father," Jess said blankly.

"What do I owe the pleasure?" Algos asked suspiciously.

"You called me, remember?" Jess said.

Was this a dream, or was she messing with him?

"I did?" he asked with caution.

Jess sighed and rolled her eyes dramatically. "I told you I was done. What do you want?" she asked, playing out a memory for them both. This was the moment everything changed between them.

Algos paused. He knew the scene. He just wasn't sure this was the original version.

"I have a mission for you," Algos started.

"What part of 'I'm done' is so confusing for you?" Jess asked boldly. She didn't move. She didn't blink. It had to play out just as the original version had, even if he altered.

"You will never be done with this," Algos said slowly. Jess could feel the doubt and self questioning. She needed to be on point.

"Well, I am. So, if there's nothing else," she said as she stood up and headed for the door.

"Why are you here?" he asked with great intregue. He was going off script. She hadn't fooled him at all. She turned around and put her hands on her hips.

"You. Called. Me. Are you going senile?" she asked, treading lightly.

He leaned back and studied her. "Nice try, Sweetheart. I know too much to be fooled with such childish trickery," he said bluntly.

Jess' wicked smile spread across her lips. "Do you, now?" she asked.

"Why are you here?" he asked more forcefully, but with more curiosity than he should have let on. "Do you think you can save your daughter this way?"

"Aw, Daddy, she's saved herself. I'm not worried about her at all," she cooed, daring to come closer and sit back down in the chair before him.

Algos tilted his head and studied her. "Did you know the dead aren't safe? Even in the dream realm?" he asked eagerly, watching her.

Jess didn't falter. "Still waiting for you to come get me," she taunted. She fed into her dark side. It was the only way to match the psychopath who was her father.

"Maybe I'll just come get Jack and Mario. Then you and Sophie can join me like you're supposed to," he said, squinting to study her more thoroughly.

Jess threw her head back and gave the most evil laugh he had heard come from her yet. "You're such a delusional, sad man, aren't you?" she said with a laugh.

"I get what I want," Algos replied with more force. Jess had hit a nerve, and she knew it.

"Not always," she taunted, wagging her finger and giving a tsk tsk sound to go with it.

"I get what I want," he said as anger boiled in his blood.

She tilted her head and faked sympathy. "Your own parents didn't want you. Your wife didn't want you. Your children don't want you, and Sophie will never come to you," she said as her eyes turned a vibrant red.

"I killed my parents. I killed my wife. I killed my unruly children, and Clarice ONLY wants me. What makes you so sure that

Sophie, who has my blood coursing through her veins, won't come to me?" he asked, raising his voice to her.

"Because your blood isn't the only one coursing through her veins, and we both know she's more powerful than you could ever dream of being. Too bad we got to her first," she said, sticking her bottom pouty lip out at him.

"You didn't!" he shouted as he slammed his hand against the desk.

"Oh, but we did," she said, batting her eyelashes. "You've lost. Again," she added for additional sting. "What's wrong, Daddy? Cat got your tongue?" Jess asked innocently.

"You're dead," he growled as he stood up.

"That's true," she said with a shrug. Jess continued to sit in the chair.

"I can kill you, again," he hissed. "And there will be no coming back."

"You have to find me first," she said with a smile.

Just as he quickly limped in her direction, she was gone. "NO!" he screamed out to no one.

Jess sat up, gasping for air.

"What did you do?" Jack asked in a panic.

"Get ready," she said while catching her breath. "He's coming."

Jack, Corbin, and Mario all looked at each other in brief terror before putting their game faces back on.

"Gather who you can. He won't be far behind," Jack ordered. The other two ran off to prepare for war. "You were supposed to wait," he whispered to his wife as he waited patiently for her to gather her bearings.

196

"He's killed enough people. I couldn't sit back and wait anymore," Jess said with anger.

"This won't save her," he reminded his wife.

"No, but it will allow us to save Sophie," she said sorrowfully. "You told me I would have to choose sides. I told you I would always choose our daughter. She's dying. I'm done waiting," Jess said with determination.

"Me, too," Jack whispered and kissed his wife on the head. "Now, go recharge. You're going to need it."

Jess got up and disappeared into darkness. Jack prayed to the man upstairs, not sure if he could be heard, but trying all the same.

Roger came up behind Tina. "Any luck?" he asked.

"It's taken awhile, but I found the folder we need," Tina confirmed. "Who hides cloning information under a folder titled 'TV Guides'?" she asked in irritation.

"Clearly someone who thought no one would go in there to look," Roger laughed. "Obviously not nearly as smart as you," he said, putting a hand on her shoulder.

"I found what I think are the results of tests, but they're outside of my expertise," Tina said, offering the laptop to Roger.

He adjusted his glasses and studied the test results on the screen in great detail, before saying, "I'm not sure either. I think it's time to call an old friend," Roger said, pulling out his burner phone and dialing.

"Hello?" answered a very confused woman on the other end.

"Elaine, it's Roger," he said cautiously.

"You said I wouldn't need to be contacted anymore," she hissed in panic on the other side.

"I know, I know. I wouldn't have contacted you if it wasn't important," Roger assured.

"What's more important than my life!" she exasperated.

"He's trying to clone Sophie," Roger said in his doctor's voice.

Deafening silence came from the other side.

"Elaine?" Roger asked in panic.

Silence.

"Elaine?" he asked more loudly.

"That cannot happen," she finally said. "Send me what you've got. I will be in touch."

The phone went dead in Roger's hand.

"Poor girl," Tina whispered.

"Agreed, but even she knows this can't be," he said in sorrow.

Tina sent an encrypted file to Elaine and then turned toward Roger. "Now what?" she asked.

"We wait," he said with a frown.

"Time is running out!" yelled one of the female cloaked figures.

"Shouting doesn't help anyway," Rebecca said, rolling her eyes as she continued to study the book in her hand that was titled *James.*

"It's now or never!" another shouted.

Rebecca closed the book and stood up. "Now works for me," she said with a shrug as she went over by the fire and sat down before it. "Leave me," she ordered.

The cloaked figures hesitated, but knew better than to argue with her. Once they were gone, she closed her eyes and took in a deep breath. "James," she whispered to no one. When she opened her eyes, she found James sitting in the middle of the library, gathering a stack of books.

Rebecca borrowed a skinny, long blonde haired and green eye girl about his age for a host. Walking in his direction, she purposely tripped and the books in her hands went everywhere. "Oh! I'm so sorry," she stuttered.

"You're fine. Here. Let me help," James said as he got to his knees and helped the stranger collect her strewn books.

"Thank you so much, but you don't have to. I'm such a klutz!" Rebecca said, shaking her head.

"It happens to the best of us," James said with a smile as he handed the books back to her.

"You're quite the gentleman," she said, batting her eyes.

"Thank you, but I'm already taken," he said, blushing and sitting back down to read.

"One lucky girl," Rebecca said, sighing.

"One lucky guy is more like it," James said with a hint of sorrow in his voice.

"Trouble in lover's lane?" Rebecca asked casually.

"She's just not feeling well at the moment, and is really sick. I'm not sure how to help her. I actually feel quite helpless," James found himself confessing to the stranger. Something wasn't right. He could feel it.

"Do you talk to her?" Rebecca asked, not missing a beat. "I hear coma patients can hear everything you say to them."

James became agitated. "I didn't say she was in a coma," he said, staring her down with suspicion in his eyes.

"Well, that's because you're not awake, and I'm here to help you," Rebecca said with a shrug.

"And you are?" James asked, stepping back.

"Let's just say I'm a guardian angel," Rebecca said with a smile.

"Sorry, Miss, but there are too many players in this game to just take you at your word that you're on the right side," he said, looking around for a weapon, should it come to that.

He felt his body being forced into a chair.

"If I wanted you dead, you'd be dead," Rebecca said honestly. "Now, what's the problem?" she asked, taking a seat across from him.

"Who are you?" James demanded.

"The name's Rebecca, and I'm a friend. Time's running out. What's the problem?" she repeated.

"None of us know a Rebecca," James retorted.

"That's because I was a player before you joined the game," Rebecca said flatly. "What's. The. Problem?" she asked again.

"Something's blocking me from her. I don't know," James said, staring at her cautiously.

"Odd," Rebecca said, more to herself. She pulled the backpack off her back and ruffled through it. "I'm not aware of a blockage," she said as she dug through the bag. "However, that doesn't mean there's not a work around," she said with a knowing smile. "Ah, Ha!" she shouted as she pulled out a purple stone on the end of a necklace.

200

"Here," she said, shoving it to James.

"What am I supposed to do with this?" James asked with doubt.

"Wear it," she said, rolling her eyes. "When she calls, there will be no wall to stop you, regardless of who built it."

James looked at the round amethyst encased in a heart-shaped silver necklace. "Why should I trust you?" James asked, still staring at the stone.

"Do you honestly have anyone else?" Rebecca asked.

"Yes, plenty of people," he said with a frown, holding the necklace up to the light.

"Do you honestly have anyone else that has given you a golden ticket to get to the woman you love?" she rephrased with a hint of irritation.

"How do I know it's not a trick that does her more harm?" he asked, looking deep into her eyes.

Rebecca put her hands on the table and leaned in. "Because the line between death and the living has been removed, and Algos has every intention of using it to wipe out everyone you love. Sophie and all," she said bluntly. "Now," she said, leaning back to study him. "Are you going to step up and be the man she needs, or not?" she asked, crossing her arms.

"You don't know a damn thing about me," he warned.

"I know a lot more than you think," Rebecca said with a shrug. "She's saved your sorry butt on more than one occasion, led Simon away to keep you safe despite it shattering her own heart to do so, and she has lost everyone in her family to still come back to you. Don't you think it's time to return the favor?" she asked smugly.

James froze. Rebecca's been busy. She knows a lot more than

they gave her credit for. But who was she, and which side was she actually on?

"Put it on," she demanded. "It will keep you safe even when she can't," she added. "Every key needs a lock to fit into. To ground it. To help it open endless possibilities, and to give it purpose. You, James, are Sophie's lock. It's time you do your part so she can do hers."

James looked back down at the necklace, but when he looked up, Rebecca was gone. He bolted upright in bed desperately trying to catch his breath. When he looked down at his hand, the necklace remained.

"Are you alright?" Tina asked as she rushed to her friend.

"Rebecca says hi," he muttered as he put the necklace on around his neck.

"What's that?" Tina questioned hesitantly.

"The sledge hammer," James said before falling back onto his pillow into a deep sleep.

"Trust No One."

Words that echoed in Sophie's ears as she worked on her second round of skimming books. Still no answered appeared. She watched John out of the corner of her eye all the same. Sophie felt a strong positive connection to him, but she couldn't exactly trust herself in here either.

John had been pacing throughout the library as he read book

after book. His granddaughter was quite fascinating, but something caught his eye that made him stop in his tracks. A chess set appeared out of nowhere that hadn't been there since they arrived.

John knew well that nothing happened without purpose. Especially if it was within Sophie's mind. Good or bad. "Do you like chess?" he asked casually.

"Ugh! Dear God, no!" Sophie whined.

John laughed at such a dramatic reaction to the game. "Why not?" he asked curiously.

Sophie sighed and rolled her eyes dramatically. "Dad used to try and make me play. So did Eddie. But the game is dreadfully boring to no end."

"I thought it was a great game of intellect?" John questioned over his shoulder as he continued to look at the magically appearing board.

"Please! Every move is fixed and predetermined," she said, putting her book down and looking at him. "There's an average of 40 moves that even have the same theme. An aggressive opening, patient mid-game, and inevitable checkmate. You can play through every move, but in the end, you will continue to repeat the same patterns, expecting a different result. Basically, playing chess is the definition of insanity. Doing the same thing over and over again expecting a different result," Sophie said, shaking her head and picking up her book back up.

"Sounds a lot like someone we know," John said out loud to himself.

Sophie put her book down. John was right. That's why she had always been ahead of Algos. His moves were predictable, despite the variation or two. He was always more aggressive right out the gate, waited for his time to strike in the middle, and expected a checkmate in the end. He kept the same game plan, expecting to eventually win in the end. That was his downfall, and Sophie's gain.

John turned around to face her. "That's why you will always win," he said with a smile.

"In theory," Sophie said, deep in thought.

"Someone always wins in chess, right? And if you know his patter, you will always be ahead," John said with excitement.

"Not always," Sophie corrected. "Sometimes, both sides can box themselves in where there is no winner. It's just a dead draw," she said flatly.

"So, like a tie?" John asked, confused.

"More like both sides resigning at once to end the game," Sophie said with a shrug.

"I don't see Algos ever resigning," John said with a frown.

"Me neither," Sophie said, matching his expression.

John turned to study the board more closely. "Hey look! You're the queen," he said, impressed.

"What?" Sophie asked, standing up and walking over to see what he was looking at.

"Yes, look," John said, pointing out the various pieces. "There's your dad, and your mom. I'm guessing that's Mario, Tina and Ben, and Eddie's the knight. You even have a king," he said, picking up the white piece and handing it to Sophie.

"It's him," Sophie whispered, but something else caught her eye on the board. "But I'm also the queen on the black side," she said with a gulp.

204

John turned back around and saw what Sophie did. Sophie was the black queen, Algos, as the black king, and even Jess and Clarice were also pieces. "Oh," he said, regretting bringing Sophie's attention to the board. "Weird that some are on both sides," he said out loud to himself.

Sophie clutched the figure of James and walked away.

"Look!" John said over his shoulder. "I think it's more because of the bloodline than good vs. evil," he offered. "Chess doesn't have a good vs. evil. They only colored the pieces to determine who gets to make the first move, right?"

Sophie stopped. She really wanted to believe John's theory, but something deep in her stomach said otherwise. She turned to face the board again. "That wouldn't make sense. I can't go first, and second at the same time," she contemplated.

"But don't both sides need to keep their queen safe?" John countered. "Maybe you're just on both sides because both sides value you as their queen? Look, your mom and Eddie are on both sides, too. I know for a fact your mother is not evil," he said with authority.

"How can you say that?" Sophie asked as her voice cracked. "His blood runs through her veins as much as it does mine!"

John looked at Sophie like her dad used to when she was hurting. "Jessica had two parents. A mother that was obviously pure good to prevent her from slipping to the other side despite being forced to leave her at an early age. You were raised by two GOOD people."

John sighed and walked over to Sophie, taking her hands in his. "Listen, Sweetie," he said in his fatherly tone. "There isn't a family in existence that doesn't have those family members they wish they could remove from the tree," he snorted. "Your father has a few on his side, too. But that didn't determine the person he became in the end. He made his own choices. Some really great ones at that," John said, winking at her. "Sometimes you just have to take the good and the bad, and make the life that you were meant to make. YOU'RE the one that decides. Not what flows in your veins. Besides," he whispered as he leaned his forehead against hers, "I'm in there too, ya know."

Sophie giggled and wiped the tears that had escaped her eyes. He had very valid points. John didn't know how to see the world through anything else but facts, and the fact was that he was exactly right and Sophie needed to accept that.

She held the piece of the familiar figure up so she could inspect it. Sophie rubbed her finger over the facial features of the white piece that was blurry in her mind, but her heart knew them all the same. She hadn't told John what had been happening when she slept. Sophie worried if she said it out loud, it would stop happening. She looked everywhere for the book of the boy who talked to her, but it was nowhere to be found. Someone had clearly taken it. She hoped it wasn't John.

She knew she could talk to the people she thought of with the books of her memories. Maybe the chess piece would be enough to at least reach out and thank him for talking to her while she was trapped. He obviously cared for her, even if she couldn't remember who exactly he was. There was still something about him. Something important. She needed to find out what that was.

"I'm exhausted," Sophie lied. "I need to lie down for a second."

John looked at her worriedly. She was sleeping a lot, and in here, that couldn't be a good thing. However, she would know her body better than anyone, and she would have to be the one to pull them both out. She would need her strength for that.

"Just a little while," he warned her.

"I know," she said with a weary smile. "You can even wake me up if it's too long," Sophie said, winking at him.

"Deal," he said, winking back. He covered her up with a blanket as she laid down on the couch, rubbed the figure between her fingers, and closed her eyes.

"Hello?" Sophie heard the voice that had been talking to her so regularly call out.

"Hello?" she called back.

Out of the shadows came the perfect life-sized version of the figurine she still clutched tightly in her hand.

"Sophie?"

"Hello?" he heard her ask with more doubt than he desired.

"Are you okay?" he asked, rushing towards her, but stopped when he saw her retreat a couple of steps back. "Do you know me?" he asked, trying to keep his panic at bay.

She looked at him for what seemed like an eternity, but never gave an answer.

"That's okay," he said with a smile. "I know you," he added with a wink.

There was something oddly familiar about him.

"Where are we?" James asked, looking around. Blackness

surrounded them, with no floor or ceiling to be seen. It was very eerie.

"I'm not sure exactly," she confessed honestly.

"I'm glad to see you're okay," he offered with a weary smile.

"I don't think I am," she replied with sorrow in her voice.

"How can I help?" he asked her eagerly.

"I don't know," she said, tilting her head back and forth as she inspected him. "Thank you for keeping me company," she whispered.

"You would do the same for me," James replied with a shrug.

"I would?" she asked, more to herself.

"You would," he assured her.

The necklace around his neck glowed. It caught her eye.

"What's that?" she asked cautiously.

"A friend gave it to me," James said, looking down at the glowing necklace. "I was having trouble getting to you."

Sophie's heart fluttered, but she didn't respond.

"I figured you were always coming to find me. It was my turn to find you, even in the dark," he said, giving her his boyish grin. Her knees grew weak.

"I know you, don't I?" she asked, gaining some confidence.

"Yes," James whispered. He felt something scratching his leg in his pocket. "Of course," he whispered softly. He stuck his hand in his pocket, and she drew back to prepare for an attack. James saw her out of the corner of his eye and froze. "I'm sorry," he said quickly, holding his hands up. "I have something of yours."

Sophie frowned in doubt, but nodded to let him pull the box out of his pocket. He slowly opened it to show her the engagement ring inside. It glowed like a beacon, and she had to cover her eyes at the brightness, but once her eyes adjusted....

She saw herself push him up against a tree and taking him in for the first time. Then Sophie saw herself standing in the kitchen with him and watching him fix her breakfast. Watching him sleep by her bed in a chair, holding her hand. Hiking in the woods. Swimming in the cove. Crying in a shed and feeling "come find me" being traced in her hand.

Sophie watched the first time he made love to her. Snuggling on the couch and watching movies. Waking up in his arms. James proposing on the night Mario was murdered. Saving her from the pool. It was one thing to read memories, but these were flooding her, emotions and all. Everything that had happened to them since they met seemed like an eternity ago.

"James," she said, as tears filled her eyes. She ran and jumped into his arms. He grabbed her willingly and kissed her passionately. Her veins glowed a bright ice blue.

"Hey, Smalls," he said with a smile against her lips.

"I'm sorry," she cried. "I didn't mean to forget." She clung to him tightly.

"I know," he said, running his fingers through her hair. "How can I help you get out of here?" James asked her urgently.

"I don't know," she said honestly.

Sophie felt her body sink faster than either of them could do anything about. The floor had become a body of water, and she slid deeper and deeper to the bottom. No matter how much she fought to swim back to the top, she just continued to sink to the bottom, wherever that was.

"NO!" she heard him scream. She watched helplessly as he stood on solid ground above her, getting smaller and smaller. He continued to scream her name into the nothingness as she sank further and further down. Sophie was lost and losing the battle.

Suddenly she felt herself hit what was obviously the bottom. She fell cross legged and sat still to look around. Then her eyes turned a flaming bright red, and her veins glowed to match.

"I told you I would get my way, one way or another," she heard the other Sophie whisper in her ears.

Fifteen

"We need more time," Mario told Jack.

"We don't have it," Jack replied, gathering supplies from the cabin. Mario heard just the slightest sound of a cane hitting the ground.

"Let's go," he told Jack, putting his hand on his shoulder and steering him in the opposite direction. He waited a few seconds before letting go and allowing Jack to get ahead of him, before he raised his hands and a stone wall appeared separating them.

Jack heard the whisper of the wall rising behind him, but when he turned around, it was too late. "Mario," Jack shouted as he ran towards the make-shift door in the middle of the wall. However, with the simple flip of Mario's wrist, Jack heard the door lock, knowing he would not be allowed through.

"MARIO!" he shouted in anger and panic.

"Jack, Buddy, I need you to listen," Mario said softly.

"No!" Jack shouted back.

"I'm gonna need you to go save our girls for me," Mario said calmly on the other side.

"NO!" Jack yelled back even louder.

"Jack," Mario said in his fatherly voice. "You're the only one that can."

"They're going to blame me," Jack said, pulling the guilt card.

"Nah," Mario snickered. "They know I'm too stubborn to go out any other way," he consoled his friend.

"Go, Jack," Mario whispered, but Jack couldn't move. Instead, he slid down the door and cried for the loss of his best friend.

"What's wrong?" Corbin said in panic as he raced to Jack, quickly noticing the new cement wall.

"Mario's buying us some extra time," Jack said between sniffles.

"But if he...." Corbin started.

"He knows," Jack retorted. He pushed himself to his feet and grabbed the supplies he had dropped. "Let's go," he said with determination and walked past Corbin and on to find his wife for the greatest fight they will ever fight.

Corbin stared at the wall and tried to push through the pain he was absorbing from Mario and Jack. "Impressive," Corbin said, looking at the wall, before he headed off to follow Jack. "Good luck, my friend," he said over his shoulder before he disappeared into the darkness.

212

DEAD DRAW

Mario walked over and took what would be his last beer out the of the fridge, popped the top, and took a giant chug. Funny how in death, there were still a few things that you could still enjoy in this realm. He closed his eyes and let the aroma consume his nose, and the various flavors tickle his tongue and throat.

The sound of the cane grew louder. Mario turned and leaned against the counter like he had done so many times in his life and death. Well, if he was going out, it was going to be on his terms. Not this asshole psychopath's. He had taken enough away from him. Mario was done letting him take anything else. He continued to swig his beer while he waited.

"What a pleasant surprise," he heard Algos sneer.

"I get that a lot," Mario said with a smirk as he took one last sip of his beer. Algos growled in irritation.

"Where's my darling daughter and schmuck of a husband?" Algos asked with impatience.

"Making final preparations for your death, I'm guessing," Mario said with a nonchalant shrug.

"You were always so delusional, Mario," Algos said with a diabolical laugh. "That's why my daughter would never choose you."

Algos was trying to rile Mario up, but just like everything else, he didn't know that ship had already sailed long ago. He always thought it was Jess that he had fallen in love with for life, but it would be her gift of her own daughter that would teach him what love really was. The love of a father. Even if he was just a stand-in.

"She got the better deal," Mario stated honestly.

Algos rolled his eyes. "So, do you want to die quickly, or would you like me to take my time?" he asked Mario bluntly.

"I've never been a fan of quick," Mario replied flatly. He needed to give them as much time as possible. No matter the cost.

"Maybe, I do like you, after all," Algos said, impressed.

"Doubt it," Mario said with a shrug.

"You know, just for you, let's do this old school style," Algos said, putting his cane down and taking off his dark grey suit jacket to roll up his sleeves.

"You sure you can handle that?" Mario asked with a smirk.

"You'd be surprised," Algos retorted.

"Very well," Mario said with a shrug, and headed to the middle of the kitchen floor. He knew Algos wouldn't fight fair. He didn't know the meaning of the word, but he got into stance all the same.

Mario put his left foot forward, carefully balancing on the ball of his foot, and put his right foot directly under his right hip. He held his left hand out at waist level, preparing to block any strikes, and placed his right palm facing up in front of his chest. He motioned Algos to come at him.

"Been playing with my daughter, I see," Algos said with a snort. "It won't help you. I trained her," he taunted with pride.

"We'll see," Mario said with a cheeky grin.

"Very well," Algos sighed as if he were bored, and took the first punch.

Mario blocked and sucker punched Algos in the stomach as hard as he could. They both heard a couple of ribs crack. Algos just laughed as he used the pain to fuel himself and clocked Mario in the

214

jaw. Mario staggered back to catch his footing and prayed the wringing in his ears would calm sooner than later. That was gonna leave a mark. Mario took stance again and ignored the pain throbbing in his jaw and eardrum.

Algos came at him, and Mario kicked him first in the side of the knee, then in the gut, and in the jaw, forcing Algos to stumble back as he took the hits. Mario didn't let up, and continued to swing at Algos. He secretly wished he had died earlier when he was in better shape, but it would just have to do.

Algos grabbed one of his hands in mid-swing and twisted it, bringing Mario to his knees as Algos spit out the blood that was forming in his mouth. When he smiled, his teeth were covered in blood. "A little out of shape, I see," Algos snickered.

"Still in better shape than you," Mario said flatly as he flipped backwards to escape Algos' grip.

Algos quickly grabbed him by the top of his head and pushed him down to the ground onto Mario's back. He lifted his leg up and kicked Algos in the face, rolling back on his hands and pushing himself onto his feet.

"Well, at least you don't have to worry about me making you any uglier," Mario said, panting. Algos yelled and came for him.

Algos tried to hit Mario on the left side, but he got blocked, which he quickly used his other hand to grab Mario by the neck and leg and lifted him above his head, throwing him onto the table and breaking it in two. "Stay down, Boy," Algos growled. He was losing his patience.

"And what fun would that be?" wheezed Mario, as he staggered to stand up. Man, he'd really lost his touch over the years. Too bad he wouldn't have a chance to work on it.

Before he had time to get a full footing, Algos grabbed Mario by the shirt and threw him up against the cement wall he created, but Mario used his feet, quickly scaled the wall, and flipped over the old man instead. He landed a lot less gracefully than he intended. Dang. Sophie made it look so easy whenever she had done it.

Algos threw a punch, but this time Mario used Algos' momentum to throw him so hard, Algos hit the kitchen counter on the other side of the room. "Now, that's what I'm talking about," Mario muttered to himself.

Algos grabbed the nearest fork in his rage and went after the man that caused him to see red. Mario grabbed it and held it up in the air as he used his free elbow to hit Algos in the throat, before using the same elbow to knock the fork out of the old man's hand.

"Ah, ah, ah," Mario said. "No cheating."

Algos spun around and kicked Mario so hard in the gut it sent him flying back to the cement wall. Next time, he would have to think of a softer barrier. Then he chuckled. There would be no next time. Even he knew it. He got to his feet quickly.

Algos started swinging at him repeatedly, and Mario did his fair share of blocking them. In desperation to get him some space, he stepped on the back of Algos' only good knee and enjoyed the shout of agonizing pain that came out. Mario would be damned if he made it easy for the old man.

He quickly walked around and grabbed Algos' neck to snap it in two, but Algos was faster and rolled out of it. "Such a slimy little thing, aren't you?" Mario sneered in frustration.

"You have no idea," cackled Algos in reply, as he pulled a small

216

knife from his pant pocket. The same one he used to kill his father with so many years ago.

"What did I say about cheating?" Mario grunted as he did his best to avoid being cut. For an old guy, he still seemed in better shape than Mario.

"It's the only way to play," Algos grunted as he sped up his strikes against the gnat that was not only irritating him, but preventing him from getting what he wanted. Enough was enough.

He covered the knife in his special concoction. It would just take a nick to take this asshole out, and a nick was what he got in. Mario felt the poison take over rapidly, but he would not go down without a fight.

However, the poison was stronger than even Mario expected. Algos grabbed his hand, crushing it, fracturing it instantly in multiple places, as he stomped on the back of Mario's leg, breaking it immediately. Mario's agony could be heard all across the dream realm.

Jack held onto Jess as she fought against him with anger boiling in her blood and tears running continuously down her cheeks. "You can't," he whispered in her ear.

Algos leaned over Mario with his demented grin, knowing he had won. "You should have picked easy," he whispered into Mario's ear as he listened to him gasp desperately for air that refused to fill his lungs.

"You should have left my girls alone," he wheezed with a smile of his own. "Now, they're pissed. And they're coming for you," he added as he coughed the blood that rapidly filled his mouth into the old man's face.

"Please," Algos laughed. "They always come home. They always come to me. I own them," he said defiantly as he enjoyed his excitement at watching the life leave Mario's dead body.

"Must really sting that everything you just said describes me to a 't' instead of you," Mario laughed as he coughed and gasped and struggled to hold on to what life he had left. "Why do you think you couldn't find Sophie for so long?" he taunted. "Jess gave her to me. Willingly. Because she loved me more than you. And so does Sophie."

Algos glared at Mario, knowing the words he spoke were true. Within seconds, Algos started violently stabbing Mario repeatedly as he yelled out, "I will have them both! You're going to be dead!"

Sixty-seven stabs later, Algos climbed off of Mario's limp body. "Now, what do you have to say?" he asked smugly.

Just on cue, the black fog circled around Mario's body and turned into a giant skeletal hand before the hand lifted him up and the fingers closed over his body to crush him into dust.

"That's what I thought," Algos said, as he dusted off his pant legs, limped to what was left of the kitchen table to grab his coat and cane. "Oh, Jess, Dear," he called out. "Daddy's come to take you and Sophie home!" He started dragging his body to the locked door within the cement wall.

Clarice woke up with a throbbing headache. "What time is it?" she moaned.

"You should be more concerned with what day it is," the doctor said over his shoulder. "Welcome back."

"What are you muttering about?" Clarice groaned as she tried to get her bearings.

"You've been out for a few days," he said as he took her vitals, but she kept yanking her arm out of his hands.

"That's impossible," she growled.

"He's right," she heard the troll say from the doorway.

"Where's my father?" Clarice demanded.

"Taking care of some unfinished business," said the doctor flatly as he continued to fight to get Clarice's vitals.

"Stop touching me!" Clarice hissed.

"I need to check your vitals," the doctor insisted.

"Just let the poor sap do his job," Eddie said with a frown.

"Why are you here?" Clarice asked, glaring at him.

"Seemed like someone should check on you," he said with a shrug, letting her know her father had never come to check on her.

"I just had a headache," she grumbled.

"Nice try," Eddie retorted. He had asked Jack about what the possibilities were. The only theory was that with Algos pulling Clarice into the dream realm, so often without her consent, was taking its toll on her mind. She's lucky she woke up. Jess was going to make sure there wouldn't be a next.

"Where is she?" Clarice asked, interrupting his thoughts and changing the subject. He watched her struggle to look around the room for her clothes and things.

"Still MIA. Where ever she's hiding, there's no surveillance there or on the way," Eddie said in frustration. He hoped she bought it.

"That seems very unlikely," she announced. "Besides, aren't you supposed to be the best at finding her?" Clarice retorted.

Eddie just smirked at her and didn't respond.

"Where the hell are my things?" she finally shouted in annoyance.

"In a locker in the other room," the doctor said, crossing his arms. "If you can get there without falling, you're welcome to leave," he said flatly.

"This should be interesting," Eddie snickered under his breath.

If Clarice could have made him combust into flames at that very second, he would be dead. Good thing she didn't have that ability, Eddie mused. Clarice stood up and gave herself a few extra seconds to steady. However, on her first step, she headed straight for the ground. She felt Eddie catch her before she hit the floor.

"Looks like you're laying back down, Princess," Eddie said with a smirk.

"Shut up," Clarice growled, but fell asleep the second he placed her back on the hospital bed.

Sixteen

Corbin felt Clarice's distress, but he had more important things to deal with at the moment. He looked around the room at the small army he had been able to gather. Those that Algos had taken that had gotten trapped in the in-between because they had unfinished business that didn't allow them to cross to either side. They weren't much, but they would have to do.

"You okay?" he asked the timid girl he knew as Giselle.

"Yeah," she breathed. "Anything for Sophie," she added with a weak smile.

"That a girl," Corbin said with a smile.

"He doesn't have Simon with him, right?" Giselle asked meekly.

"No, Dear," Corbin confirmed. "Hell's been waiting for Simon for quite some time, and was keen to get him to where he belonged," he said, putting a reassuring hand on her shoulder.

"Good," she said with a nod as she continued to shift her weight back and forth to prepare for the battle coming.

"Corbin," he heard Jess call his name with a hint of worry as more people appeared to be walking in their direction. A lot more.

Corbin followed Jess' stare and wasn't sure to be thankful or worried. He couldn't sense anything about a single one of them, and there were too many for him to fight at once. The old man, who looked like he was in his 70s, with sparkling blue eyes full of mischief and life, held up his hands as he led the group to Corbin.

"We're here to help," he said with a smile as warm as sunshine.

"And you are?" Jack asked, coming to stand next to Corbin.

"The name's Bill. I'm a friend of Sophie's," he said with the warmest of smiles and pride.

"Nice to meet you in person," Jack said slowly as he held out his hand to shake with the man that had sacrificed his life to give his daughter a ride to safety.

"There's an awful lot of you," Corbin said, impressed.

"My son has caused a lot of damage," said a woman flatly, with long red curly hair that cascaded down her back. She looked extremely in shape. "Consider us on loan," she said with a wink. "Angie," she announced to the group as she took Jack's hand.

Jess kept her distance, but watched in awe. Her grandmother. The woman that gave birth to the psychopath that was her father was standing just a few feet ahead of Jess.

The mixture of emotions was overwhelming.

Angie looked directly at her. "It wasn't my choice to give birth to such a lost and destroying soul. He took my second son against my will along with my beloved husband, but I wouldn't change it," she said, clarifying for Jess.

"How can you say such a horrible thing?" Jess asked in horror.

"Because, dear Jessica, I got you and Sophie as the result," she said with a reassuring smile. "Now," she said, addressing the group, "I think it's time that he gets stopped. Don't you?"

Everyone shouted with excitement at their pep talk from the most unlikely source, but they quickly grew silent as they heard Algos finally unlock the steel door that separated them. They stood as the army they were, to protect Sophie at all costs.

Jack grabbed Jess' hand and held it tight. She looked at her loving husband, hopefully not for the last time. Jess felt another hand take her free one. The grandmother that she never got to know. Angie gave her a warm, reassuring smile as she squeezed her other hand.

Algos burst from the other side of the wall and was surprised for a split second at the welcoming party that waited for him on the other side. "Well, hello everyone," he said with a smirk. He saw the usual suspects with a few additions, but one figure stood out the most. "Mother," he growled.

"Nicolas," she said with her own smirk. She knew he hated his birth name.

"Algos," he corrected her, showing his irritation.

"Okay, Nicolas," Angie said with a shrug, enjoying torturing her son with such a simple thing.

"Nice army," Algos sneered, looking around at all the people he had helped, one way or another, get there. "I love you think you can stop me," he sneered.

"I can," said a female voice hidden deep in the back. Everyone looked towards the back to see who had spoken. When they parted, an early twenty-year-old girl with a book in her hands and her legs hanging over the arm of the chair she sat in. Her hazelnut hair cascaded down to the middle of her back, and her blue eyes sparkled like diamonds as she continued to read *Fire Starter* by Stephen King.

"Please, Becks," Algos gave a deep evil laugh. "You couldn't even keep your own children safe!" he taunted.

"Oh, I think some of them turned out all right," she said with a smirk, taking a quick second to glance at Jess before going back to her book. She looked very bored to be there.

"Rebecca," Jess whispered, putting the puzzle pieces together. Jack and Angie held onto Jess' hands tight to keep her grounded.

"This should be interesting," Corbin said to himself, hiding in the middle of the crowd.

Rebecca smirked in response, but didn't take her eyes off her book. "You know you can't hide in the den with the lions," she said flatly as she turned the page.

"You always thought you were so cleaver," Algos said, rolling his eyes, clearly not impressed.

"You always underestimated me," she said as she turned another page.

No one knew what to do. They just watched the two go back and forth like watching a tennis game.

"You've been playing chess too long," Rebecca said, finishing her page. "You're still as predictable as ever," she said with a shrug.

"I'm bored with your games," Algos said, clearly irritated.

"You must not get very much rest sleeping in the shadows all the time," she said casually, standing up slowly and placing her beloved book in her chair. "You're looking awfully ragged, Hubby," she said with a challenging grin. Jack recognized immediately where Jess got hers and smiled.

Rebecca pushed the sleeves up of her "Be Kind" shirt she wore as she started walking towards Algos. He shifted his weight. Clearly uncomfortable to face this ghost of his past.

"What's the matter, Al?" she asked as the corner of her lips curled up further.

Algos tightened his grip on his cane, waiting for her to get closer before he struck. "You can't stop me," he said, but the doubt in his voice betrayed him.

"There's nowhere to run, my friend," she said, feeding off his energy.

"Who said I'm running?" he asked calmly.

The crowd filled in behind her as she passed. Corbin went to stand next to her, but she grabbed his hand and pulled him back a bit. "Don't," he heard her voice inside his head. Corbin froze and let the people fill in around him, keeping him hidden. Algos hadn't seemed to see him just yet. Rebecca seemed to want to keep it that way.

"Why don't you just come deal with me yourself?" Algos taunted as she continued to make her way through the crowd towards him.

"Plan on it," she said as her hair flipped around as if there were some undetectable wind circling around her. Her cheeks grew more rosy by the second. Those around her could feel the heat she was sending out and took a few extra steps back. The temperature was unbearable to be too close.

"Rebecca," Angie said with a nod as Rebecca got close.

"Angie," she nodded back, not taking her eyes off Algos. She was just shy of the darts from being able to reach her. They both knew it.

"Scared to get closer?" Algos taunted at her nervously.

"Not at all," she said as her smile grew. She looked as dangerous as Algos was. As Rebecca raised her hands, balls of glowing light filled her palms, growing so bright that it was blinding everyone, including Algos. He held up his hand to shield his eyes just in time to see the cloaked figures approaching the group.

"Looks like I'm not alone," he stated excitedly, knowing the ace up his sleeve was about to be played. To his surprise, none of them moved.

"We're just here to observe," boomed the male voice he knew well. It threw Algos off his game.

"Do you forget who you work for?" Algos warned.

"Not at all," shrieked a female voice from the other side.

"No matter," Algos shouted in frustration. They weren't his only "get out of jail free" card he had planned.

"It's time for you to go home," Rebecca said. The floor shook as she spoke.

Corbin watched in fascination. He had seen no one with so much power in the realm. How had he not sensed her power before? This was a fact that didn't sit well with him. He was thankful she was on their side for the moment, but she had been very well hidden. Corbin wanted to know why exactly.

Algos put a hand in his pocket and twisted the knife he had stabbed Mario to death with in his hands, feeling the stickiness still warm on the handle. That was the boost he needed.

"Very well," Algos said, pulling it out, and putting his hands out, palms down, and backing up. "A guy knows when he's not wanted," he said with a shrug and turned to the door. He took two steps, flicked open the knife, exposing the poisoned switchblade, turned, and swung as hard as he could.

"No!" Jess yelled, stepping in front of her mother and taking the hit. The knife caught her in the shoulder. Jack caught her as she fell back.

Rebecca yelled in fury and held out her hands, as light as bright as the sun lit up the room and she pushed Algos back through the door to the other side. "Seal it!" she demanded as she ran to her daughter's aide.

Angie and Bill held out their hands and began sealing the door with their own lighted palms. Everyone from their group did the same.

"Will that keep him out?" Jack asked desperately.

Angie shouted over her shoulder, "You will be safe from now on. The power of the heavens will not allow him passage."

Rebecca took Jess from Jack's arms. "Corbin!" she screamed over the noise.

Corbin pushed through the crowd to get to his friends. Jess' body was convulsing and her shoulder and arm were turning black as a white frothy foam dripped from the corner of her mouth. Corbin leaned down to pull out the knife.

"Don't touch the blade," Rebecca ordered, not taking her eyes off her daughter as she gripped her. "It's poisoned," she added.

Corbin nodded and carefully pulled out the knife. Everyone gathered to watch in panic. Jack took her other hand and squeezed it tightly. "Don't you leave me," he ordered her through tears.

"Corbin, you need to heal her," Rebecca ordered.

"I don't know how!" he said, shaking his head and looking at her in disbelief.

"You can, and you WILL," she warned him.

"I don't know how!" he shouted back. "If I did, I would!"

"Corbin, you can, and you need to figure it out FAST," Rebecca warned, looking up at him and piercing him with her red, glowing eyes.

Corbin looked down desperately at Jess' body, that was turning more black by the second. He closed his eyes and took a deep breath. He felt Angie's and Bill's hands on his shoulders. They were filling him with extra energy and power.

"You can do it," Jack whispered to him.

Corbin took another deep breath in and out and held his hands over Jess, keeping his eyes closed. Nothing happened.

"Focus," Rebecca pleaded.

Corbin frowned and took another deep breath in and out. After a few seconds, ice blue light grew within his own palms. They turned into ice blue flames that slowly escaped his palms and circled Jess' body.

"That's it," Rebecca encouraged.

Corbin took another deep breath in and this time, when he breathed out, the flames grew and consumed Jess' body. He raised his palms up and Rebecca let go of her daughter. Her body raised up into the air as if it were being carried in the arms of the flames. Slowly, her body rotated in mid-air. Everyone looked up mesmerized, when suddenly the icy blue light exploded and everyone had to shield their eyes.

Jess' hair blew wildly behind her as ice blue flames consumed her eyes. She stood above everyone and slowly floated down to the ground. She closed her eyes, putting her head back and taking in her own deep breath and letting it out.

Corbin dropped his hands, and staggered as his body was depleted having given all of his energy to Jess.

"Thank you, my friend," he heard her say before looking up to meet Jess smiling back at him with glowing ice blue eyes.

"No problem," he said, returning her smile and collapsing.

"Corbin!" Jack shouted, running to his friend.

"He'll be fine," Rebecca assured. "He just needs to recharge. He's not used to using so much power at once," she added.

Jess' light faded to light blue and everyone dropped their hands to see the miracle before them. Rebecca got to her feet and staggered a bit herself. Jess grabbed onto Rebecca to help her balance.

"You alright, Mother?" Jess asked eagerly.

"Just a little tired," Rebecca lied.

Jack held onto Corbin as he carefully watched the cloaked figures look at each other before nodding and disappearing, as if nothing had happened. Anger brewed within him, and he had to be sure to keep it in check.

"Get him to bed," Rebecca ordered. "He'll need lots of fluid," she added. She walked away from the crowd.

"Where are you going?" Jess asked as she chased after her mother.

"Jack, your dad will return soon," Rebecca said, looking at Jack and ignoring her daughter.

"My dad?" Jack asked in confusion.

"Who do you think keeps order in here?" Rebecca asked casually.

"John is head of council?" Jess asked, in shock.

"No better man for the job," Rebecca said with a smile.

"Where's he been?" Jack asked in desperation.

"Keeping my granddaughter occupied," Rebecca said with a shrug. "It's time I get them both back where they belong," she said, turning away from everyone and walking away.

"I'm coming with you," yelled Jess as she met up with her mother.

"You can't," Rebecca said flatly.

"The hell I can't," Jess said defiantly.

Rebecca giggled. "You're definitely my daughter," she said with a smirk. "But no. You actually can't. You won't get through," she said, putting her hand on her daughter's shoulder. "I will get her back to you," Rebecca said reassuringly. "Both of them," she added for clarity.

"Why you and not me?" Jess demanded.

"I'm more powerful," Rebecca said with her challenging grin. "But just as stubborn," she added with a wink. "If it were safe, I would let you. But it's not, and she will need her mother," Rebecca emphasized.

"I need you," Jess begged.

Rebecca tilted her head and looked at her like a loving mother always does. "I'll be around," she lied. "You definitely turned out better than I could have ever hoped," Rebecca said with her eyes filling with water. "I know you will help your sister find her way," she added.

Before Jess could say anything else, Rebecca pulled her into a massive bear hug and disappeared into thin air, leaving Jess to fall to her knees and cry. She would never see her mother again. Even Jess knew that was goodbye.

Seventeen

S ophie felt arms wrapping themselves around her, and her fury exploded. Whoever held onto her was stronger and pushed them both to the surface. Her veins and eyes were converting back to blue the closer she got to the surface.

"NO!" she heard the evil side of her scream inside her head.

As they got closer to the surface, a beam of light shot out and cracked the surface. James grabbed desperately at Sophie's hands to help pull her out of the water. Rebecca climbed out after her. She was gasping for air.

"Is this what you've been doing when you sleep?" Rebecca shouted in between gasps. "Bringing in people against their will?"

"Stop yelling at her!" James shouted back as he helped to hold

Sophie's hair back while she spit the water out of her lungs.

"It does YOU more damage than her!" Rebecca roared back.

"Who the hell are you?" James yelled.

"Rebecca!" she shouted back.

"You gave me the damn necklace to do this!" James reminded her in a warning tone.

"That's not the point," Rebecca muttered.

"Sounds like it is," James retorted as he helped Sophie get to her feet.

"I don't know how I do it, and it's not on purpose,"

Sophie clarified in between her own gasps. "Except this time," she said weakly, looking at James.

Rebecca frowned at her, but knew she was telling the truth. "Fair enough," she finally said. "But you can't do it anymore," Rebecca warned. "If they don't give you permission, then their minds unravel and they don't always wake back up," she added.

"Well, when we get out of here, you can show me," Sophie said more sarcastically as her lungs began to work on their own again.

"What happened?" James asked her, brushing the wet hair away from her face.

"I don't know," Sophie lied, but Rebecca could read right through her.

"We need to get you back and get you out of here," Rebecca said with disappointment on her face. "James, you need to go back. I've got it from here."

"If you had it, why did you wait so damn long?" James shouted at her.

"Watch it," she warned him. "I was busy keeping Algos out of the dream realm for good, so Sophie COULD come back."

James and Sophie looked at each other in shock.

"He will not have access to you other than in physical form from now on," Rebecca confirmed. "Which we need to get back to. Your body is shutting down."

James pulled Sophie's face close to his. "I'll be waiting," he whispered before he kissed her passionately.

"See you on the other side," Sophie breathed once they parted.

Rebecca made a circle of light behind him. James smiled his boyish grin and headed in the direction of the light Rebecca had made. He took one more look at Sophie over his shoulder, then walked through to the other side.

"Did he give you what you needed?" Rebecca asked in amusement.

"He always does," Sophie said as she watched him with her Cheshire grin.

"Good. Let's go. Time's running out," Rebecca ordered as she made another ring of light, took Sophie's hand and walked with her through it.

"Hello?" Roger asked urgently as he answered his burner phone.

"It's me," was all Elaine said.

"Hey, Elaine," he said, waving Tina and Ben over while putting the phone on speaker.

"You were right," she said in her doctor's voice. "He was trying to clone her."

"Was?" Roger asked for clarification.

"That's the thing," Elaine said with a hint of confusion. "Every sample taken was tainted. No embryo or mother survived the testing," she said, deep in thought.

"How does that happen?" Ben asked, confused.

"Exactly," was Elaine's only response.

"How would they get her DNA?" Roger thought out loud.

"Every fight," Tina whispered. "Think about it! There's a clean-up crew that comes to remove all dead bodies in order to not be detected. The girl is good, but I can't imagine with that kind of fighting that some DNA doesn't get left behind in the process," she said, feeling very sick to her stomach.

"But you said every sample was tainted?" Roger asked again.

"Yes," Elaine stated. "Someone had clearly made sure that the DNA was damaged and was replaced with something that would ensure death of the embryo and host," she confirmed.

"Well, you know Algos isn't the one doing it," Ben huffed.

"Eddie?" Roger asked.

"I don't think so," Tina said. "He wasn't even aware of the program, and he asked me to look so he wouldn't get caught digging."

"What if that was on purpose?" Ben asked in suspicion.

"I know we don't know him well, but biology doesn't seem to be his expertise. Tech is. Under myself, of course," Tina added with a triumphant smile.

"So, who's batting for Sophie on the inside?" Roger asked.

"I think the more important thing to ask is how long can they keep it up without dying in the process? Or are willing to?" Tina added with a frown.

"Well, it's not like she can stop fighting," Ben said in desperation. "Or make her DNA unusable or untraceable," he added in frustration.

"Actually, there is," Elaine cut in. Everyone jumped. They had forgotten she was still on the phone.

"What do you mean?" Roger asked, confused.

Elaine grew silent. She heard a sound that had haunted her dreams since she met Roger and everyone in New Orleans. "I will send you a file," was her desperate response. "I don't think I will be around to help you."

"Elaine, what's wrong?" Roger asked, frightened.

"Tell Sophie, I'm sorry. If I would have known sooner, I would have saved her sooner," she said in sorrow before hanging up the phone.

"What's wrong?" Ben asked fearfully.

"Another friend is being sacrificed for the greater good," Tina whispered.

Within seconds, the computer dinged with a message containing an encrypted file and a name of another genome surgeon with the words "Good Luck" at the end. Everyone looked at each other as they swallowed their guilt for getting another life taken for Sophie's cause and got to work.

Dr. Elaine Cox could proudly say that she had lived a life of little regret. Her only genuine regret was not being able to help Sophie before things got so out of hand. She ran her hand through her long brunette hair and looked at herself in the mirror.

She had always been a thin girl, but she had definitely lost a few pounds and several nights of sleep trying to resolve the mess that she couldn't stop. Her face was more pale than normal and her eyes sucken in. Elaine had given up sleep to come up with a solution to Sophie's DNA, never being shared with others. A serum that would camouflage her actual DNA.

Jess had allowed her to keep some vials in case Elaine needed to develop something her daughter needed in the future. This definitely qualified. Without having Sophie to test on, it was only an educated guess. Too bad no one will know of her greatest creation. A serum that would help to provide false positives should any DNA ever be obtained.

Elaine realized it was just a theory, but it was the best she could do and still live with herself these last several months, hiding in fear. The sound of the cane hitting the pavement outside the window of her apartment reminded her to drop the phone and smash it into unusable pieces. She would not be responsible for him getting his hands on Sophie.

Elaine grabbed the blue serum that she had been saving for this exact occasion out of her top desk drawer. She turned around, leaned against the desk, and closed her eyes as tears ran silently down her cheeks. In just a couple of minutes, Algos kicked her front door down in fury. He was much scarier and angrier than Elaine had imagined.

"You're coming with me, doctor," he said, panting in his anger. He was clearly already royally pissed.

"I'm not going anywhere with you," she said weakly.

"I'm not in the mood, Doc," Algos growled with warning. "I just lost my plan A, and you're my Plan B," he barked at her. He stepped towards her to grab her by the arm, but Elaine was quicker.

She jabbed the needle into her neck for the fastest reaction and squeezed the plunger hard. He watched the blue serum quickly disappear into her veins.

"NO!" he yelled as his eyes dilated and he started spitting like a rabid dog. Algos grabbed her by the arms and shook her in his fury. "You will not take this away from me!" he screamed at her face as it was already turning a quick light blue. Algos screeched to the ceiling a string of cuss words that could be heard around the world. No one had witnessed this measure of anger from him. Including himself.

Sophie woke in a gasp in the library with Rebecca still holding her hand and John bent down eagerly at her side.

"Don't scare me like that, Sweetie," John said distressed. "You're lucky Rebecca got here when she did," he warned.

"And you are?" Sophie said as she pulled her hand out of the woman's hand.

Rebecca gave her a smirk. "Well, technically, I'm your grandmother. Ugh! What a nasty word. It makes me feel so old!" she said in fake horror.

Sophie looked at John in confusion.

"Your other grandmother," Rebecca clarified. "Your mother is my daughter."

Sophie scrambled to put as much distance between her and the woman who had married the psychopath that was her grandfather.

"Sophie Lee," John ordered. "You show her some respect. She's the reason your mother's as good as she is." He gave her a disappointing look that made Sophie feel like she was back in the principal's office as a little girl.

"I'm sorry," she said, bowing her head down immediately. "But why would you marry someone so awful?" Sophie asked, staring straight through Rebecca's soul.

Rebecca sighed heavily. "Because we all had a role to play in order to get you here and to the place, you are right now. You can fight fate as much as you want, but it will always win in the end," she said in a sad tone.

Unfortunately, Sophie knew just what she meant. She had experienced the same life story herself. Rebecca stood up and looked at John.

"You need to go back," she told him with authority.

"We've been trying, but she hasn't figured out how to set us free," John said matter-of-factly.

Just then, a screech came from the other side of the door. "ENOUGH!" they heard the other Sophie scream.

But it was another voice that terrified Sophie more. "Let her go!" shouted her mini me. Sophie ran to look out the window. She saw the teenage version of herself, and the ten-year-old version of herself standing between the library door and the other Sophie.

"No!" shouted Sophie. She went to open the door, but John and Rebecca both stopped her immediately.

"You can't," Rebecca warned.

The two younger girls circled the evil Sophie in her red ops outfit, and black bobbed hair. Out of nowhere she tossed her head back and cackled like a hyena. "Look who's looking to die for you, sweet Sophie. Someone with bigger balls than you!"

Sophie's face grew red, and her hands balled up into fists.

"Well, isn't she pleasant," Rebecca said as she put her hands over Sophie's, taking her anger away. No one expected what came next. The evil Sophie sped out of nowhere and grabbed the teenage Sophie high in the air with a single hand. Her body was flailing around as she tried to escape the evil Sophie's grip, which just encouraged her to tighten it.

Her mini me, a few feet away, looked in horror and grabbed her own neck. John and Rebecca watched Sophie struggle to breathe in response. Of course, they were all tied together.

"You forget, sweet Sophie," she growled. "I have all your power, and no regret." Her grin grew wider, sending shivers through everyone watching.

"Keep her inside," Rebecca ordered to John as she flung the door open, but it was too late. The evil Sophie squeezed teenage Sophie's neck so hard that her windpipe collapsed under the pressure. Her eyes became bloodshot almost instantly, and her body went limp. Her evil twin just tossed her teenaged body off to the side as if it were a bag of trash. Then she set her eyes on the little girl, and her eyes grew a bright blood red. The little girl shook her head as she backed away slowly in horror.

240

"Run!" they heard Sophie scream behind them. The little girl didn't hesitate. She took off running in Rebecca's direction.

The evil Sophie stood and laughed with pure evil as she gave the little girl a head start. Nothing was more exciting than the hunt of a prey.

The little girl ran with all of her might, despite her eyes being blinded by tears. At the very last second, she slid past Rebecca and into Sophie's arms. Rebecca stood back and slammed the door shut. She heard Sophie's evil twin screech again, shaking the walls of the library with it. She twisted her head back and forth in front of the window with blind fury and spitting like a rabid dog.

"Well, that can't be good," Rebecca whispered. The fear in her voice betraying her. She had never seen such a thing. Then again, Sophie was like no other.

Sophie held onto the little girl as she bawled in her arms. "What's going to happen to us?" the child asked in a trembling voice.

"Nothing is going to harm you," Sophie assured her with determination. She just hoped that she could keep her promise.

James woke up in a gasp and found the entire crew surrounding him.

"You alright, Son?" Roger asked as he began checking his vitals. The purple necklace had stopped glowing for the time being.

"I'm okay," James said in between gasps. "She's coming back."

"Who's coming back?" Tina asked with dread.

"Sophie!" he gasped. "Should be any minute!"

They all watched her eagerly, waiting for her to finally wake up. Only she didn't. Then many alarms started going off from the various medical machines, and Ben and Roger jumped into action.

"What's wrong?" Donna demanded.

"I don't know," Roger answered honestly. He started giving Ben orders, along with everyone else. They took them eagerly.

James grabbed Sophie's hand. "Come on now," he pleaded with her. "You're supposed to be coming back." His voice cracked as tears filled his eyes. "Rebecca," he said, standing up. "Bring her back!"

Everyone watched with broken hearts as Roger and Ben fought to stabilize Sophie, and James kept screaming at the ghost to bring her back.

Cecil and Daryl came to restrain James, but he just started fighting them off. "I will not lose her AGAIN!" he screamed madly until Cecil got his hands behind his back and ordered him to calm down.

"Jamie Moore, calm down!" his mother ordered. "Fighting each other helps no one!"

He struggled until he lost his energy to fight any more. Cecil held onto him as he fell to his knees and cried his frustration onto the floor. Tina rushed over and held onto her friend, crying with him.

"She'll come," she whispered to them both. "She always does."

Charles!" Algus screamed in his office as he paced like a rabid dog.

"Yes, Sir," Charles said flatly as he entered Algos' office.

"Get the doctor!" Algos ordered in fury.

"Of course, Sir," Charles replied with no emotion, bowed, and left into the shadows.

"I am really sick and TIRED of people messing with my plans!" he shouted at no one.

The image of his wife and mother flashed before their eyes. The smirk on their faces. Like they were better than he was! Anger brewed dangerously in his veins. Someone was going to have to pay. The good Dr. Cox didn't help his mood or his situation, either. Even Clarice wasn't available to release his frustrations on. Well, they were going to learn.

They were going to realize he never had a Plan A without a Plan Z and all the ones in between. The memory of chess came to mind. His lips curled up at the ends. Chess. His favorite game. The only game you could have an aggressive start, deceiving middle, and inevitable checkmate in the end.

He'd played the aggressive start move off and on, pausing occasionally so that the other side never saw the inevitable checkmate coming. His checkmate. Algos was a master at the game. He had no intentions of losing now. He headed for the lab.

"How goes it, Doc?" Algos sneered as he walked into the secret lab.

The 5'8" thin brunette jumped at the sound of his voice. She hated when he snuck up on her like that. She hated he visited her at all, frankly.

Algos always carried his cane, but used it as a weapon and a taunting tool more than a necessity. Trying to use it as a warning of

doom The doctor knew this as much as Algos did, which is why he
purposely didn't use it when entering the lab. She didn't appreciate his
attempt to play with her like any of his other prey.

"Everything is on schedule," the doctor offered in annoyance.

"And how is my 'special' project coming along?" Algos asked
with eagerness.

The doctor froze. Last time Algos was told that the treatments
didn't work, she had paid the price. Not just because Jess showed no
signs of success through her teenage years and beyond, but that
Sophie did once she became a toddler. Her mother was the original
doctor assigned to that "project". He murdered her for being wrong.
Now, her daughter took her place.

"She appears to be handling them well," the doctor offered
nervously.

"Are you sure?" Algos warned.

"We won't be able to test her for a few more weeks. The serum
needs to do its job," she replied with as much confidence as she could
muster.

"You know the price if it doesn't," Algos forewarned.

"Yes," the doctor replied with a hint of irritation. Of course she
knew. She was the one that lost everything, the first go-around.
However, something still bothered her.

"What is it, Doc?" Algos demanded, watching her eyes change.

"Why still hunt for Sophie if this is her replacement?" the
doctor asked carefully, making sure not to look directly at him.

Algos smiled with a diabolical grin. "My granddaughter has
many talents that have yet to be unlocked. She has had access to the
dead for over ten years. Let's just say that it would be an easier

244

transition. However, you must always have a Plan B, C, D, etc should Plan A go awry," he offered with pride.

Dr. Liz Banks was the spitting image of her mother, with brunette hair that cascaded to the middle of her back, and emerald green eyes that sparkled when she had made a new discovery. Only Dr. Banks took more interest and less hesitation to Algos' experiments than her mother had, making Liz his new favorite doctor. Of course, he waited to take away her mother until Liz had graduated and could take her place. Always have a replacement. That was Algos' rule, and Liz was it. She cared less about the subject itself and more about the results, just like he did. He would have to reward her soon. Keep her motivated.

"It still makes no sense that the cloning never took effect," Liz announced with frustration.

"Sometimes," Algos stated, "It is just a matter of going about it differently. Carry on, good doctor," he said as she listened to the sound of the cane beating the cement floor fade away.

"Well, it's just you and me," Liz confided into the girl's ear as she grabbed another gold vial and slowly released it into the red-head's IV. "Let's see just how deadly we can make you," she said with a sheepish smile.

Eighteen

Tina tried to swallow the vomit that threatened to escape her throat as she watched their protective detail eat the chicken Alfredo that Sally made for everyone in the kitchen. James remained by Sophie's side, and Tina waited with him while Ben and Roger went to gather more medical supplies from the local hospital. If Sophie didn't wake up soon, Tina would have to face Clarice. Alone. And lose everything.

"What's wrong, Ti?" James asked her. He knew his friend well, and she was more troubled than usual.

"Just a lot on my mind," she lied.

"You always have a lot on your mind, and you never look like that. Spill the beans," James ordered.

Tina's eyes filled up with water, and she quickly tried to blink them away. "We've all made choices trying to keep Sophie as safe as possible," she whispered. "I guess I'm just worried some aren't forgivable."

James turned to look at his friend. "What are you talking about, Tina?" he pressed.

"I can't," she quietly sobbed as she shook her head, trying to get her emotions under control.

James reached out and took her hand in his. "Tell me," he softly encouraged her.

"You'll never forgive me. Neither will Ben," she said in between sobs.

"I can't help if you don't tell me," James urged. "It will be between us," he added with hope to get her to talk.

Tina looked down at her hands and weaved them in and out repeatedly. "Clarice cornered me in Vegas," she began slowly.

James took in a sharp breath, but knew better than to interrupt when she was like this. Tina waited to collect how she could confess without having him hate her. It was hard to find the words she needed.

"I was in the bathroom," she finally continued.

"Did she hurt you?" he growled. He couldn't stop himself. She was his sister.

"No," she said, looking at him and assuring him. "But I guess I led her to me somehow. I'm sorry," she said as she cried.

James stood up and pulled her into his arms. "No one is going to be mad at you for a psychopath's daughter cornering you," he laughed, as he ran his hand softly up and down her back.

Tina pulled back and blurted out, "I'm supposed to give her Sophie tomorrow." She couldn't bear to look him in the eyes as she edged toward hysteria.

James froze and thought to choose his words carefully. "And why would you do that, Tina?" he asked cautiously.

"I wouldn't!" Tina confirmed in desperation. "But I've done something really stupid, and Clarice knows it. She's holding it against me in exchange for Sophie," she said, staring at the floor in guilt.

"What did you do?" James asked more firmly than he intended. He watched her face turn from pale to green and she pushed past him to run to the bathroom. He followed her immediately. Out of habit, he grabbed her hair and held it back for her as she violently deposited what little she was able to eat since yesterday into the toilet. "What did you do?" he tried again, but another wave of nausea won the battle and he saw her struggle worse than any night spent playing drinking games.

Tina leaned back against the stall wall and closed her eyes. The cool bathroom floor and metal wall felt good against her body, that was currently on fire. She secretly hoped the lady from the bathroom was right, and it got better. If she could keep it, that was.

"What is wrong with you?" he asked as he grabbed a couple of paper towels and wetted them with cool water. He brought them back and placed some on her forehead and on the back of her neck.

"Stress," she lied as she gasped for air that wasn't tainted with the aroma of chicken Alfredo.

"If I didn't know any better, I'd think you were pregnant," James snorted, but stopped at the look of shame that came across her face. "Oh, Ti," James breathed. He reached out and brushed the hair that was sticking to her forehead away from her face. "How far along are you?"

"I think like 6-7 weeks or so. It's kinda hard to tell since I don't know when I got off," she confessed.

"Does Ben know?" he asked her, knowing the answer.

"Not exactly the right time," she said sadly.

He sat down next to her against the stall, and she leaned her head on his shoulder. "I don't know how this happened," she whispered. "We're so careful," Tina added in shock.

James laughed and took her hand in his. "Fate had other plans," he said with a smile. "You need to tell Ben so he can check you out. Or dad."

Tina shook her head. "Sophie comes first," she said with determination.

"I'm pretty sure they can handle both," James said, leaning his cheek against the top of her head.

"No Sophie, means no hope for anyone," Tina reminded him. "Time is running out. Her body's shutting down. We all know it, and none of us can do a damn thing about it," she said flatly.

James sighed deeply. "When was the last time she ever let us down?" he asked her.

Tina giggled. "That stubborn mule? Never," she replied.

"Exactly," James confirmed. "And I know this sounds weird, but I can still feel her."

Tina squeezed his hand. "It's not weird at all. I feel her too."

"So, tomorrow, huh?" James asked casually.

"Yeah, but it doesn't look like Sophie will make it. I'll have to go and buy her some more time," Tina exhaled her vow with determination.

"Why don't we all just go see how Sophie's doing and come up with a plan?" he asked her, knowing what was going to unfold, regardless. James pushed himself up and held out his hands to her. She grasped them and let him pull her up off the floor. "Hey," he said, pulling her in. "We're a team. We decide as a team, and we play them out as a team. Sophie wouldn't want it any other way," he said, kissing her on the head.

"Oh, whatever!" Tina laughed. "That girl would be off on a rampage by herself, and taking names before coming back to tell us all about it!"

"I don't know," James said with his boyish grin.

Tina rolled her eyes dramatically and walked out of the bathroom with James' arm around her shoulder while she tried to figure out how she could borrow everyone just a little bit more time and not get killed.

Sally watched her son carefully navigate Tina to a chair and wrap her up in a throw. "Hey, Donna," she called over her shoulder. "Can Daryl go out and get some saltines?" she asked, not taking her eyes off of Tina.

"Still being stubborn and not telling anyone?" Donna asked, watching Tina carefully too. Sally looked at her and gave her a motherly smile. "You don't have to have kids to know what that green face means," Donna chuckled.

250

"I think someone's finally figured out," Sally said, turning back to her son.

"I hear apricots help, too," Donna added in deep thought. "Daryl," she called over her shoulder. "We need you to grab some supplies."

"Why do they call it morning sickness if it's all day long?"

Daryl said in frustration as he came over to the women. "Make a list," he added, shaking his head. "And why haven't the two actual doctors put it together yet?"

"Doctors are only able to focus on one thing at a time," Sally said with a wide smile as she looked at her husband and Ben with loving eyes. "It's not their fault. But it doesn't help that they're men either," she giggled.

"I take offense to that!" Daryl mocked, hurt.

"That's because you're more of a girl than a man," Cecil teased as he came to join the group and see what was keeping their interest. It didn't take long to figure out. "She might want to tell him before she starts showing," he said, shaking his head.

"She's still got some time," Donna said, winking at him.

Just then, Tina turned to look in the direction from which she felt she was being watched. A smile crept over her lips as she watched the group that had been whispering about her scramble to look busy suddenly. Poorly, she might add. But it was still nice to be with family. Even if they were a hot mess of one. She just had to sneak out in the morning to do her best to save them and hope that Sophie woke up in time to save her in return.

Tina turned to watch Sophie lying in the hospital bed. Minus her muscles flinching pretty regularly at the moment, there was no other sign she was doing anything other than sleeping. "Please wake up," she whispered, before she closed her own eyes to rest.

James knew Tina planned to go before anyone woke up, which is why he never slept. He couldn't let her sacrifice herself and his future goddaughter or godson because of him. That would not be an option. His only ace in the hole was how exhausted pregnancy seemed to be for his friend, or Tina would have never let him leave before her.

James waited until everyone else was passed out minus the night shift downstairs, and he crept over to her bag and quietly dug through it until he found what he was looking for. Without even looking at it, he slipped it into his jean pocket and went back over to Sophie. He gently brushed the hair away from her face and kissed her gently on the lips.

James had already written a note and left it on the end table in the hall. He only took a bit of cash to help him get to where he needed, and left his bag next to Sophie's bed, but there was something he needed to do before he left. James bent down and pulled the engagement ring from his bag and took it out of its box.

He gently pulled her left hand into his own and slid the ring on her ring finger. He bent down and kissed her gently on the lips once more before whispering in her ear, ever so softly. "Come find me one more time." Then he kissed her on the forehead and crept down the hallway to his escape.

"We can't stay in here," Rebecca said, pacing the floor. Sophie continued to hold the little girl, that was still trembling with fear, in her arms.

"Well aware," John said, skimming the books he'd already read a thousand times before.

"No," Rebecca said with warning, looking right at him. "Time has run out."

Sophie didn't think John's face could get any more pale, but it did. She wasn't sure, but she guessed she had reached the point of never returning, like John had mentioned when they first met. Sophie looked down at the little girl trembling in her arms.

"Here," she whispered to her as she picked her up and set her back down on the couch, covering her up with a throw. She reached over and picked up the green book titled *Anne of Green Gables* and gave it to the little girl. "Read this. It will help."

The little girl looked at her blankly, all color drained from her face. She was in shock, but nodded in agreement. She snuggled down and began to read her favorite book of all time. Sophie watched her from behind the couch, but her focus was on Rebecca and John.

"I'll go," Rebecca was saying.

"You don't have the strength," John reminded her, shaking his head. "You've spent too much already and broken enough rules to get here."

"She doesn't know that," Rebecca countered. "I still have tricks she has never seen."

"No!" John ordered.

"You have to get back," Rebecca reminded him. "They used Algos to try and take over. You need to get back and restore order," she commanded.

"And you're stronger than me to keep her safe from Algos. She needs you," John retorted.

"You just don't give yourself enough credit," Rebecca said with a meek smile. They both knew he was right. "I can't sacrifice you for what might come later."

"There's no might," John hissed. "You and I both know this isn't done until he is."

Sophie looked at them both, then looked down at the little girl. Tina's voice rang through her ears.

"Some people say that when we're trapped within ourselves, sometimes that means we need to find peace from within in order to move on."

She looked toward the door. Her evil twin had gone back to sitting in her metal chair on the other side of the room, with her elbows on her knees, barely holding her head up. Her red eyes glowed, begging for Sophie to come to her.

"Find peace from within," she whispered to herself, but everyone was too distracted to hear her. It was the one thing no one had allowed her to try. Maybe because they knew it was a lost cause. But it could still be the way out. Her time was out anyway. She was going to die either way. Why not at least try?

Sophie felt something being slipped on her ring finger.

When she looked down, she saw the engagement ring that

James had been trying to give her for so long. Someone had clearly put it on her actual finger, and it was the last thing she was going to see.

It fit perfectly. She blinked at the tears that filled her eyes. "Come find me," he murmured in her ear.

"I'm coming," she whispered back as she took her hand and balled it into a fist. It made a fine weapon for sure. Something told her, if she was ever getting out of here, she would be having it cleaned. A lot.

Her veins glowed a light blue under her skin. She took one last look at the loved ones that remained in the room with her, surrounded by books filled with a lifetime of memories of people that had crossed Sophie's path. Some she had saved. Others had been sacrificed for a war Sophie never asked to be a part of. Her own innocence was terrified and trying desperately to get lost in her favorite book. And a single wooden chair that appeared next to her out of thin air. Sophie took a second and tiptoed to the door, opened it, and stepped to the other side. She took her wrist and twisted it, consciously locking the door.

Rebecca and John looked up at the sound. "Did she just..." was all Rebecca got out before they both ran to the door. Sophie had locked it from the other side. Neither of them could open it.

"Don't Sophie!" John half begged, half warned, but Sophie ignored him and began walking to the center of the room. The evil Sophie tilted her head like a predator studying her prey, watching Sophie move closer. The corners of her lips curled up in pure evil and wickedness. The moment she'd been waiting for.

"Sophie, open this door!" Rebecca ordered, but Sophie did no such thing.

The little girl jumped from the couch to run to the door. "No, Sophie! You can't!" she screamed.

"Oh, but she can, apparently," her twin sneered.

Sophie ignored her and kept breathing slowly until she got a few feet away from her twin. She put her hands on her hips and tilted her head to match her counterpart.

"You know, we could just be friends, and stop all this nonsense," Sophie offered.

Sophie's twin fell out of her chair laughing so hard.

"Or, I could just kill you and be done with it," Sophie replied flatly, rolling her eyes at the girl's reaction. It was worth a try to offer. Clearly, option two was going to be the only option in this game.

"Please!" shouted her evil twin as she used the chair to dramatically help herself to her feet. "You have too much emotional baggage to ever beat me!" she shouted out. "At least I won't have to go by your stupid name anymore once I'm free," she added with a smile.

"And what's this clever name you've chosen?" Sophie asked, less than impressed.

"Reine," the other Sophie said, holding her head up high with pride.

"Seriously?!" Sophie laughed. "Have we not read enough books to come up with something better?" she asked, laughing so hard her eyes watered.

"It means," was all her twin got out in anger.

"Yeah, I know what it means," Sophie said, holding up her hand and cutting her off. "Algos thought he was being smart by changing his name, too. It means nothing. It's just another name," she added flatly. "Queen, even in French, doesn't make you one," Sophie said, unimpressed.

Reine's eyes filled with fire and rage. Sophie just shook her head and quietly fed on the energy Reine insisted on giving her for free.

"Nice ring," Reine added sarcastically.

"I think so," Sophie said with a shrug.

"Too bad you won't get to see it in person," Reine sneered.

"I will be the judge of that," Sophie said with her Cheshire grin. She took stance and waved her opponent to come.

"God!" Reine laughed. "I guess you want to go out the same way your beloved Mario went out."

Sophie didn't move. She just patiently waited.

"Oh. You don't know?" her twin taunted. "Brunette, over there didn't tell you that grandpa took him for good?"

Sophie tried not to let the shock betray her this time, because she was most likely lying, anyway.

"What would I get out of lying to you?" Reine snorted, reading Sophie's mind.

"Rebecca," Sophie called out, never taking her eyes off her evil counterpart.

Rebecca hesitated, but John squeezed her arm in warning. She sighed heavily in response. "He sacrificed himself to Algos to save your parents," she hollered in response. "He kicked his ass pretty good, too," she added.

Rebecca knew Sophie, because Sophie was as much Rebecca as Rebecca was herself. She knew better than anyone that anger was great fuel, but only if it didn't blind you completely. Rebecca made that mistake once herself. She would not help Sophie do the same.

Just on cue, the anger boiled from within Sophie. Not at Mario. She knew Rebecca was telling the truth, because she knew Mario better than anyone. Her evil side was counting on this information, destroying her like it did the first time, but Sophie had learned that lesson the hard way. She would grieve for her godfather once she got out. Right now, she needed the extra power of being pissed off.

Sophie took one controlled breath to anchor her emotions, and once again waved her hand to signal the attack of her opponent. She knew she could flip the switch with just the right trigger word, but she would not give Reine the enjoyment. Sophie was going to have to stay herself as long as possible, although she was already growing weaker by the second.

"Oh, this is going to be fun," Reine said in excitement, and bowed before Sophie in acceptance of the challenge before speeding at her head on.

Nineteen

"Hold on!" John called over his shoulder. Everyone grabbed the closest object they could find in order to stay on their feet. Reine came at Sophie, and Sophie grabbed her by the hand and flipped her over her own head. When Reine landed on her back, the library shook violently as books fell off the shelf. Rebecca picked up little Sophie and held her close to her.

Reine smiled with anger and satisfaction as she flipped around to be on all fours. Her mouth foamed, and fire danced in her eyes as she looked at Sophie like the prey she needed to eat after months of starvation. The game was finally being played. Sophie took stance and waved at Reine again.

Reine took the invitation eagerly and took off running. This time, Sophie had to jump into the air and out of her reach, as Reine slid past her and grabbed at her feet. Reine jumped to her feet and spun to quickly grab Sophie by the neck and lifted her off the ground. Sophie's legs flailed underneath her until she finally got a footing on Reine's stomach and kicked so hard that they both slid back from each other. Both girls were panting as they got to their feet.

This time, they both ran at each other full force. Reine grabbed the sleeve of Sophie's jacket as Sophie went to slide past her, and she was instantly out of it, grabbing the other sleeve and throwing it over Reine's neck. Sophie pulled back with all her strength and started dragging Reine back with her.

"Such a kindergarten move," Reine laughed as she grabbed the jacket around her neck and flipped Sophie over her back. Sophie did a somersault and landed on her feet, purring like an extremely dangerous cat. She spun around and faced Reine. "Is that seriously all you've got?" Reine taunted with a laugh.

Sophie tilted her head from side to side as it popped loudly. "Just getting warmed up," she said with a shrug. The girls charged each other again.

Sophie bent over and pushed off with her legs, wrapping them around Reine's waist, and pulled her to the ground. She quickly grabbed Reine's arm and held it high behind her back, and stepped on the back of her leg. They both heard her fibula crack. Reine cried out, but then began laughing like a hyena at Sophie. She was thriving on the pain.

"Stay down," Sophie growled.

"I'm good," Reine said as she rolled over and knocked Sophie square on the jaw, forcing her to take a few steps back. Reine found

260

her own footing and swayed back and forth like a cobra under a snake charmer's spell, relishing in the pain that shot through her leg. "Let's go," she smiled and waved for Sophie to come for her.

Sophie started a punch-kick combo, alternating between using her legs to kick Reine in the stomach and face as she blocked the punches that Reine threw. She was growing tired quickly. She had never felt so drained.

"She's been in here too long," Rebecca warned as she watched Sophie fight for her life. "She will not have the power to finish," she warned John as she covered the little girl's ears that she held against her.

"I still know what you said," she shouted in anger. Rebecca tried not to giggle at such a stubborn response.

Sophie punched up right, left jab low, and spun to instantly kick backwards connecting with Reine's stomach. Both girls put a little space between themselves and swayed. Reine started swinging at Sophie with all her might, and Sophie did a few back hand springs to barely miss her reach. She spun and kicked over Reine's head to make her duck in order to get access to her neck, as she hung on and kneed Reine in the stomach a few times before Reine pushed her palm into Sophie's stomach as hard as she could, including some added power, that sent Sophie flying backwards and landing on her back.

Sophie grunted when she hit the ground. She rolled back and forth, trying to get her bearings as she slowly recovered and found her footing.

"You're not impressive at all," Reine said as she spit out the blood that had built up in her mouth and paced back and forth, staring Sophie down. Reine knew Sophie was no match for her. She knew she was winning and would be set free any second.

"Get up!" demanded the little girl from the other side of the library door. Sophie centered herself and attempted to give her air deprived lungs the controlled breathing they so desperately needed. A couple of cracked ribs were making it difficult, though.

"Sophie, you've got to fight power with power in here!" Rebecca yelled at her. She wasn't sure what Sophie could actually do. She was pretty sure Sophie didn't know either. But if she didn't, she was going to die, killing all of them with her.

Sophie held up a wavering thumbs up and continued to find focus.

"God," Reine laughed. "I should just kill you to put you out of your misery," she said dramatically, rolling her eyes.

"I'd like to see you try," Sophie laughed with her fading oxygen.

Reine shook her head in dismay and charged Sophie again. Sophie dropped and round kicked Reine to her back. Then she jumped on her and straddled her in one fluid motion as she continued to punch her repeatedly in the face.

Reine got a hand free and grabbed one of Sophie's fists, squeezing it as the bones in her hand shattered. Sophie punched her square on the jaw as hard as she could, then got to her feet and stumbled away, holding onto her throbbing hand.

"She's going to die," John breathed in misery.

"She's not done yet," Rebecca lied, never taking her eyes off Sophie. It was clear Sophie did not know how to use her powers in here. And it was going to cost her everything.

Reine threw her head back as she howled like a wolf howling at the moon. Her veins grew red like lava, and the fire within her eyes grew larger. She looked like a bull ready to charge, and then she did.

Sophie held up both hands to brace for the impact and used her good hand to block what shots she could before she returned the favor and shoved her good palm into Reine's stomach as hard as she could. Light shot out from her palm, shoving Reine onto her back as she slid a few feet away from Sophie.

Sophie's breathing became more shallow. She was thankful for the distance, but whatever shot out of her hands drained her even faster than physically fighting.

"Sophie," she heard John whisper. Sophie looked over her shoulder and saw Rebecca nod her approval. She looked back at Reine. She was going to have to get mad to survive.

"It's a real shame that everyone's going to have to die, because of you," Reine laughed. "I think I'll start with Tina and Ben," she added. Sophie thought of the life that grew within Tina. While Reine got to her feet, Sophie's veins glowed visibly red as it quickly covered her body and consumed it.

"I think I'll have my way with James before I take him, though," she said, cackling.

That was it. Fire ignited within Sophie's own eyes. Matching Reine, she saw nothing but red.

"Now, that's what I'm talking about," said Reine in excitement. "It's about time you decided to play," she added.

"I was born to play," Sophie said with her mother's grin shinning through.

"That's not good," John gasped.

"Let's hope you're wrong," Rebecca whispered back.

"I can let the world burn, too," Sophie reminded Reine.

Rebecca's stomach dropped. Sophie understood she needed power, but she was tapping into the wrong side.

Without caution, Rebecca knew first-hand it was impossible to come back.

The girls took off to charging at each other like bulls, and the collision brought entire bookshelves down in the library. Rebecca and John dropped to one knee simultaneously to find balance as Rebecca carefully held the girl up in the process. When they looked back, Sophie had Reine in a headlock.

"You will not touch my family," Sophie growled at Reine.

"Stop me," Reine laughed and flipped Sophie over her neck, but Sophie held on and landed on her feet, flipping Reine over her head in return. Reine grunted as she landed on her back. Sophie stood on her neck.

"I will do what I have to," Sophie hissed as she put more weight on Reine's neck.

Reine grabbed Sophie's foot and twisted, forcing Sophie to rotate in the air before sliding backwards on the balls of her feet and balancing herself on her good hand. She closed her eyes and held her head up, letting the darkness consume her like it had the night Clarice murdered Mario.

Reine scrambled to her feet, and got into the same pose to copy Sophie, but Sophie was too busy enjoying the feeling that came with getting lost in the evil that flowed in her veins.

"I knew you'd like it," Reine snickered. "But it's time I was in charge," she warned before charging Sophie again.

Sophie stood up straight and waited until Reine got right in front of her. She spun and hit Reine as hard as she could right in her spine, as discs and bones shattered. The battle shook the floor and the nothingness around them. Reine staggered to gain balance. Her lung had been punctured, and she was gasping for air.

Sophie looked down at her ring, that glowed a lot less with all the blood on it. Sophie saw the damage she had done with it on, and giggled to herself.

"What's so funny?" demanded Reine.

"You're right," Sophie said with another laugh. "I'm never going to see this ring in person." She held up her shattered hand and admired what James had given her, bloody and all.

Sophie had ruined his last proposal by running away after losing Mario. Now, it would be too late for her to have a second chance to say "yes". Her body was shutting down. She could feel it. Faster than ever with the power she was using. The window to get the hell out was long gone. There was only one more thing to do. Make sure Reine didn't get out either.

"Let's do this," Sophie growled as she stood with her feet apart and arms hanging straight down.

"NO!" she heard her mini me scream from the other side of the door behind her.

Reine used her own good hand to wipe the blood that was dripping from her cheeks and nose. The corner of her lips curled up. This was it. She was going to finally be free.

Sophie watched Reine shrug in the acceptance of the challenge and charge her once more. As she braced for impact, she did what no one saw coming. Right before Reine reached her, Sophie pulled out two wooden stakes from the wooden chair carefully hidden in the back of her pants, jammed them into Reine's neck with as much force as she physically had left, and twisted.

They heard Reine shriek so loudly that it shattered the glass of the window they were looking out. Rebecca quickly covered the little girl's eyes to protect them from falling glass as she used her other hand to grab John and pull him away from the door, keeping her eyes closed. Once the walls and floor stopped moving like an earthquake beneath their feet, they all opened their eyes to find Sophie on her knees, gasping for air over Reine's glowing red body.

All three held their breath as Sophie's veins continued to glow bright red to match Reine's. The little girl hid her face in Rebecca's shirt for fear of what was to come next. When Sophie looked in their direction, her eyes carried the red fire that had been in Reine's while fighting. Rebecca put herself in front of everyone as the door unlocked and opened, and her heart beat out of control. This was not how this was supposed to go down!

When the red fire left Reine's body completely, her body turned to ash and fell to the floor. Rebecca held out her arms to keep John and the little girl behind her, as Sophie closed her eyes and breathed in deeply to help replenish her starving lungs. "You need to go," Rebecca hissed.

"We can't get out without Sophie," John reminded her.

"You're going to have to find a way," Rebecca shushed back with the stress showing in her voice, but her face showed determination as she prepared herself for battle. She never took her eyes off of Sophie. Then something else unexpected happened.

When Sophie opened her eyes, there was no longer red flame, but an ice blue flame that burned in her eyes. Her veins lost their blood red fiery glow as they shifted to a bright icy blue. It was as if aqua blue lava was engulfing Sophie's body and devouring the red.

"Well, that's different," Rebecca muttered to herself.

Once Sophie's body was covered in ice blue veins with a bright icy blue glow around her, she held out her palm towards their direction and a bright ice blue light shot out, blinding the others. They covered their eyes immediately.

When the brightness dimmed some, they removed their hands from their eyes.

"It's time to go back," Sophie said, still glowing a bright blue, and suddenly standing in front of them.

"What about you?" John asked nervously.

"I have a psychopath to destroy," she replied with her Cheshire grin, despite the ice blue flame still consuming her pupils.

Rebecca handed the little girl to John. "Go," she ordered, making sure they passed behind her.

"I'm not leaving you," John ordered.

"I'm right behind you," Rebecca said with a weary smile. The look she gave him made him shudder, and he grabbed the girl and carried her through the portal.

"It was really nice getting to know you," he said to the creature that had replaced his granddaughter.

"Tell dad I'll be in touch," she said with a smile, still staring in Rebecca's direction. Once they were both gone, Sophie tilted her head to take Rebecca in. "I will not hurt you," she said. "But it is time for us to go."

"I can't exactly let you leave, until I know it's my granddaughter I'm letting out," Rebecca countered honestly. She prepared for an attack as Sophie closed her eyes once more. When she opened them again, it was her regular blue eyes that stared back, and the ice blue glow faded.

"It's me," Sophie whispered her assurance softly. "I just had to make peace with myself before we could leave," she said with a slight smile.

Rebecca studied her intently. "Well, this is a first for me," she said honestly. "You are definitely nothing like what I was expecting."

Sophie giggled like the innocent little girl that she used to be. "I'm still figuring it out myself," she replied honestly with a shrug. She took Rebecca's hand in her own good one. "Maybe sometime we can practice and see what all I can do. It might come in handy," Sophie said hopefully.

Rebecca dropped her hand and stared at her cautiously. Sophie held her breath.

"Sometimes madness and greatness can carry the same face, but I can't stop, no matter your decision. I didn't ask for this, but I walk this path because it is my destiny. You can fear me or love me, but this game will end, now," Sophie added softly.

Rebecca studied the girl next to her that was fire of her fire and blood of her blood. Then she wrapped her arm around Sophie's shoulder and walked with her to the portal. "Now, that will be some serious fun!"

Sophie nodded as she watched Rebecca return to the dream realm. Then she looked around her. The library of her memories looked like a war zone, but the books remained. She would just have to reorganize them. Sophie laughed at herself for thinking such a silly thought. She had more important things to do.

Sophie looked at the sky above her. "I'm coming for you," she said in a low and determined tone as she bent her knees and pushed herself off the floor. She rocketed through the darkness and closed her eyes.

When she opened them again, she was in the medical hospital bed in an abandoned hotel, surrounded by loved ones. She sat up slowly. No one had noticed she was awake.

"What's a girl gotta do to get a cheeseburger around here?" she asked dryly. "And maybe a soda," she added with a hoarse voice.

Jess gasped and clutched onto Jack's arm tightly. "Sophie," she breathed out.

"Are you sure?" he asked her.

"Can't you feel her?" Jess asked her husband in agitation.

Jack didn't answer.

"Jack," Jess demanded.

"I feel something," he finally confessed. "I'm just not sure it's Peanut."

"Of course it is!" demanded Jess. But Jack wasn't so sure.

Twenty

I t was the first time Clarice had felt like herself in a while. She couldn't remember ever being so sick, but her vitals finally came back up and she could walk out of the room without passing out. When she had finally come to, only Eddie was waiting for her. Of course, her own father wouldn't care if she was still among the living. He never had, and yet she kept hoping all the same.

Once she got dressed, Clarice had gone to his office. Algos nearly ran her over, storming out of it. "Find her!" he ordered on a level of rage that she hadn't witnessed since Jess originally left them both behind.

"Nice to see you, too," she muttered to herself as he stormed down the hallway like hell on wheels. No word of where he was going.

270

Just that Sophie needed to be here by the time he got back. Whenever that was.

Eddie had given Tina 24 hours to find what she needed after he had stealthily plugged into the system. Now, the open link was gone. He crushed the phone into tiny pieces before flushing it down the toilet piece by piece. He hoped she had gotten the information she needed. Leaving it on any longer would put his own life in jeopardy, and no one to help them from the inside.

He continued to portray his normal, miserable self while he looked for Sophie. More for himself than the enemy. He heard Clarice slowly make her way into the lab from behind him.

"Please tell me you have found her while I was gone," she said dryly.

"We found the van that we think they drove from Bakersfield," the redhead answered for him. "But it was found in a chop shop not that far away. So, either they're still close by, or someone doubled back," she reported as she squinted at the screen in front of her.

"That's not exactly a lot more than you had a few days ago," Clarice said, irritated and obviously still exhausted. Her bark wasn't as bad as her bite by far, but she was too tired to care.

"Whoever is helping her is good," the redhead said in frustration.

"Did we hire you because you were better?" Clarice snapped in irritation.

The redhead dangerously gave Clarice a sarcastic look over her shoulder. Before anyone knew it, Clarice was holding the girl in the air by her throat with one hand. "Look at me like that again, and you'll be worse off than good old Clark," she growled.

The redhead nodded desperately until Clarice let go and she dropped to the floor. She rubbed her sore throat as she got to her feet, but kept her eyes down.

"That's what I thought," Clarice retorted, before walking back over to Eddie. "She needs to be located before he gets back," she said over her shoulder. Only it lacked her usual snarl that came with the territory when Eddie was involved. She ignored his hesitance and went back to her room to lie down.

Clarice opened her eyes to find the wooden door before her. "I'm not in the mood," she warned.

"Open it," she heard Jess carry the same tone in return.

"I'm too tired for this crap," Clarice yelled.

"I know. I'm going to help you. Now, open the damn door," Jess warned.

Clarice sighed dramatically and opened the door to find her sister on the other side, inspecting her eagerly. "Stop fussing," Clarice growled as she waved her off.

"Stop whining," Jess said flatly as she continued to look Clarice over.

"I'm fine!" Clarice snapped as she went to collapse onto the sofa. "What do you want?" she asked, not bothering to disguise her irritation as she closed her eyes.

"I want to help, Clare Dear," Jess said softly, bending down next to her sister.

"Call me that again, and I'll kill you again," Clarice warned.

"Stop being so stubborn," Jess said, standing up and putting her hands on her hips. "I'll make you some tea."

"I don't want any damn tea," Clarice growled. "Now, send me back so I can sleep."

"I can't do that," Jess said over her shoulder as she prepared tea against Clarice's will.

"You can. You just won't," snapped Clarice. Jess ignored her and continued to prepare the tea. When it was finished, she joined her sister back on the sofa.

"Drink," Jess ordered. "It will help."

"Sleep will help," Clarice muttered and ignored her sister's request.

"Drink it or I'll shove it down your throat," Jess said with a sarcastic smile.

"Try it," Clarice growled back.

Jess got up to sit on her sister and hold her down, forcing Clarice to shout back, "Fine!" She took the tea grudgingly and drank.

"He hasn't even checked on you, has he?" Jess asked, already knowing the answer.

"What difference does it make?" Clarice mumbled and continued to drink the tea. It did help. She wouldn't tell Jess that.

"It should matter to you," Jess lectured.

"It's not like you can save me," Clarice retorted back.

"No," Jess said, looking away from Clarice. "But Sophie can," she added cautiously.

Clarice threw the cup down and stood up with as much anger and energy as she could muster. "Send me back," she hissed.

"Are you so stubborn that you won't let your niece save you?" Jess demanded, standing up with equal anger.

"Your brat has been the bane of my existence, just as much as you were. Now, send me back!" Clarice shouted back.

"Not until you give me your word you will not harm her," Jess said as her eyes glowed red with her anger.

Clarice threw her head back and laughed wildly. "I have already been saving her life since the day you left. Now let me go!" she ended in warning.

"You've been hunting her like a dog for most of her life," Jess snapped back.

"Well, at least there's still one of her!" Clarice shouted back.

Jess froze. "You knew?" she asked, stepping back from her sister, feeling sicker than a dog.

"Of course I knew," Clarice barked back. "You all assume I know nothing, but I'm the reason we have not turned your child into a personal army," she said sharply as she walked back towards the direction of the door.

"So, you do like her," she heard Jess say, too happily for Clarice's desire.

"No," Clarice said, spinning back around. "One of her is a big enough pain in my ass. I'll be damned if there's a hundred of her," she said, crossing her arms defiantly, but Jess was already looking at her with those stupid puppy dog eyes filled with love that she had.

"Okay," she said with a shrug.

"Seriously, stop it," Clarice warned.

"Stop what?" Jess shrugged innocently.

"Just because I had been helping to keep her as a single pain in the ass, doesn't mean I have to continue doing so," Clarice warned her, but it was too late.

"Uh huh, sure," Jess said with a shrug. Knowing that Clarice saw the danger in cloning Sophie as much as they did, and for her own reasons, had prevented their father from accomplishing it. She knew Clarice had good in her. She just didn't see it for herself.

Clarice sighed heavily and dropped her arms in surrender. "I couldn't stop it with you," she mumbled. "But I REALLY don't want more than one of her," she added quickly. "I don't think anyone needs that," she said sourly.

"She'll come for him. I need you to help keep her safe," Jess said casually, like she was requesting the dog to be taken out for a walk.

"No," Clarice said, and turned for the door.

"You owe me," Jess warned.

"For what?" Clarice snapped as she whirled back around to face her sister. "You left me! And he could care less if I lived or died. So, help me understand why the hell I owe you for ANYTHING?"

"Prague," Jess said flatly.

Clarice glared at her. Her hands bunched up into fists.

"Watch yourself," she warned. It didn't matter that Jess was already dead, or technically, family. That was a topic never to be discussed, and Jess knew it.

"Like I said," Jess said innocently. "You owe me."

"You're lucky you're already dead," Clarice growled through her grinding teeth.

"Just saying," Jess said with a shrug.

"Fine," Clarice conceded. "If our father doesn't kill me between now and then, I will keep your Satan spawn safe," she muttered under her breath.

"I knew you would," Jess said with a wink and her precious smile.

"Can I go back now?" Clarice snapped. "I'm ridiculously exhausted, and this doesn't help, sweet sister." She sensed Corbin before she saw him. For whatever reason, she took in a sharp breath as he walked towards her.

"Clarice," he said with his stupid boyish grin.

"Corbin," she muttered back.

He went to put his hands on her shoulders, but she stepped out of his reach.

"Do you want to feel better or not?" Jess asked sarcastically.

"Can you give us a moment?" Corbin asked Jess. She looked at him oddly, but left them alone. Clarice looked at Corbin suspiciously. "Listen, Clare Bear, is it?" he said with his stupid grin.

"Not unless you want to die again," Clarice said sweetly, with the warning obviously tied to it. Corbin laughed in response.

"Very well, Slick," he said with a wink. "Let me see if I can help you out a little."

"And what can you do for me?" she asked, stepping away from him again.

"I really hate it when you do that," he said, catching her off guard.

"Do what?" she asked, confused.

"Get further away from me," he said with a grin. She clearly didn't know what to do with that information, and he took his opportunity to close the gap between them. "Stop being stubborn," he shushed to her and placed his hands softly on the sides of her head.

She watched as Corbin closed his eyes and took a deep breath.

Clarice felt warmth spread quickly through her body. Her exhaustion melted away and was replaced with a newfound energy. She wasn't sure if the warmth in her cheeks and groin were from Corbin's magic trick or not, but it was an uncomfortable sensation for her all the same. She stepped back out of his reach to collect herself.

"Better?" he asked, looking at her a little too intensely.

"Yeah. Thanks," she said, unable to look him in the eyes.

He took her hand in his and held tightly so she couldn't pull away. "Your dad's pretty pissed at us," Corbin warned.

"Great. What did you guys do now?" she asked, irritated, knowing she would be the one to pay the price.

"He won't be making you sick anymore," Corbin said softly. "He can't get back in here, and you won't be forced against your will to enter. That's why you were getting so sick," he confirmed. "It has to be a willing action from both parties."

"Huh," was all Clarice could muster. The warmth had lessened everywhere but where she needed it to.

"We'll do our best to make sure you don't catch the aftermath," he said, looking into her eyes and through her soul.

"Good luck with that," she said with a frown.

"I have my ways," Corbin said with a wink.

"Can I go back now? I'm still exhausted," Clarice asked, cutting him off. He knew she was uncomfortable. He also knew why. Corbin could feel it as much as she could, but she was too scared and unsure to accept it.

"Sure," Corbin replied with a nod. He brushed the hair away from her forehead. "You're pretty exceptional, you know that?" he asked before he quickly swiped his finger across her forehead and sent her spiraling back into darkness.

She didn't get to respond. Not that she knew what to say. All she knew was Corbin Dallas was dangerous. On a different level than she was used to, but dangerous all the same.

Rebecca staggered to her bed, and fell thankfully on top of it.

"You're not okay," she heard a female voice shriek behind her.

"I'm fine," Rebecca sighed. "I just need to rest."

"You broke the rules," the cloaked figure that stood in her doorway hissed at her.

"Yeah, well, I didn't have a choice," Rebecca breathed out as she curled up into the fetal position and tried to ignore the pain that was consuming her body faster than ever.

There was a long pause before the figure bent down closer to Rebecca's face. "Is he back?" the voice creaked at her.

"I really need you to tone that done a bit," Rebecca sighed, keeping her eyes closed. "Of course he's back. I wouldn't be here if he wasn't."

"I won't be able to save you," came a softer female voice.

"Well, aware," Rebecca murmured as her body quit on her all together, and she spiraled into darkness and pain.

The hooded figure stood up and studied her for a long time before disappearing into a black fog. Then reappeared with Corbin beside her.

"Fix her!" the cloaked figure demanded.

Corbin saw it was Rebecca and rushed to her side. "What's wrong with her?" he asked the cloaked figure.

"She spent too much power," the figure hissed. "She's dying. Fix her!" it shrieked at Corbin.

"I don't know how!" Corbin shouted back.

"Fix her or be banished!" the figure shrieked in return.

"You all act like I know what the hell I'm doing," he muttered to himself. He looked at Rebecca and moved the hair from her face. He could feel the life that remained in her quickly leaving. And the pain was unbearable! Even as a secondary party.

Corbin racked his brain as quickly as possible. Even with all he had learned, he knew Rebecca was not the norm of what he had come across. "Maybe she just needs to rest?" he offered.

"FIX HER!" the figure shrieked so loudly that the ground shook beneath them and nearly knocked Corbin on his butt.

"I'm trying!" he growled as an ice blue flame flickered in his eyes in response.

"Yes! That!" the cloaked figured yelled in a less shrieking tone.

Corbin looked back at Rebecca and took a deep breath before closing his eyes. He focused on all the ghostly lives around them and unknowingly tapped into their energy. Ice blue flames circled his body as his veins lit up ice blue to match. When he opened his eyes back up, they were as bright as a lighthouse beacon. He looked down at Rebecca and held his hands out to her. Ice blue rays shot out and jolted Rebecca's lifeless body, lifting her into the air as her head hung back.

"Again!" shrieked the voice next to him. He used all the energy he had left to shoot it into Rebecca's body that grew so bright, the entire dream realm lit up. Everyone closed and protected their eyes, no matter how far out they were.

Corbin's body couldn't take any more, and he collapsed, limp and unconscious. When the cloaked figure looked back up to Rebecca, her body was gone.

"What did you do?" the cloaked figure shrieked its demand, but Corbin was passed out cold, unable to hear it as he replaced Rebecca's soul in the darkness and swallowed up the pain she had left behind.

"Sophie!" Tina yelled as she rushed over and nearly squeezed the life out of her.

"Missed you too," Sophie giggled with her dry mouth. "I really need that soda," she added.

Sally came from the kitchen with a glass in hand and gave it to her. Sophie took a large drink as she looked around the room and waited for her eyes to adjust.

"Hey, Soph," Ben whispered as he checked her vitals. "Long time no see," he said with a weary smile.

"It wasn't by choice," Sophie said, giving him a weak smile in return.

"I'm going to give you a shot," she heard Roger say next to her. Sophie nodded as she continued to sip on the coke in her hand. The carbonation was just what the doctor ordered.

Roger looked down at the yellow serum in the vial. He prayed Elaine was right, and this was going to obscure Sophie's DNA regularly so that she would never be detected again. He sighed and quickly injected it into her arm. Only time would tell if Elaine was right.

"You okay, Kid?" she heard Cecil ask from further back. Sophie nodded and kept drinking the soda.

"How about some food?" Donna asked her in her motherly voice.

"Sounds great," Sophie said softly. Her eyes were adjusting, but even with the blurred vision, she knew they were fussing way too much. "Where's James?" she asked, looking around for him. The room grew deafening silent, as no one could make eye contact with her. Tina was closest to her. "Tina," Sophie said more aggressively. "Where's James?"

Tina stood up, tears escaping down her cheeks, and guilt consuming her face. "It's my fault," she sobbed.

"What's your fault?" Sophie asked with apprehension, trying to keep her emotions intact.

Roger took a deep sigh before confessing, "He left early this morning. While we were asleep." The sadness and worry in his voice was overwhelming to her ears.

"Where did he go?" Sophie asked, staring at the sheet that still covered her.

"He had to meet Clarice," Ben finally admitted. "He was trying to buy you more time. Here's the note we found." He handed the note to Sophie and gave her a second to read it.

Sophie took her time to read each word carefully. "Come find me," he had told her. What the hell was he thinking?!

"I'm sorry," Tina sobbed again.

"It's not your fault," Ben said, pulling her into his arms. "You can't control the fact that James decided without any of us, and went into the lion's den solo," he grunted in frustration.

"He didn't just go for the hell of it," Tina said, separating herself from her husband.

Sophie looked at her friend, who was clearly in misery. "They don't know?" she asked, confused. Tina kept her eyes on the floor and simply shook her head no.

"Well, not entirely true," Sally confessed, pulling Tina into her own arms.

"Will someone just tell the boy!" Daryl shouted from the back of the room.

Ben looked at his wife and around the room. He was quickly guessing that he was the "boy" Daryl was referring to. "Tina?" he asked, taking his wife's hand in his.

"I'm sorry, Sophie," Tina said, straightening up and taking responsibility for the first time since Vegas. "James left this morning to meet Clarice, because she cornered me and demanded that I hand you over personally today," she said, looking Sophie in the eye. "I didn't intend to ever do it," Tina added quickly. "But James found out I was pregnant and went to buy us more time so you could wake up and save us all."

Tina could see the shock on Ben's face out of the corner of her eye, but had to push through.

"Some lady gave me a pregnancy test in Vegas, but Clarice knew even before I did," she said, turning to face her husband. "I don't know how I could have been so careless on both accounts, but this is where we're at, and I don't even know what's going to happen. I didn't tell anyone because I needed Sophie to be safe first. Or none of it mattered either way."

Ben looked around the room, with most of them not returning his eye contact. "Did everyone know but me?" he asked in fury.

"Relax," Daryl said, getting closer to him. Just in case. "She didn't tell any of us, either. We just happen to know the signs and weren't taking care of our star patient," he said, giving Sophie a nod. She was already taking the IVs out of her arms and pulling the sheet off of her.

"Whoa," Roger said immediately. "You need to slow down."

Sophie put her feet on the floor and gave herself a second to test the waters before looking up at everyone. "Listen," she said with authority. "He had his reasons, and it doesn't matter what they were, but I'm going to get him." She looked at Tina and smiled warmly at her. "You're not to blame for his stubbornness, or Clarice being a pain in the ass. I promise," Sophie giggled.

"You can't go get him," Roger said in his doctor voice.

"Doc, I'm the one who can," she said, winking at Roger before pushing him away to stand up. "We're going to take a second and celebrate the addition to our family, and then we have some butt kicking to do," Sophie said with firmness. "Do we have something other than coke?"

"I picked up some alcohol free champaign when I went out last night. I was guessing we were going to be celebrating today one way or another," Daryl said with a wink as he and Donna went to collect glasses and pour some drinks.

"I'm sorry," Tina said again. This time to Ben.

"I'm not mad at you," he said honestly. "I just feel like a horrible husband that you didn't feel you could come tell me," Ben replied, clearly hurt.

"I needed you focused," Tina offered with a shrug. "And I didn't want you devastated if something happened," she added honestly.

"Nothing's going to happen," Sophie affirmed. "Other than you have to run an errand for me," she added as a second thought. She raised the glass she took from Donna and waited for everyone to follow suit. "To our newest family member!"

Tina kept looking around the hotel floor. Did they not understand that they were a long way from being scot-free, and Sophie had clearly lost her mind while being lost in it. She watched as everyone took a sip like nothing major was going on.

"Drink," Sophie encouraged. "It's alcohol free," she added with a wink.

Tina shook her head in disbelief and took a sip as she was ordered.

"Relax," Sophie said with a wink. "I wasn't just sitting around doing nothing while I was waiting to wake back up," she added, before turning around to address the group. "I'm sorry I was gone for so long," Sophie announced, as if leading a small army. "But we have some work to do before this is done," she added.

Everyone nodded in confirmation as Tina watched Sophie take charge like never before.

"Daryl, you, Ben, Tina, and Cecil need to go to these coordinates," Sophie ordered as she looked for a piece of paper and pen. Sally handed her some, as if reading her mind. "Thank you," Sophie said with a smile.

"What are we getting?" Cecil asked her.

"You're not getting anything. You're destroying," Sophie said with authority. "We've given Algos some serious blows lately. We can't leave Dad's satellite as an option."

"This is for the tower?" Tina asked, staring at the piece of paper Sophie had handed to her.

"Yes," she nodded. "I found them in the cabin after Mario was murdered. I just didn't have time to deal with it until now," Sophie confirmed. "But if I have learned nothing else, it's that we are a family. And sometimes we need to help each other out to win the war," she confessed. "I can't keep trying to do everything myself, and right now I need you to help me with this."

Tina looked up and studied her friend. She definitely had changed while she was in a coma. "On it," she replied as Tina folded up the paper and put it in her bra. Sophie laughed and turned to Roger.

"You, Sally, and Donna and whoever is left are going to stay here. We might need you when I bring James back," she said with a frown. Roger hesitated, but nodded in confirmation. "I will bring him back as safely as possible," Sophie assured.

"I know you will," Roger replied, giving her an assuring smile.

"I'm assuming this is still a safe and undetected location?" Sophie asked, turning to Donna. She knew who ran the show.

"You know it, Kid," Donna said with a wink.

"Good," Sophie said with conviction.

"You'll need weapons," Daryl told her as he dragged out what they had on hand.

Sophie held up her hand. "They won't let me in with them," she said, shaking her head.

"What are you going to do?" Sally asked alarmed. "Just walk up and knock on the door, unprotected?" she exclaimed.

"She is the protector," Tina said with her own mischievous smile returning. "She doesn't need weapons." Sophie gave her a wink back. "But shouldn't I stay and help you get in and help control the doors or something?" Tina asked distressed.

"You've helped me get out of enough locked rooms," Sophie said softly. "And you're the only one that can destroy the satellite from the ground. Can you get access to the key again?" she asked her.

"Of course," Tina said. "It was never that far."

Sophie walked over to her and put her hand on her shoulder. "I really need you to take care of this. For all of us. It needs to be done right," she pleaded.

Tina hesitated, but nodded. "Of course." She knew Sophie was keeping her as far away from the action as possible. She and Ben both. And the child that was growing inside of her. Sophie was all the hope Tina needed to gear up for round whatever at this point with Algos and Clarice. She started packing her backpack with the supplies she needed and walked away to make a phone call to get the key back into her possession.

"You're going to have to keep everyone safe," Sophie told Ben. "You're the best doctor I know."

"Hey!" Roger shouted, mocking hurt.

"Sorry!" Sophie shouted over her shoulder and giggled. "I keep forgetting I have two skilled doctors on the team."

"Nice try," Roger muttered. His wife just shook her head in dismay. It was good to see everyone in better spirits, though. Sally would take it.

"I don't like you going alone and unarmed," Donna declared, putting her foot down.

Sophie collected her things. "I know, Donna, but it will be fine. I learned a few things while I was…napping," she said. When she looked up, there was a red fire glowing in her eyes. Everyone gasped and stepped back. The fire disappeared as quickly as it had appeared. "He's so predictable, it's not even funny," Sophie said without missing a beat, and continued to pack up what she needed. "Chess will truly be his greatest downfall. I'm better at it than he realizes," she giggled.

"And what's your greatest downfall?" Ben dared to ask her.

Sophie paused and then giggled again. "The same thing as my strength" She looked down at the ring that was still on her finger. "Emotional baggage," she said with a smile, and went back to packing.

The aliens had definitely taken over Sophie, Ben and everyone else decided. She was different, for sure. They just hoped for the better and not the worse. Sophie tossed her bag onto her back. "I'll be back as soon as I can," she announced.

"Don't you need to know where James is meeting Clarice?" Tina asked, confused.

"Nah," Sophie said, shaking her head. "He won't be there by the time I get there, since they have a head start. I'm going straight for Algos." She started walking towards the hallway toward the exit.

"So, where are YOU going then?" Cecil called out.

Sophie paused and looked over her shoulder as her Cheshire grin grew wider than ever before. "I'm going to pet some lions," she snickered. She was gone before anyone could say anything else to her with her cheetah speed and an overwhelming desire to get even.

Twenty-One

"**F**or the love of..." was all Clarice could groan out when she walked into the abandoned building to find James sitting in a chair waiting patiently, and no Tina or Sophie in sight.

"You look disappointed," James smirked.

"Hey, White Knight," Clarice shouted at him as she walked in his direction. "You're not saving anyone and just causing me more grief than necessary."

She had woken up refreshed, and Clarice was thankful. Something told her she would need the extra energy today, but this was not helping. It was bad enough that Jess forced her hand to keep her Satan spawn safe, but this was just plain dumb and ridiculous that this kid was causing trouble when she didn't need it.

"Where is she?" Clarice asked in exasperation.

"I'm sure she'll be coming soon enough," James said with a shrug.

"I can't go back empty-handed," Clarice warned him.

"I figured," James shrugged.

"I'm not responsible for what he'll do to you," she said flatly.

"Okay," he replied, shrugging again.

"So, you're purposely dying?" Clarice asked, looking at him with doubt. "For no reason other than her? Because you 'love' her?" she finished with a hint of jealousy, but emphasizing her point. He probably already knew, but she just wanted to be clear all the same.

"Yes," James said simply. "I do love her. She's my world. She's my family," he stressed, knowing that Clarice was her family, too.

Clarice screeched. "You know 'love' gets you killed, and half the time it's 'family' doing the job in this family," she said with a frown, adding air quotes to prove her point.

"It doesn't matter," James said, staring her down.

Clarice rolled her eyes and shook her head. "Do I have to kick your ass, or are you just going to come with me? Because I'm really tired and not in the mood," she declared.

James looked at her and gave her his best boyish grin. "Let's go," he offered, standing up and walking to her side.

"Ugh! At least wipe that stupid grin off your face. I've had enough today to last me a lifetime," she muttered as she led the way. James followed without a sound, but his grin remained.

They walked outside, and Clarice held the passenger back door open for him to get in.

"You know," James said, still smiling. "If you hadn't killed Mario, I'd say you're really not that bad, and just really misunderstood," he said, climbing in.

"I'm feeling less sorry for you by the second," Clarice said as she slammed the door.

James waited for her to get into the driver's seat before replying, "It's you I feel sorry for. A girl with daddy issues, that's going to die at the hands of the woman I love. She's pretty pissed. It will be very painful for you," he said casually as he turned to look out the car window.

Clarice glared at him in the rearview mirror, before turning up the radio as loud as it would go so she wouldn't have to listen to him anymore. She should have just put him in the trunk. What was wrong with her? Then Corbin's face appeared before her eyes. "Go away," she growled, and as soon as he had appeared, he was gone. Clarice slammed her foot on the gas pedal and sent them both flying down the abandoned highway in the middle of nowhere.

Jack kept his head bowed down as he stood before the council of death. He noticed it was a smaller council, but he was sure breaking the rules on even their end had consequences. That didn't mean they were in the clear, however.

"They broke the rules," one shrieked on the far left.

"They also saved the realm," the center figure reminded them.

Jack knew better than to speak up, but he couldn't help but

wonder if it was his father saving him after all of these years. Standing seven feet tall and hooded with their faces hidden, Jack wasn't sure if that was to promote fear or carried another purpose.

"They should still be punished!" shrieked the one on the far right.

The center figure remained silent.

"Too many rules have been broken! There must be consequences!" boomed another, shaking the ground beneath Jack. He stumbled to get his footing again before speaking.

"If I could address the council," Jack requested with the utmost caution. "We only broke rules to keep this realm safe. Balance is required for all of us to survive. We had to break some rules in order to stop those that already had. You can't play by the rules when going against a team who doesn't respect them to begin with," he pleaded.

"He's right," the central member concluded.

"You give him special treatment!" shrieked the one on the far left.

"I keep this realm balanced for EVERYONE'S sake, including YOURS," warned the middle figure. "You will respect that or find yourself with the others!"

The ground under Jack rumbled violently, and he quickly dropped to one knee for balance. He knew that speech from heart from growing up. Why had he never known that his own father controlled the realm he stayed in for Sophie?

"You will remain if you choose," the figure boomed, breaking his thoughts. "But this will be your only warning," he shrieked.

"Understood," Jack nodded without looking at any of them.

"We have other business to deal with," the figure stated. "Be gone," it ordered.

Jack found himself unable to move. He tried, but his body failed him. What was going on? He kept his head down cautiously as he fought to stand back up and leave. The other members took no notice and disappeared into a black fog and were gone. Jack sensed he was not alone, but kept his head down since he couldn't tell who had stayed. He took a chance.

"Thank you for keeping her safe," he whispered before raising his head slowly.

There was one figure who hovered over him with its head tilted. Studying him. Remaining silent.

"I'm sure she appreciated getting to know you," Jack tried again.

John hovered over the figure that felt so familiar to him, but he was already quickly forgetting. Then images of a redheaded girl in a library quickly flashed before his eyes. Sophie.

"You raised her well," the figure finally offered.

"I raised her like you did me," Jack said with a weary smile. "I miss you," he said softly. He watched the figure tilt his head in the other direction as if trying to remember where and how they knew each other. It was a tactic his father used often when trying to recall questions he or his mother asked while he was in the middle of an experiment to try to not get busted for not listening.

Maybe that was the price you paid for being a council member? You were forced to forget everyone you knew in order to stay impartial. That would be a better explanation of his father never talking to him rather than simply not caring. Even Jack knew better than that.

292

"I did well, too," the figure said without a hint of emotion as it raised its hand and set Jack free. "Just stop breaking the rules, please," he added before disappearing into his own black mist, leaving Jack alone with his thoughts.

"I'm really not trying to," Jack insisted, before walking away to find his wife and Corbin.

Sophie was fast, but they had a bigger head start than expected. She had tracked James to the abandoned building, but they were already gone. Not that it was hard to track James. He left as many clues as possible, trying to lead Sophie to him. "I'm coming," she whispered to no one.

"You're gonna need some help," she heard a familiar voice behind her.

Sophie spun around immediately.

"Hey, Kid," Mario said, leaning against a pillar with a bright gold hue around him.

"I thought you were dead," Sophie said, trying not to smile. "Again," she added for clarity.

"Right?" Mario laughed. "Well, I can't just seem to leave you behind," he said with a shrug.

"Well, I'm glad to see you all the same," she said with her Cheshire grin. "Although, it doesn't feel like I'm sleeping," she said in realization.

"Different planes, different rules," he said with a shrug.

"Does that mean I don't get to talk to you as much?" Sophie asked in sadness.

"You can always talk to me, Kid," Mario said with a smile. "You just might have to listen a little harder to hear my response," he added with a wink.

"You're always so difficult," Sophie said, rolling her eyes.

"You wouldn't have it any other way," Mario smirked.

"True," she shrugged. Then an uncomfortable silence settled between them.

"Are you sure?" was all he asked.

"Yes," she replied, knowing the reference.

"You're a little too weak to be going right now," Mario warned.

"I don't have a choice," Sophie replied. "They have James."

"I know," he whispered. "I'm more worried about you though."

"You always are," Sophie retorted and dramatically sighed. She shuffled her feet like when she was a teenager and was nervous to ask him a question.

"Out with it," Mario laughed, knowing the sign well.

"Do I get to hug you one more time?" Sophie asked, not looking him in the eye.

Mario looked at the sky before nodding. "Oh, I don't think this one time will hurt anyone," he said with a smile and opened up his arms.

Sophie ran and jumped into them eagerly. She gripped him and nearly squeezed the life out of him. If he had still been alive, that is. Mario took her in and held her firmly. She felt the warmth spread over her body, but then again, that was always Mario for her.

He hummed in her ear as he held her, not quite ready to let go, but knowing he could only give her so much of his energy without consequences. Mario regretfully put her back down and took a step back. It exhausted him to share his power, but she didn't need to know that.

"You'd better get going," he warned her in his fatherly voice.

"Will I see you again?" Sophie asked him eagerly.

"Oh, I'll always be around," he said with a smirk. "Now, go. Before it's too late," he ordered.

Sophie leaned in and gave him one last kiss on the cheek. "Thanks," she whispered. "For everything." Then she took off running to save the man she loved, who she could still possibly save.

Mario watched her run off with her ponytail flapping from side to side as she did. Just like when she was growing up. Then he closed his eyes and slid down the pillar that had been holding him up since he let go of his goddaughter. He closed his eyes in pain, and the surrounding hue faded. He would never regret the decision he had just made. Even if it was possibly his last.

"Where is she?" growled Algos from the shadows.

"Right here," Clarice yelled as she entered the lab. "I brought a gift," she added as she shoved James towards Eddie.

Eddie stared at James and tried to hide his shock. James ignored Eddie all together.

"James Moore?" they heard Algos ask, in obvious confusion.

"Yeah, well," James replied, "I thought I would check out your digs and see what all the fuss was about."

Clarice tried hard to hide her smile. It's a shame the kid was going to die. She might learn to like him after all.

"White Knight, here, thought he'd help motivate Sophie to come to us," she said dryly.

"How generous of you," they heard Algos sneer from the shadows.

"What? Too good to show your actual face?" James asked with a shrug.

Eddie could see why Sophie liked him, but he was going to be dead before she ever arrived if he didn't stop smarting off. Even Eddie knew it, and there'd be nothing he could do about it. Then again, it would also mean he could have Sophie for himself. Though he doubted she would ever forgive him if he didn't stop the idiot from dying before she got there.

"He's at least as useful as he is mouthy," Eddie cut in flatly. "She will definitely come for him," he added as he glared at James, hoping to take it as the warning to shut the hell up that it was.

"Would you like a tour?" Algos asked a little too sweetly.

"Might as well while I'm here," James shrugged. He knew he would not see much. He just hoped that if he could keep them distracted long enough, it might buy Sophie enough time to get to him before he actually died. That would definitely be ideal.

"I mean, if it's going to be the last thing he's going to see," Clarice shrugged. "Come on, Troll," she said over her shoulder as she passed him. She hoped her father would agree, but Clarice didn't have that kind of luck.

"I've got this," Algos replied sharply. "Mr. Moore, follow me," he said over his shoulder then they all heard the cane hit the ground as he moved further away.

"Like just into the shadows?" James asked, looking around. "How am I supposed to follow if I can't see him?"

"Your eyes will adjust," Clarice offered with a shrug.

James looked at her and laughed sarcastically. "Okay, then," he said as he headed into the darkness and followed the sound of the cane hitting the cement floor.

"Well, he's not going to make it," Eddie said with a frown.

"Oh, I wouldn't count him out just yet," Clarice said, folding her arms and leaning against Eddie's desk.

"What is wrong with you?" Eddie asked, shaking his head.

"We don't have enough time," she laughed before heading off to follow James and see if she couldn't save him from himself after all. Clarice turned the corner and watched James be led into her father's office.

"Looking for something?" Algos said on the other side, making her jump.

"Just looking to see where you're taking my bait," she replied in annoyance, hoping her concern wasn't giving her away.

"That's none of your concern," he warned her. "I want her alive," he reminded her.

"Yeah, yeah," Clarice said with a frown. She would not be able to keep James safe after all. Well, she wasn't obligated to, so no harm, no foul, right?

"Go," Algos ordered her, and watched her sigh dramatically before turning around and heading back to the lab. She was changing. And not for his benefit. It was time to put another plan into place. It wasn't his favorite, but he knew it would do. He turned to his office door, opened it, and slinked inside like the monster he truly was.

"I think you need to come," Giselle said, wheezing as she rushed up to Jess and Jack.

"What's wrong?" Jess asked in trepidation.

"Corbin," Giselle breathed out.

Jess looked at Jack in a panic, and they both raced after Giselle. In the middle of the realm laid Corbin's unconscious body.

"What happened?" demanded Jack.

"I don't know," Giselle answered honestly. "I just found him here, alone."

Jack bent down and picked up his friend into his arms.

"Corbin!" he shouted, but Corbin was trapped in darkness, unable to hear Jack's call.

Jack closed his eyes. His life force was low, but still there. He looked at Jess before he picked up his friend and carried him away.

"Where's he going?" Giselle asked panicked.

"To the council," Jess answered, watching her husband walk to his doom.

"What do you want?" the figure on the far left shrieked their demand.

Jack went down to one knee and balanced his friend close to him. "Something's wrong," he said, looking at his friend. "We need your help."

"This is not our concern!" shrieked the figure on the far right.

"Just because Algos can't get in now, doesn't mean he won't continue to try," Jack warned with anger in his voice.

"This is not our concern," he heard his father bellow.

"You want balance?" Jack said, looking up with anger burning in his eyes. "He IS your balance," he growled.

"Watch yourself," his father warned.

"He had more power than he knew what to do with. That's not balance. That's trouble," screamed another.

"He's trapped," said an unfamiliar voice. Everyone turned to see Bill standing behind Jack. "Someone needs to take his place," he said, staring at Corbin.

"This is not your concern!" yelled another cloaked figure.

"Someone disagrees," Bill said with a wink.

"They will know nothing but darkness and pain," John warned.

"I'm well aware," Bill declared as he walked towards Jack and Corbin. "He needs to be saved," he said with determination.

"I'll go," Jack said, grabbing onto Bill's outstretched hand.

"That's not an option, my son," Bill said with a wink and assuring smile. He pushed through Jack's hold, placed his hand on Corbin's forehead, and closed his eyes. A golden hue glowed brightly and throbbed with life. When it faded, Bill was gone, and Corbin sat up and opened his eyes.

"Go," John ordered, and the council quickly disappeared into a dark fog before Jack or Corbin could say another word.

Twenty-Two

"I can't believe you wouldn't tell me," Ben pouted. "I have every right to know."

Tina took his hands into hers as they rode in the back seat of the car that Daryl and Cecil were driving. "Honestly," she began, "All I could think about was if Sophie would not wake up, it wouldn't matter either way. And there was no reason to make you hurt any more than you already were. I couldn't do that to you," Tina whispered as she squeezed his hands.

"I know where your heart was," Ben said. "But it doesn't make it right."

"I know," she replied. "At least I have hope that there will be enough time for you to forgive me," Tina said, looking out the window of the car.

Guilt filled Ben's heart as he studied his wife's distraught face. She only did it to save and spare him. He couldn't hate her for that. Ben reached out and took her chin in his hand. "Done," he whispered with a smile. She gave him a weary smile before he pulled her into his arms. "Ready for this?" he asked her softly.

"Blowing up something?" she giggled. "Oh, absolutely!"

Ben laughed and shook his head as they raced to destroy Jack's creation before Algos got his hands on it. Tina wasn't worried. She already knew what she needed to do. No piece of data or structure would remain to give the possibility of rebuilding when she was done.

"How is Tina?" Jess asked Jack as he came to join his wife back on the sofa in front of the fire.

"Heading back from destroying the satellite," Jack informed her.

"Corbin?" she inquired.

"Resting," Jack replied. "There's nothing more we can do, but wait and see how this plays out."

Jess turned to look at her husband lovingly. "Oh, I can think of one more thing," she said with a girlish grin.

Jack stared into his beautiful wife's eyes, knowing what she wanted him to do, and why it needed to be him. However, Jack wasn't sure he could. He wasn't even sure the girl that remained was his little girl. Jack was also sure that it would give his lovely wife some peace of mind to at least try. So, Jack got up and went to do what she asked of him. He looked over his shoulder and watched Jess nod back at him in encouragement. God, did he pray she was right. Then he left her for what he hoped wouldn't be the last time.

Sophie squinted at the sky. The sun was bright and filled her body with a great dose of vitamin D. Just what the doctor ordered. She knew they doubted her, but they just didn't understand. Yes, the blood of a psychopath flowed through her veins, but it wasn't the only one that did.

She finally understood that. Everything that had happened was to bring her to this very moment. Every loved one that was sacrificed by Algos' hands would not be for nothing. Before she existed and after she was born.

The torture her mother endured against her will. The alterations to make her the ultimate killer that was passed onto her daughter, only to be taken too soon shortly after Sophie came to be. Sophie had lost a lot in a short amount of time. Her parents. Eddie. Mario. Giselle. Bill. And so many people that Algos robbed her of ever meeting.

But she had also gained more than anyone she knew. A brother and a sister, and a man that loved her unconditionally. Psychopathic grandfather and the emotional baggage that came with him and all. Mario's old biker gang remained to extend her family further. Sally and Roger were parental figures she could count on without even being blood.

And there was a world that people didn't even know existed. A realm that allowed her to still keep her loved ones close, no matter how much longer she would be allowed access to it without being dead herself. It had provided the closure that she needed to keep going. The strength to know that she would never truly be alone. No matter what happened. And that was the greatest fuel to help her fire to keep burning brighter than ever before.

Sophie wouldn't be able to save everyone. Even she understood that, now. However, it didn't mean she wouldn't stop trying. Her darkness allowed her to do what needed to be done, even if it wasn't what she desired and it meant she couldn't save everyone. But it would be love that had absolutely no limits, and that's what gave her the greatest balance of all. She would never again forget who she truly was. That's why Reine would never come to be.

Sophie would set James free. Even if she couldn't join him. Algos would be finished, once and for all, if it was the last thing she did as a living soul. Clarice would pay the price of taking Mario from her, and not making moral decisions about the life she was given. Eddie would breathe freedom again. The final checkmate would be hers. No matter the personal cost. This was how it had to be. So, Tina and Ben could have the life they deserved and raise the child that fate deemed to exist despite the misery that brought them to this point. Sophie hoped it was a girl just to give them a run for their money.

"Peanut," she heard her father whisper in her ear. Sophie smiled her Cheshire smile and sat cross-legged in the middle of the path she had been traveling on. She took a deep breath and closed her eyes.

When she opened them again, she found the familiar wooden door. "I'm coming," Sophie said eagerly as she reached out and opened the door. She found her father leaning against his desk, and giving her a weary smile.

"Don't be so excited to see me," Sophie snorted.

"I just want to make sure it's my daughter looking back," Jack said cautiously.

Sophie looked at him curiously. "Of course, it's me," she said with a giggle. "Are you, you?"

Jack's smile grew a little wider at her response.

"I didn't know inner peace would cause so much doubt for so many people," she replied, a little mystified.

"Inner peace, huh?" he asked suspiciously. "Is that we're calling it?"

"It's a long story," Sophie sighed. "But yeah," she added with a shrug. "I mean, don't get me wrong. It kinda sucks knowing so much darkness is in you, but it's good to know there's enough light to keep you balanced if you let it."

Jack studied the girl before him. "Wise observation," he said with a hint of pride.

"Well, I was taught well," Sophie said with her Cheshire smile. "Just a little too stubborn to let it sink in sooner."

Jack let a chuckle escape his lips. "That does sound about right," he said with a smile.

"Is this goodbye?" she asked suddenly.

"Oh, Peanut," Jack whispered. "I don't know," he answered honestly. "But we'll always be with you," he added quickly.

"Bummer," Sophie said with a sigh. "Yeah. That's the biggest lesson I've learned from all of this. I couldn't get rid of you even if I tried," she teased, smiling at her father.

Jack's heart melted, and he held out his hand for his daughter to take. Sophie raced to him and took his hand and stepped lightly on his feet. Jack led as he hummed their song in her ear. "We couldn't be more proud. You know that. Right?" Jack murmured against the top of her head.

"Back at ya," Sophie said, trying to fight back the tears.

"Are you sure you want to do this?" Jack asked unable to disguise the doubt in his voice. Sophie closed her eyes and let a tear escape down her cheek.

"I can do this," she said with determination.

"That wasn't what I asked," Jack replied.

"They're family," Sophie murmured. "They need to be saved. And I'm the one designed to do just that."

"Well, I'm glad to see you're in such good hands even without us," Jack chuckled against the top of her head.

"Please," Sophie giggled against his chest. "You're the reason I'm as obnoxious as I am!" she laughed.

"I mean," Jack said with a shrug, and they both laughed. "You were my greatest creation," he whispered.

"Don't let mom hear you," Sophie warned. "She might think you're taking all the credit," she giggled.

Jack sighed at the sound that always warmed his heart the greatest. "It will not be easy," he warned her.

"It would kinda be disappointing if it was," she giggled against his chest.

"The result might not be what you desire," Jack tried again.

306

"I know," Sophie said, lifting her head to look into her father's eyes. "But I know it won't be his either," she said as an ice blue flame burst in her right eye, and a red flame burst in her left.

Jack sucked in a quick breath in reaction. Sophie wasn't kidding. She had gained power even beyond Corbin's and Rebecca's abilities. Finally, she was complete. Fire and ice. The key and the protector.

"Apparently," Jack said, quite impressed as he held onto the girl they forced him to say goodbye to so long ago.

"I have to get going," Sophie said softly as the flames died down as quickly as they appeared.

Jack sighed dramatically. "I know," he said reluctantly. "Be careful," he warned.

Sophie laughed and shook her head. "I'm not the one you have to worry about," she assured him.

Jack looked his daughter up and down and realized she was right. "Go give them hell, Peanut," he said with his own Cheshire smile.

Sophie returned the same smile, and closed her eyes. The room flooded with light, and when it faded, Sophie was gone.

"I love you," he whispered into the empty space around him.

Sophie opened her eyes and took in a deep breath before releasing it. She brushed the wetness that remained on her cheeks, threw her bag on her back, and set off to save her loved ones. It was time for this white queen to take over the black king and call checkmate once and for all.

"You're a sight for sore eyes," Jess said as Corbin came and slumped onto the couch next to her.

"You're telling me," Corbin replied. He was still exhausted by whatever happened. "Where's Jack?"

Jess smiled her tale tell smile. "Giving his daughter a much needed pep talk," she replied. She knew Sophie had changed, and for the better. A mother always knows. She just hoped it would be enough.

"You guys look like a bunch of sulking teenagers," Jack said as he came in to join them.

"You hate missing the action just as much as we do, so shush," Jess replied in a fake pout.

"You're looking better," Jack said to Corbin. "What happened?"

"They summoned me to save Rebecca," Corbin said with a frown.

"And?" Jess said, suddenly looking at him with great interest.

"And nothing," Corbin said with a shrug. "One of them yelled at me and demanded I save her. I tried to do the same thing that I did with Jess, and the next thing I knew, I was looking into Jack's bright blue eyes," he said with a frown. "Next time, could you at least send a woman?

Jack laughed. "A woman couldn't carry you as far as I did. Minus my wife," he added quickly after meeting her icy glare. "I will keep that in mind next time," Jack said, assuring his friend.

"So, Rebeca?" Jess asked again.

"Gone," Corbin said with a frown. "I don't feel her anymore, at least," he clarified.

"Sophie?" she asked her husband.

"More prepared than I was expecting," Jack replied honestly. "Do you think Clarice will keep her word?" he asked with doubt. Jess went back to looking at the fire and gave no response. "Either way," Jack continued. "There's nothing more we can do right now. We're going to just have to sit and wait."

All three spirits crossed their arms in front of them and waited. There was nothing more they could do for Sophie.

They all secretly hoped it had been enough. Jess reached down and squeezed her husband's thigh.

"Let the final round begin," she sighed heavily as they stared into the fire and waited to see what moves Sophie had up her sleeves to help her survive what was coming next.

Twenty-Three

Sophie laid on her belly on the top of the hill and looked down into the trees and valley below. East of Provo, Utah, was where her enemy hid out of site in the middle of the Rocky Mountains. Sophie quickly counted ten men, some as young as herself, dressed in black ops clothing and holding various sizes of guns and knives on them. She looked to her left and saw the side of the mountain was a little too smooth with a prominent security camera to track who came and went through the unseen door on the side.

Sophie looked back at the guards that kept watch outside. Normally, killing would be a last resort, but today that would not be the case. They had chosen their fate, no matter how easily they had been deceived. There would be nothing she could do for them. Her objective was to save Eddie and James. At all costs.

She belly crawled back down the hill and hid the backpack that safely kept the essentials. James would still need supplies and money to get back, with or without her. So, she took it off her back and tossed it in the tree she stood next to. It was time to end this game.

"What the hell?" the redhead said in confusion and shock. Everyone looked up at the giant screens to see what she saw. Sophie, walking through the forest, alone and unarmed.

Clarice was standing next to Eddie and turned her head to study the girl that walked towards their entrance with no fear and dangerous black eyes that were pure blackness and focused before her.

"I think it's about to get interesting," Clarice murmured. Only Eddie heard her, but he was too busy trying to get his heart that was currently lodged in his throat back where it belonged.

Sophie walked slowly through the woods. She heard the chatter going wild on the walkie-talkies that the soldiers wore around her.

"I want her alive!" she heard Algos remind them. Her lips curled up at the corners as she continued to make her way to the entrance.

There was just no way of telling who exactly was the hunter and who was the prey, and that's the way Sophie liked it. There would be no surrender, and no escape in this ultimate chess game. It would be winner take all, including life. She heard the soldiers form a semi-circle behind her. She was correct the first time. Ten.

Sophie looked directly into the camera and held up her hands in surrender.

"It's a trap," Clarice said under her breath, although she wasn't sure which team she was currently rooting for.

"Let her in," she heard her father demand. Clarice always knew Sophie would be his doom. She wasn't so sure he saw it as well as she did, but that was not her concern at the moment.

The door that had blended into the side of the mountain wall suddenly raised slowly before her. Sophie looked in front of her and was greeted by fifteen more soldiers on the other side. She took in her last deep breath of fresh air before stepping inside.

The crew before her stepped back a few steps to let her in, while the crew behind her followed. Sophie stood still, assessing her surroundings and letting her eyes adjust to the darkness that consumed the inside of the mountain. Clearly a bunker of some sort. Most likely set up like a freaking maze for Algos' pleasure of people forever getting lost. Well, she would just have to work her way through it, and hope that she didn't get too tired before she got to the end.

"Hello, boys," Sophie said slyly. Then she heard a female cough in the far back. "My apologizes," she said with a sweet smile. "And ladies."

She felt someone stab the barrel of a gun into her back. "Move!" they ordered.

"Please and thank you would be nice," she said flatly. "Man. Does no one have manners anymore?" Sophie asked, rolling her eyes dramatically.

"Move!" he shouted at her again and pushed the barrel into her back even harder.

"Yeah," Sophie said slowly. "I'm going to need you to stop doing that."

"And what are you going to do about it?" he sneered back behind her.

Sophie smiled her Cheshire grin before spinning around to grab the barrel, flip it, and quickly shoving the barrel into his own chest. The look of shock was laughable.

"Now," she continued. "I'm willing to go with you peacefully, but you're going to have to be a lot less rude about it," Sophie said in a teacher's voice.

She heard the 9mm safety go off and felt it shoved into her neck. "Move," another boy hissed in a French accent. The man before her grabbed the gun that was now pointed at his chest with a triumphant look, and shoved it into Sophie's own chest.

"Mauvais choix," Sophie said sweetly before knocking the gun and the man who held onto it away from her chest, spinning to grab the gun at her neck, tossing it in the air, and grabbing the magazine in the other hand as she spun back the other direction and jammed into his neck and twisted. Blood squirted everywhere, but there was no time to worry about it.

Sophie quickly started spinning, ducking, and dodging bullets and swings as she took out five more soldiers. She ducked and grabbed the grenade off of the girl's belt and ran, falling to her knees and sliding across the floor. She took out the pin while she turned and threw it in their direction before popping back onto her feet and taking cover around the corner.

The explosion shook the ground and walls of the lab as everyone held on to the closest thing to them in order to keep their footing. "She's going to kill us all," Clarice growled, still holding onto Eddie's desk.

"I think that's the point," Eddie said flatly as every screen went dark.

Clarice looked at him and felt sorry for him. He was stuck in the middle just as much as she was. Only his wasn't by choice. She had done that. She had taken his freedom away at her father's orders. A strange feeling filled Clarice's heart. She didn't like it. She didn't like it at all.

Sophie took off running and headed to the next door, and kicked it down. The metal door went flying across the room and shocked the six soldiers, still trying to get their footing on the other side. Sophie took a deep breath in and took stance as she waved for them to attack.

The largest of the bunch jumped up first and charged her head on. He bowed and wrapped his arms around her, shoving her back against the wall behind her. Her body slammed forcefully against it and she moaned on contact before raising her knee to kick him in the groin and without hesitation kicked his doubled-over body into the wall on the other side of the room.

Another charged, but she was faster and ran up the side of the wall next to her before jumping up and slamming her fist into his jaw, taking him down to the ground. Every contact that was made seemed to shake the walls and floor around them as she continued to take them out one by one. When she got to the last, the younger boy crouched into the corner and shivered with fear.

Sophie stood up and studied him carefully. "Leave," she finally ordered. "Don't let me see you here again," she warned. The kid nodded eagerly and took no time waiting for her to second guess her decision. He ran past her and down the hall as fast as his legs would carry him. Good. There may be another exit.

Sophie heard the footsteps of more coming to slow her down, so she took her time and conserved her energy. She didn't know how many there actually were, and she would need to pace herself. That meant she took some punches in the process, but she needed to make sure she got to Eddie and James. Hopefully, sooner than later.

One by one, Sophie added a body to the pile left behind her. She was up to thirty-five currently. Counting made her smile and think of the first time she fought next to James. She had won, obviously. But he was cute trying to keep up with her.

Sophie found the lab and gasped when Eddie was standing next to Clarice before her eyes. He was alive.

"Hey, Eddie," she whispered.

"Hey, Soph," he whispered back. "Long time, no see."

"Yeah, sorry about that," she said, giving him a weary smile.

"Well, you're here now," he said, smiling back at her.

"I am," she said, giving him her Cheshire smile. God, he had missed that.

They listened as, what Sophie counted to be, one-hundred and seventy-two soldiers surround them.

"Seriously?" Sophie whined.

Even Clarice was in shock. "Apparently, the old man was more prepared than we thought," she said, looking around the room with Sophie.

Sophie's head snapped back in her direction. Clarice stepped back and ran into the desk behind her at the sight of Sophie's flaming one lava red eye and one icy blue. "I will deal with you in a second," Sophie warned and took stance.

"Great," Clarice muttered. She waited for the first person to charge Sophie before turning to Eddie and growling, "Run."

Eddie looked at her, confused, but the look in her eye made him take a few steps back and look for the best place to be out of the way. Eddie noticed even Clarice continued to move back and out of the way as bodies started flying around the room.

He didn't know why she didn't attack Sophie. Maybe she was just waiting for her to be worn down. However, the look in her eyes gave her away. Clarice wasn't planning on fighting Sophie. He just didn't know why.

Sophie watched a little guy jump and spin back and forth while she dodged every kick he threw out. Then he perfectly executed a flying spin-kick, catching Sophie in the gut that sent her flying to the other side of the room. The person behind her picked her up by her hair and started dragging her in the other direction while her original attacker continued to jump and spin kick Sophie in the face and stomach.

Sophie pulled herself forward, but the one that had her hair yanked her right back. When the other attacker jumped to kick her in the gut again, Sophie reached out and grabbed him by the foot and twisted it with all her might. They both heard his leg shatter to pieces before he ever hit the ground.

Sophie reached back behind her and grabbed the back of the neck of the person yanking her by her ponytail, and flipped him over her head. She slammed him so hard onto the ground that not only did the floor shake, but it broke underneath him. His spine shattering into several pieces, making it impossible for him to get back up.

Someone kicked her in the back of the knee, forcing her to fall onto her knees and threw their arm around her neck. Sophie grunted when she hit the floor. She pushed up and began slamming them both against the walls and pillars around them. He groaned with every impact. Sophie jammed her elbow into his rib cage, and he grabbed her by the neck and flipped her away from him. She rolled and immediately got to her feet.

She caught her breath as she waited for him to charge her again. He started swinging. Sophie blocked some and took hits to get better shots in herself. She used her elbows to jab him and clocked him in the jaw a few times, before she eventually just wrapped her arm around him and squeezed the life out of him. He fell to the floor and never got back up again.

A woman grabbed a pair of scissors off one desk and began swinging at her. Sophie jumped back and missed all but one of her jabs. Her arm was sliced as Sophie spun and quickly grabbed the pen off the desk next to her and jabbed it in her neck and twisted as hard as she could.

Blood ran down her arm, and she wiped the blood coming from her nose as she swayed dangerously back and forth, waiting for the next attacker. She was thankful that Algos had always taught them to attack one at a time. To wear her down in hopes of bringing her back alive. Although she was stronger and fought smarter now, it didn't mean her stamina was without limits. She looked around the room to reassess the situation.

Sophie knew her strengths, and speed was one of them. But it only came in spurts and cost her more to use it. She looked around wildly to calculate her best chances and jumped onto the desk next to her as another came for her. She began kicking and throwing the things she could grab to take out as many as she could. Sophie threw a pen like a dagger into one's eye, forcing them to fall back and hit the wall behind them. The pen went through the eye into the brain with a single toss.

Sophie grabbed a pair of scissors and threw them into another one's chest, straight through the heart. She grabbed the flatscreen like it was a sheet of paper and chucked it over the head of her current attacker, taking him to his knees and knocking him out cold. But Sophie was running out of things to throw.

When a giant started plowing her way, she grabbed the keyboard as a last weapon and began beating it over his head as he grabbed her and pushed her into the pillar behind her. It cracked and dislodged from the ceiling, crashing into Eddie's direction.

Clarice saw the projection and ran towards him, sliding on her hip, grabbing him by the shirt, and dragging him to safety with her. Sophie saw her save him out of the corner of her eye, but she was too busy to care at the moment. The giant was standing up straight and preparing to charge her again.

It looked like Sophie would need Reine after all. She closed her eyes and started screaming as she charged the giant. Sophie jumped into the air and kicked him in the ribs with her heel, forcing him to fall back a few steps. She started rotating between punching him in the gut and clocking him in the jaw. He staggered with every hit until she finally ran up the side of the wall, lunged, slid her legs around his neck and reached down, snapping his neck. She fell forward with him and jumped off just before he hit the ground.

Sophie spit out the blood building in her mouth as she swayed once more like the dangerous animal she truly was. Clarice looked from Sophie, to Eddie, and back to Sophie. "I think it's time to go," she murmured. She grabbed Eddie by his shirt, picked him up off the ground in a single tug, and dragged him behind her as she raced through the doorway and toward her father's office.

"Find James!" she barked as she continued to drag him behind her.

"What are you going to do?" Eddie yelled back in alarm, trying to keep up.

Clarice stopped, forcing Eddie to crash into her. She looked behind her.

"C.L.A.R.I.C.E!" they both heard Sophie shriek over the noise of the war taking place in the lab.

Clarice sighed heavily. "Apparently, keep her motivated," she said flatly, with a frown.

"You're not going to kill her, are you?" Eddie asked her in shock. He knew people. He knew Clarice better than she knew herself. Something had definitely changed. Whether she knew it or not, Clarice had switched to Team Sophie.

"Find James before I change my mind," she growled, staring him down.

"Whatever you say, Boss," he said, giving her his goofy smile. He winked and headed off to find James.

"Troll!" she shouted after him, but they both knew it was an empty threat. Clarice didn't know what was wrong with her. All she knew was that Sophie wasn't the little girl she had tried to drown in the pool all those years ago. She was pissed, and she wanted Clarice's head regardless of her dead mother's wishes. She sighed dramatically before running back in the direction she had just come. Apparently, today was the day she was going to die after all.

Sophie had taken out a huge chunk of her father's unknown army, but even Clarice could see she was getting dangerously tired. While she took on each attacker, Clarice pulled out the two sticks and pulled them apart, exposing a thin wire. She crept into the shadows her father used often to stay out of Sophie's sight as much as possible and took out those that stood too close to the shadows.

She watched with pride as Sophie slid on her knees, grabbing a gun from one, only to pop back up and take out as many as she could right in the forehead until her magazine ran out. Then she tossed the gun at someone's head, knocking them out on impact as she ran to tackle the next.

When only two remained, even Clarice knew her presence needed to be removed for her own safety. While Sophie was distracted by taking out the last two soldiers stupid enough to still be standing in her presence, Clarice backed away as quietly as possible before spinning and breaking into a full run to put as much space between her niece and herself as possible.

The office was empty. Eddie looked around it wildly, looking for clues. There's no way the old man would hide him in plain sight, and even Eddie didn't know all the secrets this hell was holding. He tore up Algos' desk when he noticed the bookshelves.

He raced over and started yanking the books off the shelves until he grabbed the right one and it spun the bookcase around to face a secret passageway. "This isn't creepy," Eddie muttered to himself. He took the lighter out of his pocket that he always had on him, and started making his way down the pitch black passage way.

Eventually, he started to see the light at the end of the tunnel. Literally. He slowed his pace down, since he had no weapon and no clue what lay ahead. When he found himself on the other side of the mountain with no one lurking and waiting for him, he froze.

"Oh, come on!" he yelled to the sky. He picked up a rock and chucked it out of anger before turning around and heading back in the way he came. Muttering his annoyance at not knowing how close freedom truly was, and that he was having to go back to save the boy that Sophie chose over him.

Sophie looked around, waiting for another attack, but there was no one left standing to do so. She growled out her anger as she breathed heavily, jerking her head around for her true target. Clarice.

A glimmer caught her eye, and she looked down to find her ring. Although covered in a lot of blood, it still shined with love for her. Sophie's breathing slowed down as she remembered who she really was, and her eyes went back to normal. "James," she whispered as she looked around the room for the exit, and took off running to save the man who had saved her more times than she could count.

She collided with Eddie in the hallway, and they both nearly fell to the ground. Sophie reached out and grabbed him to help hold them both up. "Eddie," she whispered her relief.

"I can't find him," he said in frustration. Sophie knew exactly who he was referring to.

Sophie thought of the chess board and the pieces that came with it. She looked at Eddie. "Where does he keep his knight?" she asked him eagerly.

"What?" Eddie asked, confused.

"He's an avid chess player like you," she clarified. "Where does he keep his knight?" she asked again.

Eddie thought long and hard. "I don't know," he confessed.

"Yes, you do," Sophie urged him. "You've seen it. I know you have," she said, nodding encouragement to him.

Eddie closed his eyes and tried to think. When he opened them back up, they were filled with wild excitement. "The basement," he said eagerly as he grabbed her hand and dragged her to where she needed to be.

Twenty-Four

E ddie led Sophie further and further into the ground. "How did you get down here?" she asked nervously. Eddie snickered. "Clarice tried to poison me. I was brought down here for the doctor to bring me back," he said. When he saw Sophie's eyes dilate again with anger, he quickly added, "That was before she switched to Team Sophie."

"She's never been Team Sophie," she growled, remembering their first interaction when Clarice tried to drown her in the pool when she was five.

"Hey," Eddie said, stopping her. "I hated her too for a long time," he told her honestly. "But something's changed. I wouldn't tell you if I didn't think it mattered," he added firmly.

Sophie looked at him and her eyes went back to normal. "I'm sorry you were stuck here for so long. I didn't know," she said in a guilty confession.

"I know," he said, putting his hand on her shoulder. They were standing outside of the door where they needed to be. This might be his last chance.

Eddie carefully brushed away the strands of hair that had fallen out of her ponytail that were covering her face. Before he lost the nerve, he took her face in his hands and pulled her in, crushing his lips onto hers and claiming it for his own. Sophie stiffened in shock, but quickly gave into the passion he was offering her. He needed this, and she would not deny him after all of these years.

He quickly wrapped one hand around the back of her neck, the other around the small of her back, and pulled her in as close as possible. She felt him grow hard against her, and she let him take what he needed.

Eddie finally pulled away to let them both catch their breath. "It's still him, isn't it?" he asked in between breaths. He looked at her, pleading for her to choose him, but she just couldn't.

"Yes," Sophie said softly while trying to catch her own breath.

The look of disappointment was heartbreaking, but Sophie couldn't lie. Not about this. Eddie stared at the ground, deep in thought, then dared to take one last look at her.

"Then go get him," he said with the smile that always made her giggle as a child. "I'll take care of this," Eddie said, nodding to the door.

"Eddie, no," Sophie said.

However, Eddie was as stubborn as her, and shoved Sophie as hard as he could in the opposite direction before sliding through the door and busting the control lock on the other side.

Sophie scrambled to her feet and ran to the door. "Eddie," she warned. "Open the door!"

He held up the remains of the keypad that he had in his hands. "You can come back and get me later," he lied. They both heard the gas filling the room.

"Eddie!" Sophie yelled as she pounded on the door, but it was reinforced steel, and not going to open any time soon.

Eddie looked around and grabbed the closest beaker labeled "flammable" and pulled out his lighter. "Soph, I'm gonna need you to go save James now," he warned, opening the lighter and watching the flame ignite. "This will not take long."

"Damn it!" Sophie screamed as she took one last look with her eyes full of tears that were escaping and running down her cheeks.

"I love you," he whispered, taking in one last look as he turned to toss the beaker towards the middle of the room, along with his lit zippo lighter.

Sophie screamed out her frustration and pain before pushing off the door and speeding away as fast as possible. The explosion went off and sent her flying.

Even shackled in chains, James' body swung back and forth wildly in the air from the pole Algos had chained him to that was embedded in the ceiling.

Algos stumbled himself from the explosion, but quickly caught his footing and regained balance with his cane. James heard the growl escape from deep in his throat. Sophie was not pleasing him, and James was thankful even if he was the bait.

"Apparently, my granddaughter is working on destroying my home," he snarled.

"That's my girl," James said with pride, trying to ignore the pain that the swinging was causing in his wrists as the shackles dug deeper into his skin.

"I love how you think you're going to survive this," Algos sneered. "Or that you think she will not be mine when this is done," he added.

"My bet is on her," James smirked as his body finally slowed down to a standstill.

It wasn't long before the metal door that led to the room they were in went flying across the room. Algos intuitively side-stepped in the nick of time. When he looked back, he saw the hurt and anger radiating from Sophie, with tear-stained cheeks and blood dripping from her nose and various cuts on her body.

"Well, you've looked better," Algos laughed at the sight of her. Her misery excited him like nothing he had ever felt before. "I take it Eddie didn't make it after all," he said with a hint of disappointment.

"Don't say his name," Sophie hissed as she stepped into the room. She didn't look at James. She needed all the focus she had left for this final battle.

Algos let her walk into the middle of the room without moving. "You're looking tired, Sophie," he snickered. "Ready to just give up and join me? It's inevitable. You cannot possibly win," he smirked.

Sophie tilted her head back and forth, popping her neck loudly, before stepping into stance and waving him on. She was done talking. She was done with him taking lives. She was done. Period.

"Let the games begin," she said with her Cheshire smile as her eyes dilated larger than James had ever seen. One eye burst into a blood red flame while the other burst into an icy blue flame.

Algos' excitement grew. "You are a treasure," he whistled in great fascination and pride. "I trained your mother," Algos reminded her as he took stance and held out his cane as if preparing for a fencing match.

The two circled each other once again as if an animal stalking their prey. Algos giggled like an obnoxious hyena as his excitement grew. She was better than he could ever have imagined. Algos charged her with his cane in front, and she waited until the last second, grabbed it, spun, and cracked it against the small of his back as hard as she could. It shattered into several pieces. He stumbled forward until he caught his footing and turned around.

"Well, that wasn't very nice," he said with slight irritation.

"Just evening the playfield," Sophie said with a shrug.

"Are you, now?" he sneered as they circled each other again.

Sophie stopped and stood up straight as she watched him from over her shoulder. "Wrong move," she heard him whisper with glee. He charged her at once. She jumped into the air and did a spiral kick to hit him in the face, but he grabbed her foot and sent her whole body spiraling into the air. She landed on her hands and toes face down, before jumping up just in time to block some of his swings.

Sophie was tired, Algos could tell. This would be too easy for him, and that disappointed him terribly. Sophie ducked to miss a swing and spun to shove her fist into the small of his back as hard as she could. He stumbled forward again. She was becoming predictable.

At least, that is what she wanted him to think. She was learning. Quickly. That it was actually him who had a certain set of moves. She was just getting to know them.

Algos came at her with several jabs and kicks before spinning to get behind her and throw an arm around her neck as he grabbed her hair and yanked her head back. He ran towards a pillar with her head first.

Sophie ran with him to collect speed before racing up the pillar and flipping over his head and carrying him with her to have him land on his back while she fell on top of him and jammed her elbow into his rib cage and shattered four ribs. He groaned in pain as she rolled off him to get to her feet. Algos was gasping for air, and Sophie was breathing just as heavily.

"Enough play," he said furiously as he got to his feet. She was swaying back and forth like the dangerous animal she was, waiting for his next attack. James held his breath, fighting the urge to call to her and distract her. He had never seen her like this. As scary as it was, he knew she was doing it to save them both. He was going to have to remember never to get on her bad side.

Algos charged Sophie like a bull, and he drove his fist into her stomach, pushing her back with great force into the wall behind her. It cracked when she hit, and her own spine fractured with a couple more ribs to match. She fell to the ground with a thud.

Before she could get back on her feet and stop another attack, he grabbed her throat with one hand and held her high off the ground. Her feet kicked wildly beneath her, fighting to get some sort of footing. He used what strength he had left to attempt to crush her windpipe.

328

Sophie grabbed at his hand and arm, trying to force him to let her go.

"Not getting along with your new pet?" Clarice asked as she came into the room. Sophie looked in her direction and became madder by the second, but she had nothing left to give. She looked at James with tears of apology in her eyes.

"You may have been right," Algos said. "She's more trouble than she's worth."

Clarice threw her head back in a cackle. "That's a first," she said, coming to stand right next to him. She tilted her head at Sophie to study her. Only it wasn't Sophie who looked back at her. It was Jess. Clarice took in a sharp gasp at the sight, but remained by her father.

"Help me," she heard Jess whisper in her ear. Clearly a trick. Clearly, her sister did not know her as well as she had always claimed.

"So, what are you going to do with her?" Clarice asked casually as she turned her back dangerously to her father and took a few steps away from him.

"She's obviously been tainted," Algos said in great disappointment. "I will have to just destroy this one and start from scratch," he said with a shrug, as if Sophie were just a mere science project and not a human at all.

Clarice nodded her head. "Yeah," she murmured. "That's what I thought."

Algos didn't feel her take his trusty switchblade from his pocket. He didn't hear her open it while he spoke. He didn't hear her quickly spin behind him before jabbing it into the back of his neck and twisting it as hard as she could. All Algos felt was the numbness that quickly consumed his body, forcing him to let go of Sophie and fall to his knees before falling face first.

Algos couldn't talk. He couldn't move. She had taken him out just like he had taken his own father out. Like some sort of poetic justice, he thought. Then he saw something walking towards him. A tiny blurred figure. As it got closer, it bent down and got right in his face. A little boy in a red jacket, with ash brown hair and blue eyes, was staring back at him innocently. "Train go fast," Peter hissed to him before his eyes turned red, and the most sinister grin crossed his face. He jammed his hand into Algos' chest and ripped out his heart. It was the last thing Algos saw, even though no one else did.

Clarice had stepped back from the body, and watched her own father's nasty poison take over his body and eat itself from the inside out. Sophie was busy gasping for air and getting to her feet to prepare to take Clarice on.

"You're free," Clarice told her flatly, not even looking her in the eye. "Go."

"I'm not done yet," Sophie warned.

"Sophie Lee," she heard her mother warn. "Please!"

"You killed Mario," Sophie said, ignoring her mother's warning.

"Yeah, and I can't bring him back, now can I?" Clarice retorted as she bent down and grabbed the keys from her father's jacket and tossed them at Sophie. "Get out!" she barked and left the room. She paused only for a second. "You're not my concern," she added over her shoulder. "Tell your mother I kept my promise and to leave me alone." Then she walked out of the room, leaving Sophie feeling conflicted about letting the murderer of her godfather leave without any harm like she had promised.

"A little help here," James called out to her. Sophie reluctantly took her eyes off of Clarice and rushed over to grab the only chair to stand on as she unlocked the locks and helped him get his feet back on the floor. He rubbed his wrists, trying to get feeling back into them.

When he looked up, Sophie was still staring at the door after Clarice. "Hey," he whispered, pulling her into his arms. "There's always tomorrow if need be," he reminded her.

She looked back and gave him a weary smile. Sophie threw her arms around his neck and pulled him eagerly to her as she crushed her mouth against his and claimed every part of him she could with her own body.

After getting a taste of her, he reluctantly murmured against her mouth. "You've done a lot of structural damage. And personally, I would like to take this elsewhere so I can give you a proper welcoming," he chuckled.

Sophie giggled in response and it was music to his ears. "We have to find our way out first," she said with a frown. As if on command, a hidden door opened to the right of them that showed light on the other side.

"Man, I hate this place," James said in frustration.

"Agreed," Sophie said with a frown. They leaned on each other and limped through the door to the outside world.

Clarice opened the door to her father's office. Someone had torn through it. Most likely, Eddie. Eddie. Clarice cursed under her breath at his own stubbornness and stupidity over the girl that never wanted him. She had hated him for so long, but in the end, he had proven to be the only one to actually care if she lived or died. Not even her own father could do that.

She stepped over the mess on the floor and ran her hand lightly over the familiarity of the red leather chair. Clarice cleared off the mess in it and took a seat. What was she supposed to do now? She had spent her entire life following her father like a loyal dog, and where had that gotten her?

Clarice looked at the mess on his desk and found the usual single photo of Jess sitting on top. He didn't even care enough about her to keep a photo of her. He only truly ever cared about Jessica. The golden child. The one that was supposed to be the answer to all of his dreams, but instead gave birth to his greatest downfall.

She turned to see the screen that showed Sophie and James still stuck in the room she had just murdered her father in. Clarice reached over and pushed a blue button under the desk that opened the door that would lead them to their freedom. She had done what Jess wanted. And here she sat. Alone. Still.

Clarice looked over to her right and opened the top drawer. She was looking for his usual stash of booze, but found a blue jewelry box she had never seen before. With great curiosity, she pulled it out and opened it. A piece of paper fell out and onto the desk. She put the box down and picked up the note.

To the daughter I always knew would replace me when the time was right. Don't let me down, C.

-Your loving father

Clarice gasped and dropped the note. *What the hell?* After

332

everything. After years of torture and degradation. The belittling and the persecuting. He wanted her to replace him if something ever happened? She was the one that killed him!

Clarice looked down at the shiny gold necklace that sparkled from within the box. She pulled it out and held it up to look at the charm. An infinity sign with a slash through it. To match the ring that remained on his dead finger.

"Sir! Sophie's getting away!" called someone over the speaker on his desk.

Still holding the necklace, Clarice pushed the button and responded flatly, "My father's dead."

"Oh," she heard him breathe. "Ma'am, what do you want us to do? The target is escaping," he said urgently.

Clarice continued to study the necklace.

"Ma'am?" he tried again.

Clarice pushed the button. "Let her go," she said aggressively. "We have a new target now."

"Ma'am?" he asked in confusion, but Clarice was too busy putting on the necklace as she leaned back, crossed her legs on her new desk, and put her hands behind her head.

"Round two," she murmured with a smirk. "Don't mind if I do."

If you have enjoyed "Dead Draw" please be sure to leave a review:

If you want early access to future books be sure to subscribe to my newsletter at:
www.chasingstormi.rocks

-

Summer '22

Fall '22

<u>Acknowledgements</u>

The Sophie Lee Trilogy would never have existed if it hadn't been for several people in my life. My mother, for putting the original seed of writing a fiction book into my crazy head. It was her comment that I later mentioned to Shyera McCollough when I was so desperate to find balance in a world that was quickly spiraling out of control due to the Covid-19 pandemic.

When discussing possible writing topics, I mentioned a story that had been started and never finished in middle school. I laughed telling her that my mother mentioned that my writing draws people in and I could be like Nora Roberts with a fiction novel. She was immediately invested and insisting that this story needed to be told.

Once a few pages were written, I shared it with my friend, Mario. He insisted it needed to be a trilogy. I couldn't believe he thought it was going to last that long when it wasn't even a full chapter yet! However, the thought intrigued me way too much to pass it up.

I found myself leaving "Easter Eggs" for what I envisioned to come as Sophie continued her journey. Writing *The Key* allowed me to have another thing to bond over with my father. He was the first to read the rough draft of *The Key* with my mother a close second. Before I knew it, my mother was offering up ideas to wrap up the trilogy with *The Key* not even being finalized yet! Thus, my parents quickly became my creative writing team.

When it was time to get started on *The Protector*, we sat around the dining room table and tossed around ideas and what I was stuck on. It is truly a blessing to have such a supportive team for my current journey. I love that my father is still sending me text messages of their ideas that never stop flowing!

You, my readers, also keep me going. I wasn't sure if you were going to love the story as much as I did, but you eagerly proved me wrong! At first, your excitement was a little overwhelming. It made me want to write an even better second book. I hope that you enjoy it as much as I enjoyed writing it.

This story took an unexpected turn, as usual when the story is writing itself. I found myself diving deeper into the world that Jack and Jess remain in to keep Sophie safe. The world Algos wants to crumble in order to gain total control of Sophie and her abilities. This new inspiration is thanks to the OG Storm Chaser.

It is a difficult journey to be on when the person that supported you the most is slipping before your very eyes. The woman that never hesitated to tell me how proud of me she was and how much she loved me now has a time clock that seems to be running out quicker and quicker as the days pass. I strongly believe that loved ones never truly leave us when they pass on to another plane, but I wasn't quite ready to be done hearing her stories or praises.

Thus, the dream realm unintentionally grew. Rules became more defined as you meet the Council of Death, and learn the ultimate punishment for breaking the rules of this sacred place. Although it has become another battle ground to face off Algos, it was inspired by the beloved OG Storm Chaser. The woman that will always hold my heart, and never be far away even when the clock runs out. She may never fully understand how much she has inspired this story to grow, but I will always be grateful to everything she is and more.

Sadly, just a few days prior to this book launching and being available in your hands I had to say goodbye to her. She made me promise to keep writing and helping others share their stories, and I will keep that promise. It took a while for her to finally be set free, but I think that's just because it took God some extra time to take on her full orneriness and warn Elvis that his biggest fan was coming for him.

I sit in the rocker and look at the empty hospital bed that lays before me. The room doesn't feel as empty as I thought it would, and neither does my heart. But there's an extra added twist that has presented itself for *Dead Draw* as I sit here soaking up the energy of happiness that remains in this room long after she's been gone.

I miss your physical presence, but you will live on in my books just like you live on in my heart. I love you OG Storm Chaser.

Always,
Your Little Stormi Dawn

CPSIA information can be obtained
at www.ICGtesting.com
Printed in the USA
LVHW050949010623
748483LV00007B/106/J

9 798985 699920